Dawn
of
Forest Black

Volume 3

ARMANIS AR-FEINIAL

Dawn of Forest Black

1. A Plagued Elf
2. Two Worlds
3. Siren's Call
4. The Stone of Immortality
5. A Nymph's Love
6. Ranger's Dilemma
7. Blenheim
8. A dark Elf's Snare
9. Temple of Corela
10. A Curse
11. The Death of a King
12. The First Trumpet

The Hidden Fae

The Hedgehog
The Nihilistic Neverending Nightmare
The Tragedy of Ted Anderson
Murphy's Law
The Thing About Apples
Lira
Keneira
To Tedward

Ranger's Dilemma

CHAPTER 1

Young Blood

Teyerien stared at the ceiling of his room, yawning as he listened to the rooster crow in the distance. Living near the farm, he never had a reason to procure a bird that would alarm him to wake. He wiped the sleep from his eyes, wincing as he felt a strained muscle in his back. He did his morning workout, consisting of no small number of pushups and sit-ups before hurrying outside, and doing some sprints between the trees until he worked up a sweat. It was so early in the morning that the color of the sky hadn't even changed. When he was finished with his workout, he gathered some clothes and sheets to his personal watering hole to launder.

Back in his home, he took off his gear: his leather cuirass, swords, bow and all, before heading out to report to the Guild.

Dashing through the streets of Kerina, he saw that the festival was still going strong. He wanted to visit, take his brothers with him, and have a nice little fun time with the general populace, but he doubted he'd get that opportunity, what with all the crazy things happening lately. Missing persons reports, Cadrasar deciding to pour out from their lands, those filthy orcs, and of course, this more recent issue with Malitu. He wondered what that was all about.

He also wondered where Yun had been. He'd returned twiddling his thumbs for her to get back. Being placed at the head, albeit temporarily, was putting a toll on his nerves. Walking up the hill, he noticed that other early risers were there, practicing their archery. There was smoke nearby coming from the forest, the familiar stench from Eahemien's research projects that he gave him permission for. Yun might not appreciate it, but perhaps his brother's innovation might come in handy much later. Shaking his head, pushing the doors open, he walked in the hall, striding towards Yun's office. Taking his keys out, he let himself in.

Sitting carefully at the desk, he looked over the reports coming in from the Rangers who had filed them. There appeared to be some force of unknown identity putting things together in Cadrasar. While this phenomenon, as he understood it, wasn't new, it did account for the increased activity coming out from the dark lands. He twisted his lips in thought. That same report also included a sighting of a dragon. *I thought they were extinct.* Though he shouldn't be surprised, Yun said that there might be a small number of them left.

Taking out his quill and a piece of parchment, he wrote down on his to-do list.

1. File the assignments together.
2. Assign expeditions.
3. Catalog a census.
4. Take account of inventory.
5. Account who is wounded.
6. Account who is dead. Account the disability list.
7. Arrange a meeting with Gergo for additional supplies.

Though that last one was easier said than done. Even he knew relations with the royal family and the Rangers' Guild hadn't been great as of late. Definitely not during a time he remembered.

A knock on the door pulled him out of his thoughts.

He put the assignments back and walked to the door. Opening it, he saw Supesien standing there with that great smile on his face. There was now more activity with the hall. Friends were sitting next to one another, waking up over morning tea, and the scent of sweet rolls filled his nose. Looking down, there was a wooden plate with one such roll, handed to him by his brother.

"Hiya!" he said in his usual cheery tone. "Good morning and let the sun not shine its light through our blessed leaves."

"Do you always wake up like this?" Teyerien pointed to the mangled hair as he walked back to his desk.

"You've known me all my life," Supesien shut the door behind him, taking a seat. "Of course, I do, and I don't usually have time for silly questions, but I'll entertain another one."

"But of course," he took a bite. The sweet roll was glazed with honey, sweet to his lips. The dough was soft and filled his tummy. "That's good."

"You can thank Yorna for that one," Supesien winked. "She knows how to bake, and on such short notice."

"Yes," Teyerien said, looking at his brother. "Have you asked her the question yet?"

"No," he frowned. "Not yet. But I will."

"But when?"

"I don't know," he shrugged. "I'm waiting for the right moment."

"Time is short," Teyerien said. "You deserve to be happy."

"You're beginning to sound like a human," Supesien cackled, pointing at him. "Oh, Carmielle, dearest time, where is your sting! I've got all the time in the world."

"Until a skirmish decides your time is done, or disease takes you," Teyerien reminded him of the very real reason elves' lives weren't limitless. They may have aged much, much more slowly than humans, but they weren't immortal, still susceptible to injuries and disease, just as much as the rest of Alkathos was.

"Supesien, we're not immortal."

"I know that," Supesien said, frowning. "And I'm happy."

"You're content," Teyerien reminded him. "Look, I'm only looking out for you. And besides, whatever happened with Lorana?"

"We were only ever friends," he reminded him. "Could you imagine? Her drowning herself in books and me in combat or adventure. She'd never know if I'd make it home alive one day or not."

"Yes," Teyerien said. Another reason why they were almost strictly forbidden from mingling too close with others outside the Guild. Susceptible to large amounts of heartbreak, and no doubt, revenge. "Well, you do you, I guess."

"When is Yun getting back? Did she tell you?" Supesien took a bite of his roll.

"No," Teyerien looked back at his desk of work. "She never does. Look, Supesien, I've got a lot of work ahead of me, now. I don't have time to talk. Get out."

"Sure thing," Supesien smiled weakly, walking towards the door. He opened it before calling out, "Borga, leave Eahemien alone. He's got approval this time!"

Teyerien listened for the door to slam shut before he compiled the risk reports to get them properly filed and organized. That was one task done and out of the way before Yun would return. Probably the one she cared about the most, it seemed, whenever she got back. She always said, "Make sure to file the reports by runes so I can easily track them."

Grimacing, he put the files in the filing cabinet, thankful there were no other disturbances.

What must have been two turns of the hourglass passed undisturbed. He sighed, leaning back in his chair for a brief break from filing. He still had so much more to do. There was no way this was going to all be done by the time Yun arrived and she'd chew him out if it wasn't. She always did. She always told him, "If this isn't right, communication is lacking. And that's how people die!" Another reminder of life's frailty was exactly what he didn't need. Looking out the window at the courtyard, he saw his two brothers sparring. Laughing as their wooden sticks swung through the air, hoping for one of them to make contact as they danced and pivoted. A dance, yes, this was a dance. All swordplay was. He wondered if he was too hard and too abrupt with Supesien. The youngest of the three was always helpful, if sometimes annoying.

Supesien's expression grew serious, and he motioned for Eahemien to stop. A high-pitched flute sang through the air and calls for attention were screamed from the yard.

Djit.

He jumped up from the desk and walked out of the office, locking it firmly again, following. the crowd of elves hurrying out of the Guild Hall. The main doors shut behind him as he got in line.

Yun and Yara were approaching. All the elves stood straighter at their approach, but only he seemed to see the bandages around Yun's waist. He wondered what she ran into that wounded her of all people. He just hoped he didn't have to find out personally.

She paced, inspecting everyone with those icy eyes. The silence from everyone else was so quiet, he heard the mouse moving over the plates of the Guild Hall, scurrying around for crumbs most likely. Her steps were graceful, despite the wound she had, which looked like it needed serious care, but she walked as if it didn't bother her.

"Teyerien," she pointed at him.

"Y—yes," he said.

"Don't stutter," she said. "Come with me. I've something important to discuss with you."

He followed her to the Guild Hall as Yara leaned against a tree. He knew she'd been injured but not by its severity. The muscles inside her belly must still be stitching themselves back together. The doors swung open, and they stepped inside. The door swung closed, the creaking of the wood scratching his ears, and he hissed as they did. She led him to the office, and she closed the shutters. She looked over at the files, going over them piece by piece, scanning them to ensure some sense of order.

"The census?" she asked as she sat down. She motioned him to sit. "Where are the census reports, Teyerien?"

"I haven't had time to do it this morning," he said. "I'm—"

"Teyerien," her fists slammed against the table. "You need to be faster. This is a breakdown in communication. When that happens, people die. Do you want their blood on your hands?"

"No, but I—" he stammered. "I'm sorry."

"Don't be sorry," her tone softened as she looked into his eyes. "I need you to be better. Can you be better?"

"I can try—"

"Can you be better?" she interrupted him.

"Yes," he said. He'd have to be.

"Good," she leaned back in her chair, folding her hands over her chest. "Now as for why I brought you here privately." He didn't like the sound of this. "I'm going on a pilgrimage. A little elf made some mistakes, and he must atone."

"Dorio?"

"What?" she shook her head. "No. Dorio did nothing wrong, and don't interrupt me. I'll be taking Yara with me, and we've got to pick up some friends along the way. I'll be leaving again immediately. Same thing, make sure to do the reports, file them, and for Carmielle's sake, do the census!"

She's leaving again?

"But Yun, you've just arrived!"

"I know that," she laughed.

"But how long will you be gone?" he asked.

"I don't know."

"I can't do this," he pleaded. "Not without guidance. I need help. This is too much to handle by just one elf, how you do it is beyond my comprehension."

"You get used to it," she sighed. "After all, I won't be here forever. It's a sad state of affairs when you really think about it. Besides, a number of elves should be returning from their expeditions shortly and keep you busy with reports from Cadrasar and other problematic portions of the world. Now, I need you to be better. Can you find it in yourself to do it?"

"Why me?" Teyerien. "Why not Atori? She's more experienced than I am. More qualified for this job."

"She's short tempered, and if you tempt her with a bed she'll take it," she shook her head. "Teyerien, I'm going to be completely honest with you. Almost anyone else could do a better job at this than you."

"Then why pick me?" he shook his head in frustration. "You just admitted it! Why me?"

"Because you won't mess it up," she pointed. "Now, to Corela I go."

"But you just contradicted yourself! Help me understand!" he cried.

"You have until I return to make sense of that," she smiled. "You can figure it out. Just read. Just write. Just think. At this point in time, that's all I require of you. Can you do that?"

"Expedition requests?" he asked.

"Approve at your discretion," she smirked. "I trust you."

But I don't trust myself. This is too big a job.

"But Yun—"

"No," she waved her finger at him. "I won't be around forever. You need to take responsibility. Now, I take my leave, and remember the census!"

Teyerien went through the guild and took a census of the injured and those too weak or sick to go on assignment. At best, with those still returning from their expeditions, he was running the Guild operating at twenty-three percent capacity. He still cataloged them as best he could with the limited time he had during the day. Spending several nights sleepless to ensure everything was done right, he felt the bags form under his eyes, and spoke to no one, and ate the minimum. It was all required of him, and it was running his body ragged.

There was a knock at the door of his office one afternoon. Bolting, he nearly tripped on the way down, and opened the door, looking up at Supesien, who smiled not. There was a grave and concerned look on his younger brother's face.. Supesien pushed him back into the office and shut the door behind him.

"This just won't do," Supesien said, taking a seat. "What are you doing?"

"I'm—"

"No, no, no, no," Supesien pointed at him, scowling. "What do you think you're doing?"

"I'm doing my job," Teyerien said. "It's just that—"

"Just what?" Supesien leaned forward. "Just what?"

"There's just too much—"

"Then delegate!" Supesien said sharply.

"But Yun—"

"I don't care about Yun right now," Supesien snapped. "Neither should you, she isn't here. She's been doing what you're failing to do for at least twenty years. She has a process. You don't. She can do it herself; you can't. You simply aren't her, and you shouldn't bother trying to compare yourself to her."

"But—" he stopped himself from his objection. What was his objection? And he felt like a child now, his younger brother chiding him when he scolded him just days ago.

"What do you have to prove?" Supesien said, combing his hand through his hair. "What do you have to prove to her?"

"I need to be able to do it," he said. "She's counting on me."

"You've given us short assignments," Supesien sighed, leaning on the windowsill. "Do you have a to-do list?"

"Yes," he answered, looking at the pile of reports on his desk. They just kept coming.

"Give it to me," he said, taking the sheet of parchment Teyerien handed him. Supesien's eyes widened. "She has you doing all of this?"

"Yes," he said. "It has to be done."

"How the hell does she do it?" Supesien shook his head. "Alright, you need to get some rest. If you keep goin' at it, you're gonna make a mistake."

"No," Teyerien said. So much was riding on his shoulders. He walked to the desk, trying to compartmentalize the next assignment for himself. "I have to keep going."

"No," Supesien frowned. "If you keep going like this, you'll make a mistake. And then someone will get killed. Do you want that blood on your hands?"

"No," he grumbled. "No, I don't."

"Get some rest, go to the tavern, get a drink or something," Supesien shook his head as his eyes read the first report. "Look, Teyerien, you can ask me for help, and I'm sure Eahemien can take a break from his research time and time again to help with something. There is no need for you to do *all* this alone." A deep sigh departed from his brother's lips. "I can handle some of your clerical work for now. Just go get some rest. Hell, take the day off tomorrow. You *definitely* need it."

"Fine," he hesitated before walking to the door. "Oh, when you file, make sure to file them by runes."

Supesien looked at him, eyebrows furrowing, as if he didn't understand the simple request. "What kind of lunatic *wouldn't* sort by the runes?" he asked. "Damnit, Teyerien, no wonder you're so stressed out. Delegate. Delegate. Delegate!"

CHAPTER 2

Induction

The next morning, Teyerien showed up at the Guild a little late after sleeping in with what could only have been the best night of sleep he remembered having. With the stress, added by his own insecurities, it finally caught up with him. He would go in with really small expectations as to what he would do today. Just get a to-do list for Supesien for the day, and call it a night..

Walking into the Guild Hall, he heard many ramblings and mutterings at his presence. They often didn't like him when he was leading, perhaps because he tended to approach things far too conservatively and refused to accept large expedition requests. Rangers liked adventures, that was what they were all here for. That, and Carmielle often brought the curious, but *he* stamped out their curiosity.

Seriously, Yun, what were you thinking, putting me in charge?

He went to the office room and walked in. Supesien was sleeping, boots on the desk. Teyerien kicked them off, and Supesien greeted him with a wave and a yawn.

"I told you to take a day off, ye need it," Supesien hissed.

"I came to give you a to-do list," Teyerien put the quill on parchment, and he noted the files were already filed by rune order. "How did you do that already?"

"Seriously," Supesien shook his head leaning forward. "You get caught up in all the details a. A goblin's lair is more organized than you are. It's simple. Now, hurry up, get me that list and be on your way. You still need to be—" Teyerien sneezed. "See! Now you're sick! Get the list and go back home!"

As Teyerien wrote the list he heard a loud ruckus outside. There was violent banging on the door, and the plaque of Yun fell on the other side of the door. Several muffled shouts and screaming were on the door. He and his brother hurried to the door, opening it to reveal a human man, armored heavily with rusty steel. The pommel of his sword had seen better days, dented and sharp where it didn't need to be sharp. This man was also covered in sweat, panting heavily, as if he'd just run from Malitu.

"Someone get this man some water!" Supesien called. "Now!"

"What are you—"

"I seek an audience from the Guild Master," he said. "I require aid."

"You see," Teyerien looked closely at the man's shoulders, they slouched. "This is the first time I remember humans sending an emissary to us for help. This is going to be good. In."

Teyerien ushered the man into the office. Supesien and he took their seats as an elven ranger came by with a tankard of water, which the man drank immediately. He returned the tankard, and the elf left the office, shutting the door. Teyerien grimaced as he opened the shutters, permitting the sound of the singing birds to sooth his mind. If nothing else, let this be done, and then he can go back to bed. Or that festival.

"Before we get started here," Teyerien leaned forward from Yun's seat. "You should know a few things,"

"Yes," the man said. "I'm aware humans are not kind to you elves up there in the north especially, but this is different."

"National and racial lines can wait, human," he narrowed his eyes. "But that's not what I was talking about. What I am talking about are the decision makers you're looking for. The Guild Master, she isn't here, so you're dealing with me."

"I see," the human bowed his head. "Forgive my intrusion."

"Let's start with your name first," Teyerien moved his hand in a welcoming gesture. "Then we can determine if apologies are necessary."

"Name is Verk," he said. "I come from Kenderhell."

"Ah," Supesien smiled. "The good old fortress of Grento. Quite rich, I understand, in resources and debauchery. Oh, I remember I was up there a decade ago, and some stark lunatic thought it was an excellent idea to start an uprising. That wasn't you, was it?"

"No," he said, and a shadow of doubt seemed to cross his mind. "But I was involved, though, a lesser man was I back then. I've a family now, two children, a boy and a girl. The shadows come and go with the times, I suppose."

"Suppose indeed," Teyerien shook his head. "Now, my name is Teyerien, you'll be dealing mostly with me for the time being until the Guild Master returns. Now, why speak to me now instead of waiting for her? Well, excellent question. We don't know when she'll be back, and I'm in charge here till she returns." He folded his hands over the desk. "Now, tell me, racial and national interests aside, the Kenderhell I know is in Grento, which means we would have to traverse through Core Crest just to get to you. We have a long-standing agreement, I assume you would know, not to meddle in the affairs of humans unless explicitly asked."

"And you are asking for our help," Supesien chuckled. "Congratulations on noting your shortcomings."

"But the people of Core Crest will not stand idly by while we simply just walk through," Teyerien explained. "Kenderhell is the wall that protects the rest of the civilized world from Cadrasar. Why now?"

"I'm not sure where to begin, really," Verk frowned, a look of shame upon his face as his eyes seemed to search the room. "I come on my own."

"Well, that look is useless, that is," Supesien scoffed.

"Let me finish, please,"

"You've come knocking on our door for help, and from my ears I could tell you made quite the racket gettin' in he'e. You deal with it as it is," Teyerien snapped. "Please continue."

"As I was sayin'," he said. "The city itself is a sludge of corruption. We can't do it ourselves. The Assassins' Guild have their hold on public office. They have been in control for the last decade. It was they who started the uprising. We trusted them when we shouldn't have, and now we deal with the consequences, but now it's gotten so much worse. Taxes get hoisted up and shipped away towards the west, we assume to the Assassins' lair, and whatnot."

"Assassins," Supesien hissed. "You want us to get involved with the Assassins? Do you e'en know what yer askin' o' us? This is a straight-out Guild War is what it is, and we won't e'en get paid fer it!"

"That's not it," he insisted. "We can tolerate our regime, that was our decision. That's our responsibility," he sighed. "But there is something out of Cadrasar coming over our plains, and we don't know what it is."

"Then maybe scout ahead and find out what it is." Supesien offered the suggestion sarcastically. "Teyerien, either he's wastin' his time or—"

"The Assassins' Guild have thwarted all our efforts to do just that," Verk hissed. "They don't even know I'm gone right now."

"Huh," Teyerien said, lips twisted in confusion. "You're a horrible negotiator, and we haven't even talked about money. So, let me get this straight, you want us to march through two lands of humans, possibly three lands, of which we have agreements to not interfere with their affairs, and while one might, if given the right conditions, might be amiable to us, the other one or two might not understand we've been requested. And now you say you've been taxed heavily, and I'm led to believe you're not going to be able to afford to pay us."

"I understand it's all up in the air right now, and it's not necessarily in your best interest to help, but we're desperate. I can't even talk to Core Crest about this, they'll laugh in my face," Verk said.

"Well, Supesien seems to be getting his laughter from ye all the same, so what good would it have done anyway?" Teyerien sighed, considering this request, and he felt sorry for the man, but he couldn't risk something that might get the elves into more trouble than they already were.

"Look, I understand your desperation, but even now, I don't really have the resources to spare just to send some rangers over, especially if they won't be reimbursed for it. You understand, don't you?"

"I do," he gritted his teeth. "I know you can't meddle in the affairs of men, but perhaps of Cadrasar. This is Cadrasar! You deal with Cadrasar, don't you?"

"Yes," Teyerien said. The man had a point, they did thwart Cadrasar's plans, even though he didn't know who was pulling all the strings from behind that barbaric land. But supplies didn't just manifest themselves out of thin air. However, there was always the risk that a human wanted to deceive them to make the elves look like the monsters of the world. Wouldn't have been the first time. "Humans asked us to interfere, and yet, it involves Cadrasar, and none of the reports tells me of any circumstances whatsoever to be indicative of the idea that forces came so far out to west as far as Kenderhell. You do know how this might look, right?"

"Yes," he said. "I do, but I'm of no Guild. No faction that might have the influence to attempt to deceive you."

"We don't know that," Supesien shook his head. "We just met you, and we don't know what to make of this request."

"And besides," Teyerien said. "It's not like we could take this on anyway."

"But—"

"We don't know what it is you want. We don't know you. You seemingly want this out of charity. And we don't know what sort of foul thing you are needing saving from. Obviously, you don't represent all of Grento," Supesien scoffed. "Which means we'd be violating several agreements to do what you're asking us to do. I don't know what to tell you."

"We've the people to scout for what that is, but not the supplies, and certainly not without people asking whoever it is we send out questions," Teyerien leaned back in his seat. "That's the last thing any of us need. Now, if you came here knowing what it was, my answer might have been different."

"But the lands of the north!" the man slapped his knees. "You weren't there—"

"And you were?" Teyerien replied, seeing the expression of the man of utmost horror that implied he saw some unspeakable horror. But there was no supernatural force, element, or creature in all of Alkathos that he knew of that would impose that limitation on mortal souls. The expressions rarely lie, save for a very talented bard. "Look, Verk, if I get the supplies I need, I will at least send someone to check it out. How far east from Kenderhell are we talking?"

"Now, that's expensive," Supesien commented. "Considering there'll be no reimbursement. Unless of course we get involved with a Guild War."

"Yes, yes, yes," Teyerien shook his head. "Just what we need. Word to get out that the elves initiated an international Guild War."

"A two month's ride," Verk answered.

"I'll tell you what," Teyerien said. "Don't leave. You'll have my answer within a day or so."

"The longer we wait the closer and closer it gets!"

"I said what I said, Verk," Teyerien pointed his finger at him. "You're fortunate to get that much from me, and don't make me change my mind, else the horses will be turned to meat tomorrow. I am not about to get a few people killed because of lack of preparedness. You might be willing to sacrifice a few elves, but I'm not. In fact," he pointed out the window. "I'm inclined to let your city fall to whatever horror you're seeking safety from. Do I make myself clear?"

"But—"

"Do. I. Make. Myself. Clear?" he spoke coldly, pointing a finger at him.

"Yes," he said reluctantly.

"Good, now don't leave," Teyerien said, and turned to Supesien. "Think you can get me an audience with Gergo?"

"You know me, I'm quite reliable," he smirked.

"Good, make sure our guest doesn't leave."

"Sure thing," Supesiensaid. "Now get outta here. Forgive us, he's been sick recently. Now, there will be refreshments."

CHAPTER 3

The Scuttlebutt

After leaving the Guild Hall, he hurried back to his home, removed his traveling gear and donned on a tunic and casual trousers and casual boots with his coin purse. With the strings kept loose, he tied them up firmly, contemplating the previous day's events, what with Atori coming about Dorio. She left, and Xelanai and Solistus were decidedly unaccounted for. What a time for that to happen. They were resourceful enough to make a trip to scout to see what that evil thing was that was about to plague Kenderhell.

No matter. There wasn't much he could do about it now. And then there was the burning of the Library. Such a shame, there were so many good books in there. A smile crept upon his lips as he looked down the road. Elves wearing various colors of tunics and trousers were walking to and from each tent. There was an acrobat not fifty feet from him, the gentle breeze of her swinging from tree to tree with a hidden strength inside that body which could only be described as divine. The movements she made in the air sent several cheers and cries for an encore. The acrobat obliged, flipping around and vaulting herself higher onto the wires. . He turned, his ponytail swishing over one shoulder as the smell of freshly baked sweet rolls hit his nostrils, causing his stomach to growl. Children were running around, and as he got to the stand, he felt something bump into his knee. Wincing, he looked down, seeing two children, a boy and girl, looking up at him. l The girl had a grimace on her face as she looked angrily at the little boy in front of her, and she darted into him, grabbing his trousers as he crawled away.

"Hey," Teyerien said, turning, and he grabbed them by the shoulders firmly. "No fighting. This is a festival."

"But he—" she pointed at him. "He stole my sweet roll! Give it back!"

"She lies!" he hissed.

Teyerien shook his head. He didn't know enough information to make a judgment call to discern who was right or wrong in a game of he said she said. He turned to the boy, giving him a scolding flick on the head, and he scurried off as the little girl yelled after him.. He couldn't help but wonder about the justice of it all, permitting the boy to run unchecked and unchallenged if the little girl was telling the truth. But he was taught better than that, and he wasn't about to spend his day off acting as a judge.

"I'll buy you a fresh one," he smiled at her, taking her hand. "How's that sound?"

"But he really did steal it," the little girl insisted, chin wobbling. "Well," Teyerien smirked. "I didn't see it. But a fresh one is much better than one that's had more than a few hands all over it, wouldn't you agree?"

"Yes," she spoke softly. " Thank you, sir."

"Of course," he went to the stand, smiling at the baker. "Two sweet rolls please."

"Absolutely," the baker replied in a high-pitched tone. There was a metal cage behind her on which the sweet rolls rested, still kept nice and warm. With metal sticks, she took two out, placing them on a leaf. Each roll was the size of a large book. "Kinasian tokens, please."

"Of course," he said, dropping them into the baker's hands, and they traded the rolls.

He handed one roll to the little girl, who took it gratefully. Steam rose from it, and the girl's eyes were delighted as she grinned widely, revealing a missing tooth. Her chestnut hair was tied neatly into a series of braids, and those brown eyes were quite adorable. She took her first bite into it, and the honey smeared over face. Looking up, she licked her lips from the excess honey.

"Thank you again, sir," her eyes were lit up with joy.

"You're welcome," he petted her head. "Where's your ma and pa?"

Taking another bite, she pointed to a stand. There were garments being shown there, and a male and female elf were there trading coins. He smiled, taking her hand, keeping it firmly in his grip so she wouldn't get swept away in the hustle and bustle of the crowd. "What's your name?"

"Mora," she said.

"I'm Teyerien, nice to meet you," he said.

"You too, mister," she squeaked, taking another bite into the roll that was too big for her face. Hopefully her parents wouldn't mind.

Teyerien cleared his throat as he approached the girl's parents. Her father noticed the pair first, and his smile was relieved as he saw his daughter. Her mother let out a cry, hugging the little girl and lifting her into her arms. Mora wrapped her legs around her mother's waist, continuing to munch on the sweet roll. "Oh, goodness, we seem to have lost her," Her father nervously scratched the back of his head. "Thank you."

"Best take care to look after your children," Teyerien smiled, holding back his ire towards such careless parents. "Especially in a place like this. Not everyone else is so benevolent."

"Can't argue with you there," he put his hand out for a shake. "Name's Brevien, and you are?"

"Teyerien," he shook his hand, but he wanted to get on with the rest of his day. "Now, if you'll excuse me, I've a sweet roll to enjoy!"

He turned from the family and walked down the road, bringing the sweet roll to his lips. Walking down the road, he listened to the cheers of people, and he found himself watching a bard playing a song in a dialect of elvish he didn't understand, but the stressed and unstressed syllables meshed perfectly with the strumming pattern of the lute. The dancing was filled with turning, kicking and cartwheels. A number of the observers threw coins to them, smiling merrily.

There was an archery contest going on. Hearing the thunk of arrows striking wood, he passed by, finishing his sweet roll, and eating the leaf in which it was wrapped. He didn't need to see more arrows fly, and he certainly didn't need to be showing off his prowess with the bow. Truth be told, he was self-conscious of his own ability, for he was far from the best archer in the Guild. Yun had that under her belt. But he was not so naïve to understand that even the worst archer in the Guild was leagues above any hobbyist.

He sniffed the air to see where his nose might lead him this time. More honey, and wine, apparently. There was a large, brightly painted wooden tavern that looked well-kept.

There was no sign on the tavern as he approached. Teyerien figured it was one of the ones travelers used. He carefully scanned the doorway, rubbing the frame of it with his hands. Smooth and soft, and whoever operated this establishment took great care to ensure only the finest experience for his guests.

Stepping through the threshold, he almost felt drunk with the scent of the wine permeating every square inch of this place. The tables were round with chairs at them. There was an odd design carved into it, one he didn't recognize, and he felt compelled to move himself toward the bar and sat down on a stool which had a fluffy cushion for his bottom. There was lots of chatter, and the clattering of dishes filled the air. This certainly was no Dripping Bucket, as there also seemed to be an elven maiden singing. Though, this one was far more calm and soothing than what was outside.

The bartender came over to him. She was a tall, burly elf, and she put a menu in front of him. Teyerien took the menu, noting a film coating it to give it a shine, gleaming in the light of numerous candles hoisted on the walls. There was a full menu here, and so many options to choose from. He hoped none of this would make him sicker than he already was.

"What can I do ye fer," she asked. "Some Mead? Beer? How's about some red wine? Or, if yer boring, ye can just get a tall glass of water."

"You certainly know how to make people feel welcome," he looked up to her. "How's the mead sound?"

"I dunno, yer drinkin' it," she replied, leaning forward with a sneer on her face.

"Alright then," he laughed. "I'll take a mead, thank you."

"And anythin' ta eat?" she asked.

"I'll take a look," he said, turning his eyes to the menu.

She walked away.

The menu was vast. There was a wide array of options, involving several garden salads with their own ratio of exquisite vegetables. Some of them couldn't even be grown in Kerina, not even in the northern part of Kinasa. The soil was too basic. There were several entrees consisting of roasted boar with various herbs, which the menu claimed to be from Korilya. How would they get those here? Was that a—was that a roasted human hand? Well, this *was* a traveling tavern apparently. Nice to see they went all the way into Cadrasar.. There were chicken legs, wings, turkeys, hams, pigs, and apparently humans were on this menu. *Oh my god!*

The bartender came back with his drink.

"Hey, I'm just goin' with the roast chicken and honeyed bread, if ye don't mind, call it a day," he said.

"You really like yer honey, now doncha?" she smirked.

"I do like good honey," he smiled.

"My name is Awilda," she said. "I'll get that right out fer ya."

"Thanks, I'm Teyerien, and you'll be taking care of me today," he said.

"In more ways than one," she snickered as she disappeared to the back room.

"I don't know what that means," he said, taking to his tankard of mead. Sipping it, he could smell the herbs and spices infused within the drink and it was like no other mead he had tasted. There was a divine level of sweetness that could only be manufactured by Carmielle herself, and with a sharp bite of an aftertaste. It was the perfect blend of bitter and sweet which he couldn't escape from, nor did he want to, as he continued sipping away, almost by himself as several other stools squealed on the floor. Looking to his left and right were elves on either side of him, talking away about miscellaneous things of which he didn't have any real interest in.

Though his ears perked up at the mention of Kora's name.

"Sister, what news brings you from the south?" said the male. "Blenheim, was it?"

"Aye, Brother," she said, turning her gaze to Awilda who served them with haste. "It fares as does all things. The king's soldiers, however, at least as far as I've noticed, have been carrying wagons of stones. Know you anything about that?"

Stones? What the hell were they doing with stones? And what was it about these stones that gathered her interest to say something about it. What were the soldiers doing? Was it by direction of the king? Or was there something foul in the air that would corrupt the heart and soul of an elf to treason? So many questions, so Teyerien enjoyed his drink but kept listening. He smelled the chicken cooking from the back, and heard the crackling fire as the ovens roared, cooking, and the sound of sizzling meat entered his ears. "No, nothin'," the male replied. "Though a little birdie told me that Kora was on her way back up north."

"That princess, free as always, was she?" the female said. "But why is that news?"

"Ye didn't he'e it from me," he brought his voice down. "But she left on horseback, and she just got back to Kerina 'erself. Trust me, somethin' foul brewin'."

"An elf left on horseback," the female snapped. "What's so abnormal about that? Left for another venture she had, trust me, nothin' to be worried abou'."

"I don't know 'bout—"

Teyerien's concentration was on the food that was dropped before him, and Awilda winked. "The'e ye a'e," she said to him. "Some roasted chicken from the spices from Korilya, best in town I dare say."

"Well, this is a city," he reminded her. "And where did you procure that paprika?"

"Korilya," she smiled. "We get our spices from all over the world, we travel ye see."

"I can see that when you offer human meat as a meal," he said. "Ain't none of us want that."

"I see, I see," she frowned. "Well, we go to Cadrasar too, those orcs are easy to please."

"And entertain I'm sure, but they don't like us elves very much," he cut into the tender chicken meat and put it to his lips. The taste was decadent.

"It doesn't help when the Rangers' Guild take to cuttin' 'em up in pieces for practice," he ignored that one. "Not good for public relations an' all."

"I see, I see," he replied. "Now, please leave me to my meal an' drink. It looks tasty, Awilda."

"Hey," a firm slap on his back. "Awilda was it? I'll have what he's having. Mead and all."

"You sure? It's got a bit," Teyerien turned to Supesien behind him.

"Of course, I'm sure," he sat down next to his brother, and was greeted with a tankard. Supesien wasn't wearing any garb that would identify him as a ranger, much like him. "I thought I told ye to get some rest? No matter. I've got some news for you, an update, if ye will."

"'Twas as good a time as any it was to see the festival. I'm rarely here for it," Teyerien said. "And when I am, I'm always drowning with work."

"Yeah, ye are," Supesien frowned, bringing the mead to his lips. "Oh Carmielle," he coughed.

"I told ye," Teyerien laughed.

"Anyway," Supesien said. "Eahemien is working on the census now. The reports are all filed away from today, and I already got a head start on the ones for tomorrow. I got you and me a meeting with Gergo first thing in the mornin'. Of course, he'll be none too happy about it, seeing as it's us and not Yun to push around."

"She never lets him get pushed," he frowned.

"Nay," Supesien replied. "That won't stop 'im from tryin' ta push us, though."

"Well, if he's amiable," Teyerien chewed on his chicken, whipping some fat from his lips. "Perhaps we'll have our answer for our friend soon enough. How is he?"

"I've got 'im a room at the Dripping Bucket," Teyerien briefly interrupted him with a cackle. "Don't worry, Teyerien, I told him not to stay up too late. Might get stabbed."

"Might get stabbed anyway," Teyerien chuckled.

"True," Supesien's lips twisted into a smile.. "Then whatever is wrong with Kenderhell isn't our problem."

"No, but you bet the humans would cry for blood when they found out."

"Yeah," Supesien sipped again, pursing his lips. "Anyway, Eahemien is also workin' the inventory tonight. We'll find everything we need, and then when you return, it should be as simple as delegating tasks. Remember, when you don't sign us up for longer expeditions now, we can help. Otherwise, we're just twiddling our thumbs like little children."

"Thank you," Teyerien sighed as his brother's meal came.

"Paprika?" he said.

"Yes," Awilda replied. "We're a traveling tavern. We get spices all over."

"Awesome! We'll wave you over if we need anythin' else, thanks!" he turned to Teyerien as she walked away. "So, there's that."

"Hey," Teyerien motioned with three fingers for his brother to come closer, and when Supesien lent a closer ear, he whispered, "Have you heard anything troubling from our reports lately? Anything about stone shipments?"

"Sadly, I hadn't had the time yet to read them all," he whispered back. "But there'd been no such scuttlebutt. Why?"

"I just heard a rumor about the king's soldiers transporting wagons of stones," he returned closer to his food. "Just before you came in."

"Eavesdropping' eh?" Supesien sneered. "Now, that seems something to be worried about. We're seein' the king tomorrow, so we can ask him."

"Sure," he said. "When you went to ask for an audience today, was there something unusual?"

"You mean besides the fact that Kora ran out without so much as a word, stole a horse and rode it off into the sunset?"

"We don't see the sunset here," Teyerien reminded him. *Well, that explains the brother's thoughts on Kora, sudden disappearance is likely to raise questions. Even hers.*

"It's a phrase," he shook his head. "Seriously, ye need to read more. No wonder I find Lorana better company."

"Do you know why she left in such a hurry?" Teyerien asked.

"No," he replied. "I didn't want to get in the way of that. We're already on thin ice with the royal family as it is. No need to add more wood to the fire. But I did notice that Gorda didn't seem to be his usual self. Seemed plagued by something."

"What of our sister? Is she still there?"

"As far as I know," Supesien laughed. "You're asking a lot of questions. I'm sure we can get these questions answered tomorrow."

"I guess, tomorrow then?"

CHAPTER 4

Trouble with the Tree

Teyerien had his Rangers' garb on as he yawned in the early morning. He skipped his workout this morning before he came in, and while looking at the office for all his tasks, he put his to-do list together. Drafted it out before looking at the reports that were left from this morning. Many were placed neatly in one pile about an inch thick. Still a lot, but he didn't have time to deal with it right this moment, for there was a meeting to attend. There was a knock on the door.

"It's open," he said.

Supesien walked through it. Taking a seat by the window, he stared outside, elbow propped up on the sill. There wasn't much to be said, save for Teyerien to put the final touch on his to-do list, and tacking it to the desk; it would wait for him to return. Sighing, he stood from his desk and walked over to Supesien, placing a hand on his shoulder as they watched the elves outside spar with one another. The sight and noises meant today was just another ordinary day; no one suspected anything otherwise. "Ready?" he asked.

"Ready as ever," his brother turned to him. "Let's go and get this over with."

"Census come in yet?" he asked.

"Eahemien is on it right this minute," Supesian said. "It'll take some time, of course. Always does."

"And what of our friend?"

"Oh, that poor fellow? I don't know. Want me to send someone to check on him?" he asked.

"That shouldn't be necessary," he said. "Besides, that will take more time than I want to spare right now. I feel the bugs jittering up my spine."

"Confidence, Teyerien," he stood, hands on his brother's shoulders. "You could stand to use a little more of that. Besides, remember, Yun chose you. Not me. No one else. There has to be a reason. There always is. Remember now," Supesien led him out the door. "This is the royal family we're dealing with. They smell fear like it goes on every meal."

Teyerien and his brother left the Hall and walked to the Royal Tree. The morning was bustling with excitement, and he noticed that there were several horses drawing wagons. The contents of the shipments were covered as they rode through the west, east and south of Kerina. Guards were cloaked, faces hidden, but there was no mistake. It was all coming from the Tree. It was all the armor of the Guards. Supesien spoke as if he went to the tree yesterday in person. Did he somehow miss this? The horses clopped their way and the wheels creaked as they moved further and further away from his sight. There was an uncomfortable churn in his stomach.

The guards at the city gates had their faces veiled. He noted there was a chain around their neck, leading to something that might be a necklace, but the source of value being on display was decidedly not where he could see it. Teyerien felt an unusual dread about their presence as he walked forward over the bridge to the stairs. They let him and Supesien through without delay.. The torches were dimmer than he remembered them being the last time he was here.

King Gergo sat on his throne, leaning to one side, his chin propped up on his fist. The crown of roots were around his head, and he wore darker clothes than usual. Arenia wasn't here, nor was Kora. No Gorda either. They were all gone. The usual attendance wasn't here apart from several armed wizards and soldiers, as if prepared to put an end to some assassination attempt.

Really? Like he was here to do that.

However, he did notice something peculiar, and regrettably it wasn't the first thing Teyerien noticed. The skin of the king was purple. He noted the chain around his neck, and there it was, hanging above his breast; a purple crystal hanging in a golden cage laced with silver upon it. It shone an unnatural light in the room that he imagined dimmed the light of the flames.

"You've my attention," Gergo's haughty voice spoke.

"Your Majesty," Teyerien said, offering a bow. "I've been receiving reports of unusual activity. T. The Rangers' Guild does not have the necessary provisions to embark on such a quest, which would lead me well into Grento. I come to seek provisions."

"I see," Gergo said. "And you bring elves into Grento for this expenditure?"

"Yes," Teyerien stood proudly. *At least look confident!* "Normally I wouldn't approve meddling with the affairs of humans, but the origin of this horror is close enough to Cadrasar, it might be worth looking into. Since it comes far enough away from Kenderhell, it is well understood that lest we pull ourselves into direct conflict with the Assassins Guild, there will be no reimbursement."

"No," Gergo said. "I will not sanction this under any conditions. Human affairs are their own unless explicitly asked for."

"But a human did come down here seeking our help," Teyerien said. "They have requested intervention."

"Strange that I have not heard of this," Gergo snarled.

"Not unusual for people to prefer the Guild over the Royal Tree," he replied.

"Is this human a king? Politicians? Or of any such individual that would have the authority to sanction our immediate involvement in their affairs?" he asked.

"No," Teyerien answered, flustered, as his brother put his hand on his shoulder. Trading a nod, he turned to readdress the king. "There are certain restrictions placed by the Assassins' Guild that prohibits such bureaucracy. As such, this investigation is outside their scope. And since it pertains directly to Cadrasar, that is within our ability and rights to investigate should we so choose. Please, I urge you to consider our supplies. We don't have enough for that."

"I see," Gergo said. "Denied."

"King Gergo," Teyerien said, approaching silently to the floor. There was no activity from the guards, though he was aware of one such elf, masked as everyone else who seemed to have their hands a little too close to the pommel of his sword for Teyerien's liking. "I know relations between the Guild and the Tree have not been favorable with one another in recent memory. I urge you to reconsider and help repair whatever broke our bond."

"I suggest," Gergo shook his head. "That should this be of any real importance to you, and your Guild, you will come up with the necessary sum to procure your supplies. Just like everyone else ought to. Now, you can—"

"Where is Kora?" he asked. He didn't know the answer, but perhaps Gergo wouldn't have noticed. "Surely she could be around and hear my case."

"She is not here," Gergo scoffed. "Nor will she hear your case. My answer is the answer you have, now if there's nothing else…"

"Would you satiate my personal curiosity then?" he asked, thinking of the shipments.

"Go on," Gergo waved his hand to permit him his inquiry.

"I've seen shipments coming from this Tree," Teyerien said. "Additionally, yesterday I heard a rumor that soldiers, our soldiers, were shipping stones throughout all of Kinasa. What *will* you tell me about that?"

"You trust rumors where there should be facts," Gergo said. "As far as shipments coming from the tree, we're developing healing salves for some of our healers down south." There was a snarl on his face. "They need them, I make them here. We're shipping those out so everyone can have them."

"And of the Rangers' Guild? Why have you excluded us from the distribution?" Teyerien asked. He heard an uncomfortable growl from Supesien.

"I suspect you have your own stock," Gergo replied. "Do you not have your own stock of healing salves? I can provide them to you."

"I'm merely questioning why you wouldn't check in with us—"

"This is the Royal Tree," Gergo growled "I answer to one person, and one person alone, and you are not him, now is there a point to—"

"Your skin," Teyerien frowned. "What's wrong with it?"

"We deal with enough racism from the rest of the world," Gergo said rather calmly. "I'll not tolerate it within the confines of my forest. Now, you've overstayed your welcome. You have your answer, and that is no. If you should run out of healing salves for your expedition, you may come to me, but I'll not provide you rations. You purchase that yourself!" He pointed to the door. "Out."

"Gergo, the Guild demands—"

" I said *out*," he said coldly. "You can leave now willingly, or I can have you escorted out. Your choice."

"Gergo—" a hand touched his shoulder.

"We were just leaving," Supesien smiled. "Forgive my brother, King Gergo, I'm afraid he hadn't quite had his mornin' breakfast. Gets a little cranky every now and again. Please permit him a pardon, will you?"

"Indeed," Gergo said, and the doors were pulled upon.

"Come on," Teyerien whispered to him. "What do you think yer doin'?"

"See that? Poor little elf doesn't have enough food. Let's get breakfast," Supesien said, turning his brother's shoulders to the door. "We'll get some nice adorable little eggs in our bellies and finish the rest of our days' work. Thank you kindly for your hospitality, Your Majesty. Pleasure, as always."

"Get yer honeyed words outta here."

"Honey!" Supesien said, rubbing his tummy. "That's the stuff. Yes, come on brother, let's go get some honey. Nice little sweet rolls, perhaps? Oh, I wonder if we've got some of those left."

"I don't like this," Teyerien whispered as his boots echoed through the throne room, and out the door.

His brother led him past the guards and shared some kind words before crossing the bridge. His nerves were on edge with the encounter, and he wanted to kick himself, for he feared he didn't represent the Guild well in the presence of the King. It wasn't his first time dealing with him by any means, but this seemed different. What was with masks? What about the stones? The healing salves. The rumors. There was much going on, and more horses were still pulling heavily guarded wagons away from the Tree down the streets and weren't stopping. What exactly did they expect to find in the forest of Kinasa?

"What are you doing?" Teyerien backed away from his brother.

"Look," Supesien pulled him close as they continued to walk so he might whisper privately in his ear. " Let's get back to the Guild and talk from there. I fear unfriendly ears are listening to us now. We can't be seen here. Come."

He nodded. Nothing about this meeting went according to how he imagined, not that he imagined any success for additional supplies, but still, nothing short of more questions and now, it seemed that it would be wise to hold off on expeditions for the foreseeable future. Damnit.

Yun, what would you do?

He trusted her to make the wise decisions, but she was still out on that pilgrimage with what's his face. *What would you do?*

A Ranger's Dilemma

"I still don't understand why Yun didn't choose you," Teyerien said as his brother sat across from him in the office. The shutters were closed and so was the door. Perhaps in quieter times, this would have been a little more welcomed as the flames of the candles lit the office. They had already told Verk they'd received no help from them due to supplies being as low as they were, and they weren't getting help from the Royal Tree. "You're much better at this than I."

"Yes, well," Supesien leaned back, boots on the desk and arms crossed. "I was approached, but I turned it down. Didn't want the responsibility."

"And here you are," Teyerien replied. "Playing the role of my trusty advisor."

"Yes," Supesien said. "And if you screw this up, it's still your fault, not mine. I was none too pleased at the appearance of our dear King."

"Was he like that yesterday?" Teyerien said, taking out some parchment.

"No," he frowned. "But he didn't seem well enough either. Teyerien, something is going on underneath our very noses, and we ought to find out what."

"Curiosity didn't bode well the last time," Teyerien frowned, quill in his hand.

"Let's write down what we know, shall we?" Supesien replied.

"Absolutely," Teyerien replied, the quill ready to take notes.

"Alright, so yesterday at the traveling tavern you overheard some people speaking about shipments, caravans even holding stones from Elven soldiers. They claimed to have been from the Royal Tree," Supesien began to recap as Teyerien took the quill to the page and recorded their meeting. "Kora has departed on short notice without telling anyone where she was going. She is not here. Left in a hurry by the sounds of it, from both the rumor in the traveling tavern, and simply with Gergo not being forthcoming with that kind of information."

Teyerien continued to jot down these notes. He heard the shuffling of wheels and feet coming from outside. There was something wrong, something seriously wrong, and he didn't know how to handle this. More eyes and ears would be needed, depending on the action he needed to take. There was only one path, and that was forward. Now, exactly where did that lead?

"As we saw, there are shipments and caravans actually coming from the Royal Tree," he continued. "Healing salves, or so the king claims. We didn't see the contents of the caravans or shipments, and we won't unless we order them. According to our finances, we don't have the necessary funds to purchase one, unless His Majesty Gives it to us willingly, and if he does, there's always going to be some fine print, and conditions involved with it."

Teyerien knew his history. He knew historically King Gergo had been written about as a generous King. He knew others who were much older than him confirm the king's character. But that hadn't been his experience. Perhaps he was that way with his direct subjects, but perhaps not so those that didn't answer to him. The Rangers' Guild did not answer to the Royal Tree. Never had, and never would unless personal and political interests happened to overlap with one another. In recent history, that had never been the case.

"That being said," Supesien glanced at the ceiling as his brother continued to write down notes. "Someone is lying or making assumptions. We don't actually know what's in those shipments. These things can't be verified. Unless we hijack one."

"We can't do that!" Teyerien whispered harshly. "What you're suggesting is a direct act of treason."

"Teyerien," Supesien shook his head. "We have an oath to uphold. Don't tell me you've forgotten it?"

"No," Teyerien said. He remembered the day he was finally permitted to take it. The Rangers' Creed was one not so easily abandoned.

"Then what is it?"

"I'll serve the will of Carmielle throughout my days," he began. "Though death takes me, I will serve her, and to her alone do I owe my allegiance. Through these great lands, though a crown may command the citizens of Kinasa, I'll serve Carmielle alone. As a ranger from the Rangers' Guild, the oldest organization since before nations formed, I will protect the forest of Kinasa, and those who dwell within them, and I answer to Carmielle alone. No crown shall govern me save for the holy covenant between me and the Guild, and the Guild to Her."

"It is impossible," Supesien said. "For us to commit crimes against the King, for we don't answer to him. We are separate from one another, as we should be. Always remember the oath we swear. And concerning His Majesty's seemingly depreciating condition," he continued, urging Teyerien to write down notes with a pointing finger. "He is sick. His skin changed color, and the queen is nowhere to be found. The soldiers, for whatever reason, are hiding their faces. What if," Supesien bit his lip. "Whatever is inside those caravans made Gergo sick? What if he gave those things in the shipment to the soldiers and they are also sick? Then they are going to get the whole dwellers sick!"

"Supesien," Teyerien remembered his observations. "There were chains around the soldier's necks, and the same chain on Gergo. An amulet."

"Yes, I noticed them too," Supesien spoke gravely. "What if these are amulets, which depending on the vantage point could be seen as stones, are in the caravans being distributed through all the dwellers of Kinasa? Then they will get sick and fall under the same haughtiness we witnessed today."

"We can't just start a rebellion, Supesien,"

"It wouldn't be a rebellion," he sighed. "And we need proof anyhow."

There was a heavy knock on the door. Teyerien gave it a scowl and blew on the parchment to dry some of the ink before putting it inside the desk. A knock sounded again, heavier than the last one, and a voice was muffled behind it. Looking at his brother, Supesien glared at the door with a suspicious gaze.

"Well, this is unusual timing," Supesien said. "Better have a looksie."

Supesien went to the door which was banged on a second time.

"Alright, I'm coming!" he opened the door.

"Teyerien, Supesien," came Eahemien's voice. "You need to get out here now!"

"What is it?" Teyerien said, coming to the door and opening it wider.

"Some damned King's Guard came in with this letter," he answered, passing a scroll to Teyerien. "They just dropped about three hundred chests. We didn't open a single one of them."

"Why didn't he just give this to us while we were there?" Teyerien scowled, undoing the green ribbon.

"Probably already enroute," Supesien reasoned.

"If that's the case, he should have said something," Teyerien looked at the letter.

To the Rangers' Guild and to whomever it concerns,

This is a mandate through all those dwelling inside Kinasa, and the Guild is not exempt from this mandate under any condition. This decree nulls and voids any and all agreements currently in place whether that be to our Goddess Carmielle, to any temple inside the forest boundaries, and transcends any promises made to the races of the world. I am leading our people forward into the future, a future that none have seen before. There has been enough intolerance to our people. That will come to an end with this decree. This future does not include the Rangers' Guild, and they are thereby disbanded if they do not follow this decree and will be banished from the forest of Kinasa indefinitely.

I have sent you three hundred large chests and inside these chests are one hundred amulets. These are my gifts to you should you want to stay in the forest. To continue living in the forest, you must wear these gifts, for these amulets are a sign of dedication to the land of Kinasa. All elves must be in compliance or will be banished. Failure to comply with banishment will be immediate execution. Enforcement of this mandate will take effect seven days from the reception of this notice.

Signed,
King Gergo.

"What?" Supesien said, snatching the parchment from him. Eyes scanned the contents inside it, and Teyerien heard the sounds of murmurs. Looking past his brother Eahemien, he noted several elves whispering to one another, and with the voices crossing over one another, he couldn't rightly tell what who was saying.

"Supesien," Eahemien said. "Can he do that?"

"No," Supesien said. "This Guild is older than the Royal Tree. He cannot do this. Teyerien!" he looked up. "You need to dispatch a messenger to Yun. This is serious!"

"She's on a pilgrimage," Teyerien shrilled.

"Then we know she's going to Corela," Supesien replied.

"We are not permitted to interrupt a pilgrimage," Teyerien said. "For any reason."

"Rules must be broken in certain circumstances, this qualifies," Supesien pointed a finger at his chest. "And this is going to require certain actions that even you are not authorized to make." Supesien snarled, stepping into the hall and grabbed the collar of a ranger close to him. "Oi. You, get yer arse to Corela, find Yun, and give her this parchment. Immediately!"

"We don't even know what these amulets do," Teyerien said as the elf took the parchment and dashed out the door with great haste.

"While our messenger is out," Supesien said. "Let's have a looksie."

"You really should be in charge here, Supesien," Eahemien brought his tone low. "Sorry, Teyerien, but it's the truth."

"Don't I know it," Teyerien shook his head before running out the door to see the shipment dropped on their doorstep.

The chests were layered in rows and columns on the training ground. Many elves were still gazing clearly, disturbed by the sudden activity. Arms crossed, they were, as they chatted among themselves as to what this meant, and there was no one among them that dared point to Teyerien for immediate guidance. These chests were undoubtedly from the king, holding the Tree's emblem engraved on the top of them. Teyerien felt a jab to his heart, none looked to him, save for Supesien, who took the reins from him. What would Yun think when she heard? When poor Teyerien allowed leadership to be ripped from him so suddenly, and those talking amongst themselves had their eyes *fixed* on Supesien?

His brother walked over to the chest and he followed. There was an unnatural dread radiating from it, and it was of a kind Teyerien only remembered once, and that wasn't that long ago in the Throne of the King. There was something foul at work, and it certainly had something to do with these amulets. Who created these? What about them created this aura of terror? Where did they come from? He knew they were being transported by the king and his soldiers, and Teyerien could assume that the King's army was equipped with these things, but where did *they* get them from? Or from whom?

Supesien opened the chest and immediately his eyes gaped open with the purple aura of fright illuminating his face. Hissing, he slammed the top of the chest shut. Kicking it hard with his boot, he turned and hurled vomit on the side of the chest. "Oh, Carmielle," he said, wiping excess spit from his mouth with his sleeve. "Oh, Carmielle, that was so foul. So foul."

"What was it?" Eahemien came to him.

"I don't know," he snarled. "But it's evil, whatever it is. We need some kind of wizard—"

"Carmielle," a voice called. "No. No wizards!"

"We don't have the capacity to find out what these things are," Supesien said, and utter shock wrote itself upon his face. "And we need to find out. We must."

"Eahemien," Teyerien put his hand on his middle brother's shoulder. "Are you still friends with the wizards at the library?"

"You mean the ones that hate us because we cut it down from burning?" Eahemien said. "There might be one I can find. I don't know how versed they are in enchantments though."

"Any wizard is good enough," Teyerien said, and immediately heard the chatter with tones of discomfort. "Go, find them."

"Sure," Eahemien darted away like a gazelle.

"What are you thinking?" Supesien asked kindly.

"A wizard would have the knowledge of what to do with these things," Teyerien said. "Never doubt the network of a wizard."

"You trust them now, eh?" Supesien said. "Well, you could have treated Lorana a bit nicer then."

"Is she still—"

"No, she's gone," Supesien laughed. "Besides, do ye think she'd help us after what ye ordered us to do to that Library?"

"It was burnin' down!" Teyerien said, before turning back to the elves of the Guild. "Everyone, I don't know what the next seven days are going to look like for us. But be prepared to answer my call!"

"The call for what?" a voice cried in the crowd.

This wasn't going to be easy to accept for anyone. He knew that, and even now, his hand trembled with hesitancy. For too long have the Rangers been in the shadows being the snake and the King the heel. For much too long have their calls for additional supplies within reason been denied. For too long, and the Rangers, he knew, were getting sick and tired of all the politics, especially with a king, a royal family who seemed to have forgotten it only existed because the Guild allowed them to exist. And with such things comes an understanding, but now that understanding had been nulled with the blatant request for the king to liquify the Rangers' Guild into his personal army.

Supesien was right. He served Carmielle. And Her will always was and always would be to protect the forest, and those that lived inside it, no matter what the cost. Evil had a way of corrupting even the soil of the ground, and the divine soil of Kinasa was not immune to such toxins. Such things would certainly destroy the tree. And yet, blinded currently by whatever it was these amulets did, he couldn't be certain how deep the soil's taint had already been achieved. Was the water safe to drink? How long until plants started dying and the animals left them? Save the forest. Save those who call it home. But should those two interests come in direct conflict with one another, and to follow the oath meant breaking a single part of it, could he bring himself to do it?

No. That was a terrible question to be pondered, for it wasn't up to him. Rather, could he compel the whole of the Guild to follow him into that lunacy? For with all things came balance, and it was about to be tilted in one way, and madness was on both sides of the scale. The promise to Carmielle, oh Carmielle, why did he have to be presented with such an impossible, albeit fundamentally critical task? If all the citizens of the forest elected it was in their best interest to burn the world down, would the Rangers' Guild let it burn? Or could he compel them to kill everyone in the forest? He feared he was about to find out. And this was a decision that only a cold-hearted killer should have to make.

CHAPTER 6

Diagnosis

"Supesien," Teyerien said in his office. It was a late night for them all. He knew the Rangers were busy stockpiling supplies they couldn't spare. There would be no expeditions for them in the foreseeable future. Which was exactly what Cadrasar would have wanted. *Could they have planned this?* A land of undead corpses, orcs and goblins who bred each other like rabbits. No. They weren't organized, and too stupid to do something like that. "What did you feel?"

"The amulet is magical or cursed," Supesien answered gravely, sitting on his chair, legs crossed. "No matter what the origin of it is, nothing good can come from it. There was something in there though, as if it was devouring my mind. I'm unsure. The sooner the wizard gets here, the better. What could be takin' him so long?"

"I don't—" he was interrupted by a knock at the door. "Come in."

Eahemien pushed the door open, and a beautiful elven wizard walked in. A green cloak, a staff, silver hair, and blue eyes, and he almost swore she was a spitting image of Yun, carrying the old historic line of blood that made its way in only so few of the genetic lines throughout the years. Her lips twisted into a sneer as she pushed past him, and then scowled as she struck the bottom of his desk with her stick.

"You've got some nerve book burnin',' ' she said.

"It was that or the whole forest," Teyerien said. "And you are our wizard for this evening?"

"Manuille," she gave a light bow. "And to what do I owe the dishonor of appearing before the esteemed Rangers' Guild? Surely nothing that you require magic for."

"That is exactly what we need right now," he said, leaning back. "Have you heard any rumors of amulets? Being delivered to dwellers by the King directly?"

She curled her lip again, tapping her cheek with her finger as she looked up at the ceiling.

"No," she said. "Amulets? You're concerned with jewelry?"

"Not just any jewelry," Teyerien said. "If the curiosity of wizards has any sway, you might be interested in this. Come."

He led everyone outside. There was a crackling bonfire, on which several deer were cooking. The flesh permeated the air, and several pots were filled with boiling water. Some bread was baking, but nothing extravagant as sweet rolls. *Sourdough,* he thought. The Rangers sat, eyeing them intently, but not a word was spoken among them. Taking his little following to the chests, he tapped it with his foot.

"Manuille," he said. "We've been given this gift from His Majestyand are required to wear it within seven-days' time. Supesien here opened the chest, and he got sick. He vomited, and he thinks it's evil. We all do."

"The King is demanding this of the Guild despite your history of not liking magic?" her eyebrow raised.

"It's not that we don't like it, we have a healthy fear of it. Some of us use it, but sparingly. No one I know here does," Teyerien said. "Any and all of us who do are out on expedition right now. But I doubt they have the knowledge and expertise to discern what these are."

"Amulets," Manuille opened the chest, and she vomited, pushing herself off the side. "Oh, rats piss! That's foul!"

"Do you know what it is?" Teyerien said.

"I've not yet appraised the stone," she coughed. "And I'm not sure I want to."

"Manuille," Teyerien said. "We've heard rumors that these things are being transported to all the people of Kinasa. I assume everyone must wear them to continue living in the forest as part of the King's decree. We need to know what this does."

"How reliable are these rumors?" Manuille asked, eyeing carefully the dark aura of the amulets.

"A rumor at a tavern," Teyerien confirmed. "Paired with my personal witness of unusual transports coming from the Tree."

She pointed at him. "Since you burned books, you'll get the amulet. Come, I need to prepare."

Teyerien shook his head as he reached into the foul odor of the chest and pulled out the amulet by the intricate chains. The aura was filthy, and he felt like he'd need a long bath as he followed Manuille through the yard with her bag and staff. The host of rangers followed, for just like he was, they all wanted to know what they were going to be dealing with. Hissing with the stench, the wizard drew a circle in the ground with her staff and tapped it several times before going into her bag. Pulling out white dust, she decorated the circle with it, and there were stars and moons illuminating the circle.

"Put it in the middle," she said.

He nodded, bringing the artifact to where she directed it. The gem of the amulet laid there, and he backed away as the wizard pointed her staff at it. She chanted in an arcane language he couldn't make out. The voice was strong as it echoed off the ground, and suddenly, it felt like her voice was sending thrums through his blood. The end of the staff lit blue, and her eyes too became radiant like the sun, and the light from the bonfire was inconsequential. The staff seemed to shake in her hand, and the spell stopped.

"Teyerien," she pursed her lips. "This is magic beyond me. Perhaps someone from the Wizards' Council might be able to discern it."

"We don't have that much time!" Supesien snapped. "That's more than a seven-day run! We now have six days. We need to know what this is and what it does. Today!"

"Manuille," Teyerien said. "Forgive my brother. He isn't usually like this. But, he's right. Time is something in short supply. Can you tell us anything about it? Anything at all?"

"I can tell you where it's from," she said. "But that's it."

"Then speak," Supesien hissed through his teeth.

"This comes from the plane of the Abyss," she replied. "But I can't tell you where in the Abyss it came from. I can't tell you who made it. I can't even tell what sort of properties it might have."

"The fact that Gergo is getting something from the Abyss is more than enough!" Supesien growled. "We don't give him seven-days. We don't even give him a warning!"

"Supesien," Teyerien snapped. "Calm down. You're not yourself! What is it in the amulet that caused you to behave so irrationally?"

"Teyerien," Supesien walked to him, hand firmly on his shoulder. "Carmielle is clear, there can be no negotiation of any kind between us and the realm of the Abyss. It cannot be. Kinasa cannot have anything to do with the amulet, and to have them distributed is blasphemy."

"But—"

"No, no buts!" Supesien pushed him. "No, we must act now. Cut off the supply from its source."

"Don't behave so rashly," Teyerien warned. "That's how mistakes get made! I don't want another Sterilus Island incident."

"What do you suppose we do then? Hmm?" Supesien roared. This was not his brother. "We don't even know what it does!"

"I'll find out," Teyerien said.

"How?" Supesien said. "It's beyond Manuille. She said so. How will *you* find out what it does?"

"There are more ways to find out how things work," Manuille said. "The thing about magic is it must be realistic."

"What do you suggest?" Teyerien said.

"Put it on," she said. "Normally I'd advise against ill measures, but considering the amount of time that is on the table, it's a necessary risk."

"I'll do it," Teyerien said.

He walked to the circle until a firm hand grabbed his shoulder. There was silent chatter, and his heart jolted as he turned to a scowling Supesien. He had completely changed. Why? Was his exposure to the amulet earlier this morning significant to change his personality? Or did he have such a fear over the cursed object that was affecting his ability to think rationally? He couldn't tell, but perhaps he'd find out soon.

"Are you insane?" Supesien said. "You never use magic without knowing what it does! It's a rule even wizards have to make sure it doesn't go off in their face! Don't do that!"

"Like Manuille said," Teyerien replied. "We don't have many options, especially with no time on the table. It's a risk, yes, but a necessary one. And one we can't afford not to take!"

"Say it's as bad as all that," Supesien exhaled heavily. "We go in and cut it at its source and this risk will be for naught."

"But we can't very well do that without evidence," Teyerien said. "When Yun gets back—"

"Yun isn't here!" Supesien snapped. Teyerien brushed his brother's hands away. "And when she gets back, there must be a forest left, and a Guild for her to return to."

"There will be—"

"Will she be back in less than six days?" Supesien said. Teyerien gasped. "And what if she does get back? What do you think she'll believe when you leave this with her?"

"That's what the messenger is for!" Teyerien said, turning to Eahemien. "Restrain him! He's not himself."

"That messenger won't catch up with her in seven days, much less get back to us with some magical solution!" Supesien said, pulling away from the grasp of his brother. "You're being rash, Teyerien. Do you think she'll approve?"

"There is but one choice," Teyerien said, reaching down to the amulet. "And that is forward." He turned to everyone watching him. "If something happens, and I'm unable to remove it myself, take it off me."

Fear filled him as the dread came close to his chest, wrapping the chain around his neck until the stone rested firmly upon his heart. The terror forced his heart to beat, and he felt sweat dripping down his head and into his garments. His eyes gaped open as his hands stretched from his body, constantly twitching as if to play a piano. He hissed as his vision began to fade into nothingness.

He was surrounded by darkness. It was heavy and oppressive as it pressed on his shoulders like a boulder. It was a warm darkness, oddly enough, and he couldn't tell what sort of substance he was stepping in, but it was a liquid, thick and slow moving as he pulled each step to move further into one direction of the dark. He was alone here, and there was nothing at all, save for him and his mind. He felt at home here, and not in his tree, and there was a solace in the solitude surrounding him. Turning his head in four directions, the darkness was endless, and his boots made no noise in the sludge he trekked in.

On his right there was a bell. Turning to it, he saw a silver stand, A bell rang as something tapped it, ringing in his ears, clear and melodic. Soothing. Turning, he walked towards it. The sludge was heavy, but soon he came out of it, climbing on black rock, and the bell, mystically lit, he squatted next to it, hand touching the rod, which was impaled in the ground. Soft, and another bell rang, and he turned. Squinting his eyes so he might see in absolute darkness, he saw a trail of bells.

Before taking another step, he looked closely at the ground at his feet with the limited range of the light emitting from the bell. He didn't understand how or why the bell was radiating light, but as the only source of it, he'd not question it, lest he broke it and found himself stumbling blind in the abyss again. Rocks were layered in a film, glimmering, and there was sediment inside the film, and it appeared to move. He hissed, jolting his head upright, and a chill crawled up his spine, and he shivered, trying to get the uncomfortable sight out of his head.

He walked between the lights. An eerie wind passed by, whipping through his hair with each step he took on solid ground. Clicking his tongue, he pushed his way to the next bell, but even as it rang, it seemed farther and farther away. Looking down at his feet shrouded in darkness, he couldn't tell what was happening because the bell seemed to be running from him. His hands shook in frustration, but he knelt down and touched the surface, and the nasty film was moving as if he was standing in a stream in the direction of the bell.

Standing upright, he began to run, but as soon as the first foot departed the ground, he slipped. He stood back up, and the bells still rang their tunes, but the light from them departed, and he found himself in utter black. He brought his film coated hands to his tunic and shivered in the cold this world brushed upon him. Fear and trembling was in his heart, and it felt like there was a hand reaching inside his chest, caressing his heart uncomfortably. He darted forward, but the hand never left him, still learning to know Teyerien's innards like a lover might touch his ears.

"Teyerien," a voice called.

"Who are you?" he shouted, turning in the direction of the voice which was behind him. "Show yourself!"

"I cannot be seen, and your eyes cannot pierce the veil of this darkness, little elf," the voice grew low, and a sinister sneer was behind that voice. "I cannot be seen, and neither can you."

"Who—who are you?" he stammered. His hand reached for the pommel of his sword. It wasn't there when he grasped for it.

"Carmielle has been lying to you," he said. "All this time."

"No," Teyerien replied. "Who are you? What do you want?"

"I want what was promised to me," the voice growled. "Can you not see? This forest is mine. It doesn't belong to Carmielle. She lied to you, for generations and generations. Can you not see?" the voice crept closer to him. "Can you not see?"

"No," Teyerien answered, inching away from the voice. He tried to control his breathing. "What do you want?"

"I want what is mine," the voice growled again. Teyerien felt a slimy substance touch his cheek, and he inched from that. "I want the forest that Carmielle promised to me, Teyerien. That's it."

"And what of those inside it?" Teyerien remembered the promise he swore to uphold. If nothing else, he could hold on to that.

"Did you mean the oath you took to Carmielle?" he said. "She won't keep your promise to you, she never does. I could show you what happened, and how false a deity she really is."

"No," Teyerien wiped whatever it was that touched his face again. A feminine chuckle filled the air. "No, you're lying, and I won't believe you. Whatever weapon formed against me will not prevail. Nothing of the sort!"

"An argument that gives one license to abandon rational thought," the voice growled.

"Oh," the female voice shrilled. "Look at his pants, can ye see it? He done pissed himself!"

"Terrified, trying to look dauntless in a place where you can't see anyone, or who or how many voices are speaking to you," each word this time sounded different. "I was there, Teyerien, at the forming of the world. I saw it all and the grandeur, but Carmielle took things from me. All I want is the forest as my own."

"There is a very good reason why Carmielle ate all you gods!" Teyerien snapped, slapping another slimy substance from his face. "For only she looks at us as having value. The rest of you treated us like we were toys for your own pleasure."

"Now, had ye not abandoned the path that would transcend ye into Godhood, we'd not treat ye like wee little playthings to be toyed with, now would we?" the female said.

What? He didn't understand.

"You mortals are such silly things," she said. "You eat; you sleep; you die, and most of you stark ravin' lunatics believe in an afterlife. Do ye know what? Yer souls get bound to the earth into little ghosts to be called upon by some spell caster whenever they see fit or want to commune with the dead or some other frivolous bother."

Where was he? Why was he here? What were these voices vying inside his head? Speaking such blasphemous thoughts that would no doubt get him hanged if anyone knew. But these were his thoughts? Were they? He often doubted Carmielle, and didn't have the steadfast faith Supesien had, but to be brought back here? In the confines of his mind? There was no telling what foul thing he could think of. And what of these promises? Who were these voices supposed to represent in his mind?

"And yet," the low growl voice came. "You still hold onto life, and an ideal that there is an afterlife you go to. And live forever. When in actuality—"

"All mortals have been destined to ascend to Godhood," the female voice intervened. "Wouldn't that be nice? Perhaps challenge Carmielle for Her seat? And like Her get caught in the endless struggle of life and death everlasting."

"Why would anyone want that?" Teyerien asked. Was he serious in considering his doubts?

"Because with Godhood comes power– you can do whatever you want with it. Create worlds, more worlds and cease all matters of conflict," the female said, and she touched him with a slimy substance. He didn't shy away from it this time. "Wouldn't that be nice to be molded into one of us? Would you like that, Teyerien? No more questions, when what you say is absolute."

"Risks. Risks. Risks," he put his hand to his forward as he bent his neck. Something that felt like a hand touched his belly.

"Your body is a husk," she said. "Flesh is very moveable. You're like a jar of clay, really. Why don't we break the jar, and like clay, mold your flesh? Wouldn't you like that?"

"Don't give him the option," the growling voice said. "Enough doubts causes leaps of errors."

Looking down, there was a green light floating above his belly, and it touched and weaved its essence through him. He felt an uncomfortable sensation of his flesh being removed from his body. Oddly enough it didn't hurt him. Or so it seemed as he slowly started to twist his head as the skin was being pulled away from his bones. The woman with a feminine voice showed herself. Purple skin, dark hair with blood red eyes glared at him. She touched him, caressing his cheek as she looked down at what was happening to his body. His heart raced as his feet tried to move, but looking down, it was just the muscle, and no muscles or tendons which he could force to move. He gaped open his eyes.

"Don't worry, little elf," she cooed. "Don't worry, we'll make you better. Wouldn't you like that? A nice new body, one that can allow you to take what you want?"

Her tongue caressed his cheek, before swirling into his ear. Unable to move from his stance, he could tell the tongue was snaking its way through his brain, turning it to mush as purple sludge climbed into his boot, forming the flesh around him. A muffled sound he heard as his sanity was being hurled into questioning. Another muffled sound.

"Teyerien!" a voice more clear, and a piercing cry screamed into his ear like a squealing pig.

"Manuille, put the fires out!" a voice that sounded like Eahemien's shouted.

"I told you, I told you, but you didn't listen!" a voice that sounded like Supesien shrieked.

"I'll do it," and Manuille's voice spoke with panting breath.

Teyerien opened his eyes. Lots of fires, the trees were ablaze. The smoldering embers were around, and ash rose from the ground. Sitting up with a splitting headache, he turned to his side. Here were several corpses right by his feet, and several other groans besides. Hissing himself, he looked up to Supesien who frowned at him while he prepared several bandages for the wounded. *What happened?* Eahemien hurried with medical supplies to help aid the injured while several other elves muttered something he couldn't understand, for the bells' tone were still ringing in his ears. Sitting up, he looked to his own body. Several cuts he had, and his hands were shaking with several cuts through the fingers.

"What happened?" he asked.

"Do you not know?" Supesien snapped as Manuille cast a spell to conjure water to spray at the trees. "Do you honestly not remember?"

"Supesien," Teyerien said. "I have a splitting headache. Just tell me what happened?"

"Your skin turned purple," Supesien snarled. "You laughed and cast spells. Magic you wielded with a fury I've never seen before."

"Tell me," Manuille came to him after the fire had been put out. Leaning against her staff, she stared into his eyes, as if researching some specimen. "Have you been trained in magic before?"

"No," Teyerien said. "I cannot wield it."

"The burned trees would like to differ," Eahemien shouted. "Do—"

"What?" Teyerien put a hand to his head. That wasn't possible. He had no training in the arcane, couldn't even speak or read the language. All of these things were beyond him. So what did they mean to imply? That he was a wizard among rangers? No. He simply wasn't proficient. "That can't be. Supesien, you know I don't mess around with magic."

"No," Manuille said. "You speak the truth; however, in determining the use of such proficiency to such a degree that is beyond terrifying, only someone high up on the Wizards' Council would be able to do what you've done today."

"What do you mean?" Teyerien said, the memory was still fuzzy.

"The amulet compelled you to do this," she said. "I cannot appraise the item, but I need no magic to tell me what I just witnessed."

"I told you, Teyerien," Supesien said, pointing at the dead. "This is on you. I told you! I warned you we shouldn't mess around with it. And some of our friends are dead! The trees are desecrated! Who knows about the birds and their nests."

"We needed to know—"

"Purple skin," Supesien sighed. "You've somehow gained mastery over the arcane. You became haughty, like Gergo of late. Manuille confirmed herself that the amulet originates from the Abyss."

"Teyerien," Manuille closed her eyes. "What do you remember?"

He told them everything he remembered. Everything from putting on the amulet and the dream he had. They all listened intently to what he had to say. He wondered where the amulet was. His hand stretched to his neck, and the chain was removed. His hands still trembled.

"What happened to it?"

"I ripped it off," Supesien said. "And Manuille destroyed it, speaking of such things, Manuille, can you destroy the rest of them?"

"Aye," she nodded grimly. "I can do that."

She walked away.

"Now, Teyerien," Supesien said with an unusually haughty snarl. "What are we going to do? This amulet changed you immediately. What happens when they get into the hands of the general populace?"

"I think you know," Eahemien said. "We all witnessed it. We can't let this happen. Otherwise, accident or not, the people will burn down the forest."

"You said it yourself, Supesien," Teyerien said. "We have to cut the supply off at its source."

"We don't know how long these things have been transported for. They could have made it to all corners of Kinasa, and it might be already too late," Eahemien said.

"No," Teyerien said, feeling a confidence swell through his veins he remembered not being there. "While we live, there is still hope. Supesien," he grabbed his brother's collar. "Get pigeons and send them flying to all elves on expedition and recall them immediately. Send runners to all our branches immediately and recall everyone here," he turned to his middle brother as Supesien swore and retreated into the Guild with haste. "Arrange scouting parties. Go door to door. Tell everyone. While we have time, Kerina will be warned."

He will save one remnant, if that. The oath was coming in question, and now, Teyerien knew he'd have to break part of the oath to secure the other. Would they follow through with him here? For with such great travesty came the end of all things. The laughter would fade. The honey rolls would no longer be baked, and the festivals would stop. Music was silent, and all manner of good things would be laid to waste. Even now, he struggled to find a ground on which he could ethically carry out what he just set in motion. Could he be compelled to save the forest by killing all who lived within it? Or would the forest burn into oblivion?

CHAPTER 7

Dark Elf

The Rangers of the Guild stockpiled months' worth of supplies and rations. Water, healing salves, and everyone was equipped with a surplus of them, with a stock hidden underneath the Guild Tree itself, in case the surprise simply wasn't enough. There'd be no telling when their limitation of good grace would come to its end. Teyerien walked the courtyard, seeing the fruits of his labor, and that of his brothers. Runners scoured through all of Kinasa, and Eahemien was leading the efforts to warn all the citizens of Kerina to evacuate immediately. To whatever end, and with whatever risk, the supply of the curse of these amulets must be cut off at its source.

He walked silently, thinking of Atori, Solistus, and Xelanai, unaccounted for. Well, he knew, but on paper they were missing, searching for Dorio. Likely in the north. Carmielle, why did Atori have to be far away at a time like this? She'd know what to do and how to execute it. *Damnit Yun!* He thrust his fist against a tree. *Why me? With all this, Atori was by far, not even close, a better option.* Not much he could do, except stay the course.

He'd not be alone for long, for Manuille advised she knew some wizard friends of hers who might be able to help on such short notice. After all, it was hard to research freely when the fires started roaring all around them, and the darkness of the Abyss encroached upon him. He felt empty, but clean, oddly enough, for the Amulet revealed certain parts of himself, and while still holding onto his lack of confidence, he held more of it than before. If things went according to plan, and they rarely did, he'd have the Royal Tree by a week's time. He'd remove the amulet from Gergo or have him killed.

No. Gergo must have been weak with his own insecurities to be pushed so far to make pacts with demons and devils. The supernatural often were beyond understanding, and knew the hearts of mortals, able to weave words to make them believe something they wouldn't have considered under different circumstances.

"Teyerien," came a high-pitched voice from behind him.

"Yes?" he turned, hand on the pommel of his sword.

An elf stood in front of him with the King's armor on. The emblem of the tree on the pauldron. A sword at his waist, a crossbow tied to his back. The hair was dark, just like any other elf, but the eyes were bloodshot red, and the skin was purple. One hand rested outward, and Teyerien sensed a foul arcane magic emitting from it. The dark elf smiled, and the purple skin confirmed it. Though he wasn't masked, Teyerien now understood why everyone was masked. It was to hide the color of their skin, to hide their true nature.

"The Rangers' Guild is being fined," he said. "Sorry, sorry, My name is Gorgonus, the accountant of the King."

"Heavily armored for an accountant," Teyerien said.

"Sometimes we have to wear the helm of a collector," Gorgonus smiled, offering a light bow. "You've destroyed Royal property."

"I don't know what you're on about," Teyerien frowned. "But we owe allegiance to Carmielle, and her alone. No one else. Now, if you're done bothering me, you can leave me now with your life."

"I'm afraid you misunderstand," he said, throwing one of those dreadful amulets, and it called him by name. "You don't have much choice in the matter. This is the King's forest, not the Rangers Guild's Forest. You understand that much, don't you?"

"I understand this is Carmielle's forest, not the King's." He took his sword and picked the chain with it. Wrapping it around the blade of his sword, he swung it back to the dark elf who presented it to him. "I ain't touchin' that."

"Teyerien," he said. "It is not just for the destruction of property. Do you care to explain why citizens of Kerina are leaving in droves? If you seek to undermine Gergo, that is an act of Treason."

"I swore an oath to Carmielle," Teyerien scowled. "Not Gergo. What he is doing, and yourself, is an act of treason against Carmielle, the Goddess of the elves. You may leave now or die. Your choice."

A black fire blew out from Gorgonus' hand. A sharp twang, and Teyerien threw his blade up to intercept the fire, and the steel of his blade disappeared. Heart pounding, he ducked and spun behind a tree. The cackling echoed through the forest. Teyerien took his bow, notched an arrow, and loosed one at Gorgonus, who deflected it with ease using his bracer. Another stream of black fire came, reducing several trees to nothingness, and the wisps of the forest were disappearing.

"You can come out now, little elf," Gorgonus said as Teyerien hid behind another tree. A whole lot of good that seemed to be doing. *Probably wasn't the best thing to be so far away from the Guild Hall.* "Gergo is not without his graces. Come."

"I'll serve Carmielle, thank you very much," Teyerien shouted, loosing another arrow. More black fire roared at him, and he ducked, knowing full well that a single ember touching him would kill him. That fire was dangerous, and he still didn't understand what it did, just that whatever it touched just ceased to be. It didn't even burn anything!

Suddenly convicted, he realized he was allowing the forest to burn. The first part of his oath was in question now. What was more important? His life, or fulfilling his oath? Could he keep his life and still save the forest? Were these short casualties of trees necessary to achieve that oath? And to maintain it? But his personal conviction told him to fight him head on. After all, he had one sword left. He ducked behind another stream of fire before finding solace behind a rock. Amidst wolves howling, he drew his blade so the sound of its drawing would be masked behind it.

He put his ear to the boulder, listening for the sound of the flame and ironclad footsteps as they trampled upon the forest floor, breaking twigs and sticks, crushing dry leaves. He looked forward as he felt Gorgonus' presence drawing near, and saw a rock which he grabbed and hurled, striking a tree. Immediately, he heard the flames scouring the trees. He jumped from his cover and thrust the sword at Gorgonus, who parried it with his bracer. The fire blasted near him, and Teyerien avoided the blast by flipping and kicking Gorgonus in the chin as he ran at the dark elf with his hunting knife, and they sparred, blades twanging in the air. He hurried and pushed the dark elf into the tree, bringing his hunting knife to the dark elf's throat, but he ducked. The knife was stuck in the tree.

He grimaced, taking his sword and throwing several precise strikes meant for piercing, hoping to undo some of that dreadful armor, but to no avail. Another blast of flame crashed at his feet, he danced around in a circle with great grace to avoid the flame where a crater of emptiness appeared. Grimacing at the strike of the forest, Teyerien dropped his sword and grappled with the dark elf from behind. Bending over backward, he thrust Gorgonus into the ground, head first, and he heard something crack.

Teyerien rolled and kicked Gorgonus in the face before more flames emitted from the metal itself. He took his sword and thrust it when Gorgonus rose, impaling him. He twisted the blade and pulled it out, kicking his opponent once more as he fell to the ground, bleeding. Gorgonus put his hand on his wound, panting, but a smile never left his face, and a dark aura surrounded it. And suddenly, everything went black.

He looked up and right at the echoing of the dark elf's cackling. It seemed to come from everywhere, and his fear took him. Unable to see a tree, he was caught in a snare, and who knew if the trees were there or not. If he just ran, he could run into a tree, rendering himself useless. The darkness absolute was the same hue as the flame, so he could hear it, but wouldn't be able to see where it was coming from or going to. His heart pounded and sweat beaded on his face. He turned, hearing the rattling of chains. *No!* If Gorgonus put the amulet on him, and with no one to interfere with it, it was over, and his soul would be devoured.

"What's wrong little elf? Scared? I was scared too once," Gorgonus said. "The encroaching enemies of the dark, Assassins, orcs, goblins, the wretched things. But with this, they can't hurt me now. They can't hurt anyone. Take the gift, Teyerien, take it, and you'll see just how liberating it is. Take it. He felt hands on his shoulders. "Just do it, it's okay. Carmielle won't fault you for it. After all, she gives us these things."

"Get out of my head," he turned, the blade swirling around in the black.

"Teyerien! Is that you?" a voice called from the Abyss.

"Friends," said Gorgonus' voice. "Maybe they'll be more receptive of this gift."

"It's not off—" he shouted. "No, Manuille, wait!"

The darkness of the veil shook.

"Again!" her voice shouted. Teyerien heard several other voices shouting and screaming. Unable to see where they were coming from, he wasn't sure if this darkness was a manifestation of the amulet, or just a very powerful illusion. He breathed heavily as the darkness shook again, and a bright crack appeared. He saw Gorgonus, and the spirit of him behind it, a devil in his heart. He drew his sword and impaled Gorgonus again, who shrieked as the light came in, and orange flames tore open the veil. "Teyerien!"

"Die!" he cried, twisting the blade.

The dark elf snarled, blood spilling between his lips, punching Teyerien in the face, and disappeared in a veil of smoke as the veil came undone. Teyerien panted as Manuille came for him, and he collapsed in her arms. The darkness was just like before, trying to compete for his soul. The veins of his exposure to it craved the dreariness, it craved its corruption. What was happening to him? Looking back on it, perhaps testing the amulet wasn't his best idea.

"What was that?" she asked.

"It was—" he panted. "A dark elf. The amulet. It turned me to one, you saw," he homed in his sight on the rock which landed at the base of a tree. He noticed several other wizards with perplexed looks on their faces. "We're running out of time."

"Good thing I brought friends then," she said. "Come, we need a plan then. Don't go anywhere by yourself. You're too important!"

He felt the slap hard to his face. A gentle rebuke, but a smile crept upon his lips as he looked at her. "Thanks. I absolutely needed that," he looked up with still exasperated breath and saw what looked like several hundred cloaked wizards. These dark elves were apparently very powerful with the arcane. He just hoped it was enough.

The Last Morning

Teyerien woke up with a start in his office. Creaking of wheels turned as the chatter outside died down to a dull roar. He stood, stretched, and donned his armor immediately before getting the rest of his combat equipment ready. The sun had yet to rise, and while it now could be seen with the hole in the clearing which he only had himself to blame for, the stars still shone. There was going to be no safety for anyone left inside the city, and based on reports from Eahemien, only one out of every three families took their warning seriously. Grimacing at the onslaught to ensue, he took himself outside, and glanced at the wizards fixing their morning tea, and the rangers eating their morning breakfast. Eggs and roasted chicken, who knew when they'd get to eat like that again. Or if.

"Teyerien," Supesien came to his left. "The Kings' guard came and started manufacturing their own siege weapons."

"Siege? For what?" Teyerien asked, perplexed. "We're just a guild. We've got no fortress—"

"Those siege weapons are enroute down south," Supesien said gravely. "Eahemien reported this to us. They're going South."

"To the temple," Teyerien's eyes gaped open.

"No," Supesien shook his head. "He'd not need these weapons for a temple, even one as big as that one. He intends to go further south. Zinasa."

"The other land," Teyerien shook his head to acknowledge his understanding. The arms' reach of who or whatever it was that was manufacturing this mess had grown long, and bold. And without sufficient help or warning, Zinasa might suffer the same fate. Which was why, now more than ever, they had to cut the source off: the Royal Tree. "Walk and talk with me."

The two walked through the camps, and Manuille walked with them, listening in on their plans while Eahemien was still taking account for supplies. The hue of the sky turned lighter as the sun was beginning to rise, and Teyerien hoped that if dark elves were anything like orcs, they didn't like the sun. But that darkness he felt was supernatural, what if their power and prowess with the proximity use of their magic could blot out the sun? There was no telling exactly how strong they were. Just much stronger than he was, and perhaps even strong enough to defend with ease this little band of wizards they scrounged up.

"Teyerien," Supesien broke the silence as they walked through the camp unhindered. "I have several companies enroute now scoping out the defenses of the forest to alert me of any significant change. It should be no surprise to you that there was some dissent. I straightened them out, but still. We could expect some of us not to comply with Carmielle's wishes."

"Indeed," he said. No surprise at all. It was still considered treason, and when they wrote the history books, whoever won, it would be seen as a traitorous act, no matter who read it. "It's not an easy thing to do. We've got—"

"Consider yourself lucky you have some spell casters among you now," Manuille said. "If you'd not gotten into that fight with the dark elf, they still might not have believed me. It's all we can hope for."

"And when help does arrive," Supesien said, his tone dropped unusually. He was normally in high spirits, but these last few days he certainly wasn't that. "It's almost inevitable it will be too late."

"What of the Tree's current defenses?" Teyerien asked.

"Fortunately," he touched his chin. "Many of the soldiers are out delivering these cursed objects. As such, there are only a small number of the Kings' Guard around. However, based on your report and Manuille's eyewitness account, we still need to exercise extreme caution."

"Yes," Manuille replied. "I highly doubt casting spells to craft an Abyss-like darkness is all they can do."

"And the fire, it doesn't burn," Teyerien reminded them. "It just forces something to cease to be."

"I still don't know what that means," Manuille replied. "But, that being the case, it doesn't sound like a spell that a novice would know, and I'm no novice by any means."

"So, what of the defenses," Teyerien said. "Supesien, get yer head together. You gave me a rough idea of numbers, but how many? Where are they in proximity to the Tree? Where is Gergo?"

"Apologies," he replied as Teyerien climbed atop a stump. "They are currently patrolling the streets and delivering the amulets to citizens. I've no word on how that endeavor is faring. However, Gergo, I've seen no reports of him, so we can presume him to be in the Tree."

"If only we could set that on fire," Teyerien scowled.

"Doing what we're doing is enough," Manuille said. "After all, history will not look kindly on this Guild after today."

"No," Teyerien shook his head. "It certainly won't."

And it's all my fault.

He stood at the stump, and Supesien and Manuille stood below him, looking onwards to the elves, getting ready for war. The bonfire was fading and he could see several disturbed, distraught, and terrified gazes in the crowds, such is the subtlety of war. They all knew the risks of expeditions, and it involved killing things, and creatures, but rarely did it involve things that which they've permitted their souls to accept as sentience. There was little they could do to prepare for the emotional turmoil each of their hearts were about to face, and it was only going to end in countless bloodshed and loss of life.

Kerina was just the beginning. He knew that, and while these incidents and amulets would be scattered throughout his homeland, every inch of it, he knew it was going to be far from over, even if he succeeded today. Yes, even if. Did he doubt it? Of course, he did. That was who he was, a doubter. He doubted they would succeed here, and even so, how much of the forest soil could recover from the spill of blood? The iron in it was enough to contaminate the soil, and the trees would drink from that moisture, and be corrupted.

"I know," he held his hand up high as he spoke loudly. "That this is far from what you want to do, and I know many of you are personally convicted, as I have been these last few days. I want you to know that though your hearts are breaking, mine broke first. Trust me when I say this wasn't an easy decision to make. Now, suffice this all to say, we have an oath to make, and an oath to keep. We swore," he breathed deeply, looking at those eyes. To see if anyone would dissent, and if those eyes would soften or harden, any change of any range of emotion would be welcomed. "We would protect the forest of Carmielle, and the people and creatures inside it. Now, I fear that we are coming to an impasse, and I've decided. This is one oath in two parts but now the two parts are in direct conflict with one another. We must decide. I have already decided that the forest is our priority, and it requires this to stand or else the trees will burn.

"I have seen the darkness. I've seen the Abyss, and many of you were here when I fell into madness when I put on that amulet and burned the trees. I assure you, I've no memory of that, and though what was described to me as a mastery of the arcane, I promise I cannot repeat those feats unless I wear the amulet, which we've wisely destroyed. Those amulets are being distributed to the rest of the people of Kinasa, and now I fear, will extend to Zinasa. Unless we cut it off at its source, the forest of Carmielle will inevitably burn. The source of these amulets come directly from the Abyss, and is being administered by Gergo," there was some chatting amongst friends in the crowd. Good, this was better than them just leaving, so he'd accept that much from them. "Listen, we are going to be fraught with despair, and we take it gladly as we forsake our comfort. I'm no diplomat with honeyed words that can sway or save you. You know this. And I also know that this expedition, this battle I'm ordering may seem like a jump for power, trust me, I don't want that, but without removing the King, the amulets will continue to be distributed, and with it, the power and corruption of the Abyss," he remembered the people who refused to leave. "We must give our all to this endeavor. Any and all costs will and must be paid for the forest. Yea? Come. Let us fulfill our oath, and the forest may be replenished, but it can't be replenished if there is no forest to return to. You with me?"

There was just silence. Well, he did manage expectations as to not expect such flowery language from him. Time was of the essence, and they had to move, and get prepared. Supesien requested the order and moved them in ranks. Companies departed in droves as they prepared for what many would still consider a traitorous act, for on the Royal tree would they march. There was a fine line with what his conscience dictated to be right and what was actually the correct path to take, and on that fine line Teyerien marched with them. All it took was a single person, a single reason, a single mission to light the flame of treason, and Gergo was all that rolled into one.

Manuille was no combat mage, and by his estimation, all of these wizards were proficient in spellcraft, however, they were mostly researchers pulled away from their studies to join together in a common goal, if even the motives were different. There was little telling where this morning would take them, and he took with himself Manuille, and a score of other elves. He dared not risk taking Supesien and Eahemien with him, for where he was going, it was doubtless he wouldn't see tomorrow.

Teyerien looked out from above the trees, swaying carefully in the wind. The streets of Kerina were quiet this morning, the Rangers hiding behind the trees and the bushes, prepared to strike against the king at his command, and his own host, bows poised to loose upon the dark elves should they be present. The only problem was, they weren't there, and that was enough reason to be unsettled, for they were the only thing preventing the king from death. Clicking his tongue, he climbed down from the tree, and snuck carefully towards the bridge leading to the tree. Listening intently, he heard nothing. No steps, no breathing, and no whispers. Just silence.

He walked across the bridge. Gazing up at the tree, he touched the door, and it was firm, but there was that menacing aura of corruption behind it. He'd been in this tree, and the corruption that was inside those accursed amulets permeated the air, the soil, and everything the Rangers were designed to protect, but alas, not here. This was a different forest. He heard rustling leaves behind him. He jerked to attention immediately, and his small host of elves came to him, the ones of whom were going to be with him to kill the king.

"He's not here," Teyerien reasoned. He couldn't be.

"Teyerien," a loud voice boomed from the tree. There was so much power behind it, it pushed him on the ground like a violent wind, his hair whipping behind him as he fell. Helped to his knees by Manuille, he looked up at the tree. The top of it, leaves and the branches themselves grew darker, and a black soot seemed to fall from them. "I gave you a chance, and you come upon my door armed to the teeth as if to lay me under siege. It won't work."

"Your Majesty," he hissed. "You've tried to give us something that is a curse, not a gift. You will damn this forest to the ground! Come out and put an end to your madness."

"Madness," Gergo's voice boomed. "You know nothing of madness."

"I put on the amulet," Teyerien shouted. "I saw the madness. This isn't us. Just take it off!"

"No," Gergo replied. "The amulet is the source of my power, and we'll bring it forward. I lead us into the future where we will not fear the peoples of the world."

"We weren't afraid of them!" Teyerien bellowed. "They simply didn't like us, and who would? With us meddling with their policies and procedures too often and for far too long? They just don't want us in their affairs. Sure, they may be racist over there, but there is no need to make a pact with the Abyss."

"I made no pact," Gergo said. "I am as I've always been, Teyerien, can you say the same? No, you cannot. My grace has its limits, and what you're doing is an act of high treason, punishable by death. Now, so that history will not write me as a tyrant, you may retreat back to your guild, and receive another shipment of amulets, which you destroyed. Now, go."

"No," Teyerien said. "I've seen what it did. Gorgonus showed me, and it cannot be allowed to stand. You will not rid this land of Carmielle!"

"Carmielle?" he said. "A false God."

Teyerien gasped.

Well, that all but confirmed it. The amulet fed the wearer doubts, and they weren't necessarily their own, but disguised as their own individual thoughts through allegory. Read far into it, one might start to believe the demon or monster feeding them such lies without restraint. Whatever it was, was powerful enough to pull the strings of Gergo, and the question ran through Teyerien's mind, if he killed Gergo, what then? Will he take the place temporarily, and be battered with the thoughts of the monster who undoubtedly lived in the dungeons beneath the tree? No chains are more powerful than that of the illusion of freedom. He'd seen that play out before. Once. It ended horribly for everyone involved.

"Now, take your false God out of my forest," Gergo snapped. "You and all who serve that pointless oath."

"This isn't your forest!" Teyerien pushed, hearing ironclad steps behind the door. "This forest was built by Carmielle for us specifically. It doesn't belong to you!"

"I've had enough of these petty squabbles," Gergo said. "You've made your choice, and now, I, King Gergo of Kinasa, sentence the entire Rangers' Guild to banishment, and death, effective immediately!"

The front doors were kicked open. King Gergo leaned forward on his throne in the back, and a host of heavily armored elves marched outside the door. Teyerien swiftly took his bow, loosed an arrow at the king which burned aflame as soon as it passed the threshold into the tree. Black fire shot out from one of the branches, and several arrows were fired from behind him. The fiery substance soared at him, and with nowhere to run, Manuille put her staff up, a bright white light shone, blinding the dark elves, and the flames wouldn't come into the light, just resting there as they smoldered with nothing to consume. He moved his feet off the bridge as the host of elves came out with their spears and shields, pushing their weapons forward, forcing the rangers off the bridge and into the common area of the tree. Arrows flew, and they couldn't pierce the metal hide of these elves.

What was he doing? A spear nearly stabbed him. Ducking to the side, he grabbed the shaft of it with his hand, and pulled. The dark elf broke ranks coming close to him, and with his sword, he pierced it, screaming as he echoed the cries of the creature, before kicking him to the bridge. As he was pushed back, him and his company, he saw several dark elves running from the Royal Tree in all directions, evading the arrows being fired at them from the trees and bushes. More flames came scouring at him, he jumped out of its way, and Manuille screamed as she saw the elves behind her disappear out of thin air, leaving him with only half his company left.

"Push at them!" Teyerien said. "We're of the Guild. We can take them. Manuille," he said. "Anything to support would be great!"

"I don't—" she stammered. "I don't have anything against this! I don't know what this is!"

"Teyerien," said a ranger, grunting as a spear struck his side, and he threw the spear away, and stabbed the dark elf who impaled him. "We should depart now. We can't fight out in the open like this."

"What's happening to his arm!" Manuille shrieked.

A foul stench in the air, emitting steam, came from the wound. Blood dripped from it, swiftly coagulating as it struck the ground, and the arm came undone. The ranger screamed as he took his hand and tried to patch it, only for the arms to be consumed by whatever it was that touched the blade that struck him. It wasn't long before the elf was in a puddling mess on the ground, unrecognizable.

"Fall back!" Teyerien ordered. "Get to cover, and don't you dare get struck! Find cover behind the tree, and we'll regroup."

"What are you thinking?" Manuille followed him amidst the fray of blood and violence. There was no doubt. The battle just started and it was already beginning to look like a massacre.

"We need to warn everyone," Teyerien said. *Damn you, Yun. Damn you.* He clearly was in way over his head.

CHAPTER 9

A scene of Disaster

The ground was painted liberally with blood. Teyerien ran over the bleeding and dying corpses of elves and dark elves alike. Dark elves were generously struck with arrows that made them resemble pin cushions. A fitting end as they lay by the trees, and others crawling for safety, blood streaking out from their wounds as if they were a paint brush. His heart grieved to see so many elves dead, burned or boiled, and their gear lay on the ground, lifeless as their bodies.

Metal creaked and clanked. Arrows loosed upon the twang of the bows endlessly pouring into flesh. The sound of flesh being cut open filled his ears as too was the shrieking of the dead and dying. Panting, he heard the rush of footsteps. A dark elf, unarmed, came running at him with a dagger, the bloodlust in their eyes was something that he couldn't ignore. Another verification could be made about the nature of the demon controlling all this, and it was filled with the thirst for blood, elf blood in particular. It didn't care if it was dark or wood elf, or the high elves. As long as it was an elf, it could be satisfied. He cut the creature down, and the knife fell to the ground.

He climbed up a tree, Manuille behind him. He pulled her up as she nearly fell from the branch, her cloak torn in several places. Grimacing, he looked back at the disaster, and there was nothing stopping the dark elves now, the rangers in complete disarray, fighting within themselves whether this order was right or wrong. Still, the faces they were killing were all familiar. These weren't some mindless orcs and goblins; faceless they could kill without consequences. These kills would have consequences that none of them were emotionally, or mentally prepared for. These scars would be unseen, and they would never recover.

"I need you to send out my voice," he panted.

"Understood," she nodded and cast the spell without question, a green light shone by his lips.

"Rangers," his voice boomed out so that all could hear. "Do not let them cut you. There's poison on their blades. One slice and you'll be dead in under a minute. Stay fast, and remember, Carmielle is with us! Don't let them shroud your minds with doubt!"

He looked down as he finished his message. Elves were casting spells to utilize the elements with ease. Shrouding the field with no small amount of smoke, the rangers were able to retreat, but at a cost to the caster's life, being ripped to shreds like they were a piece of meat by the much faster, feral dark elves. A cackling fire, he heard, and he looked behind him. Several balls of fire were soaring his way, and before he could do anything, he grabbed Manuille by the shoulders, and the flames struck the tree.

The temperature was hot, scalding as it neared his face, the flames scoured around them as Manuille cast a spell to protect them from the flamers, but the tenacity was too severe for her ability to protect them from all fire as it caressed their flesh, hair, and clothes. The wood on which they stood creaked and swayed. Snapping. Weightless they fell, and he collapsed to the ground, but on him, Manuille landed. He grimaced as he came to, she was still alive, and the screaming refused to stop. More trees caught fire and collapsed, but in the midst of it he heard something peculiar as he rubbed his eyes, the vision of what he was seeing more clear.

The sound of rocks falling in mud. First there was just one, and then another. And another. He saw the trees were ejecting black silhouettes in the distance as he couldn't right tell what they were, but his fear gripped his heart, now disoriented. Manuille pulled him up from the ground, slapping him across the face with a hot hand. He looked carefully at the scene still, more blood and corpses, and the screams became muffled.

"I need to get to Supesien," Teyerien said. "We work fine together."

"You should have done that first," she said, and they ran through the thicket of burning trees, and passed through the orgy of mindless violence. Now, the regular dwellers were involved, those still sane enough to know not to trust the dark elves. Women and children were running as their husbands and male mates tried to fend off the dark elves with the aid of the rangers. There was a large, organized ground of Rangers using fallen trees for cover, and hiding in the fire, striking through the flames directly. That was something Supesien had the guts to do.

He hurried over with Manuille, cutting down the unarmed, feral dark elves. Manuille cast a spell behind him that sounded like the earth shifting, and a shadow was cast over him. Looking behind, a sturdy wall of bark formed, and separated him from those that would chase him to end his miserable life. He deserved it. Carmielle knew, for this was a bastard's plan. Everyone who died tonight was on his head. The sounds of rocks in mud didn't stop, and as he neared the trees, he found several bodies on the ground, splattered, bones broken as their flesh was torn open. Screams he heard from on high, and he looked up as children, and women vaulted from the windows of the trees to their death. Their bodies splattered entirely on the ground on impact.

"Get off me ye bitch!" Supesien's unusually vulgar language filled his ears.

He followed, fearing the worst, and behind a burning log, his brother was pinned against the ground. Eahemien next to him, hand on the neck of the dark elf while stabbing with a hunting knife, blood sprayed into the fire, which the body was pushed, flailing in the heat with high-pitched shrieking. More elves were running behind the logs, loosing arrows into the fray. An armored dark elf tackled Teyerien from behind, the impact bruising his waist. Grunting, Manuille thrust the staff she had into the dark elf, knocking him on his back. Supesien's loud voice shrieked as a blade struck at the opening of the neck.

"Well, this is a bloody mess, now, innit" Eahemien said.

"Yeah," Teyerien coughed as more cries for battle came into his ears. The metal rang, and his body ached. Looking down, he saw a girl elf, severed at the impact of the tree atop her. She had chestnut colored hair, and in her right hand was a sweet roll. *Mora.* He gritted his teeth. *Meaningless. Meaningless. Meaningless. It's all meaningless.* Carmielle, there was no denying it, had abandoned them. *But why?* "Supesien."

"Yes?" he said, leaning against a burning log. The fear of him catching on fire didn't seem to concern him. "I need you to take command here and get everyone out. Leave the forest."

"The oath—"

"I think we'll die if we uphold the oath today," he said. "Live another day, but there's a plan. If I can kill the king, then I can delay them."

"But we can't get in the tree—"

"I can create a diversion," Eahemien panted. "I have an experiment; it could create a crater big enough to diverge the dark elves here."

"Yes," Supesien said enthusiastically. "You beautiful bastard, go get that device up and runnin' now. I'll arrange a retreat. We'll go to—Malitu! They still owe us."

"It's Gergo," Manuille said. "He'll suspect something."

"I don't care," Teyerien squeaked, pointing at Mora. "She was just a kid. And he killed her. I'm going to get in that Tree, find that bastard king, and kill him!"

"Do you think that would work?" Supesien said.

"It has to," he said. "It must. Manuille, thank you, but protect my brothers and the rest of the elves. Get as many out of here as possible. Let's pray, and hope Carmielle is in an amiable mood to spare those we sent as messengers."

"Understood," Supesien stood from the stump and walked, shouting orders.

"Wait," she said to him, her hand resting upon him, and a brown light glimmered on his flesh. "That comes off in two turns of the hour glass. It gives you protection against getting hit, so you should be okay getting cut. That black fire though, I doubt, so be careful."

"I will," he smiled as he ran off, looking back, he added, "Thank you."

To Kill A King

Teyerien looked at the tree, silently creeping around it. He peered through the flames of burning wood, and there were still many dark elves patrolling the forest. Counting them all, he saw a total of fifteen. Ten armored, and five of the feral dark elves that would prove problematic for him. However, the doors to the tree were wide open, and there was no adequate space for a distraction for which he could provide to get them away from the tree and slip through unnoticed. However, he also knew he had a finite amount of time at his disposal with this protective casing around him, and he needed to do something.

Clicking his tongue, he looked closer at the Tree, the soot falling down like snow onto the ground. The tree was now sick, the Royal Tree of all things was supposed to last forever, but now, disease and poison rested at the soil on which it ate and drank. Sighing, he wept silently, wiping tears from his eyes, considering the lengthy weeks he spent fighting now. There wasn't much time for anyone left, and he hoped, perhaps with a fool's hope that maybe, just maybe there was enough remnant at bay to which some form of recovery could be realistic.

He took one steady breath. The air was refreshing at least, if even the stench of foulness in the air was almost worse than the mushy pits at Cadrasar. The poison in the soil, there wasn't much left, not in the ways of purity. Good and evil, they are tangible, tonight was proof of that, but what he realized as he got his foot ready to jump into the fray, one last time, was this all became possible because this world wasn't black and white, it's far more nuanced, and was more gray. The grayness of morals is what made these things possible, and what frightened Teyerien most of all, that had he been in Gergo's place, after seeing Mora's corpse displayed on the field, would he have done any differently? He couldn't say things would be different.

He jumped off the ground. Running swiftly, he bashed into the first dark elf, a blade cut against his skin, but it didn't pierce or cut into his flesh, the poison worthless. He took his hands, choked the dark elf out before slicing his neck, warm blood drooling on his hands as a feral dark elf came, clawing at him. Dancing back, he sliced at the elf, the purple skin flayed open and the blood poured on the ground. Gritting his teeth, he avoided an attack by a spear, and cut the dark elf's neck, striking hard against the spinal column. The blade was pulled back, and he twisted his body hard for another strike, lopping the head off. The spear came free, and he grabbed it with haste, hurling it into another armored elf.

He turned his gaze towards the door and the elves in front of him made a shield wall, and the other four feral elves descended upon him. He grunted as they came at him with their knives and claws, but he ducked, and wove, permitting gentle scratches against his bark-like hide, and hurled them off the bridge as he took himself across it. One feral elf remained as it crawled on his back, took a dagger and poked his neck with it. Twisting his body, one hand on the collar bone of the creature, he hurled the body into the wall of elves, forcing them to separate. He threw himself into the fray, kicking shields with fury, growling, and screaming with his rage, he pushed past them. His blade, no doubt, dulling, he heard a snap.

The blade came free as it struck against the shield of the last standing elf. Spinning, slicing through the air, he took his hand, grabbed what remained of the blade, and stabbed the final elf with it, and Gergo was right there watching this happen. Panting, Teyerien reached for one of the spears, and approached the king with haste, with limited time to spare now, he needed to make this count. He hurled the spear through the threshold, and it burned in as it passed through the air. Grimacing, he took another blade from one of the corpses, and ran at Gergo.

Fire emitted from holes in the walls. He evaded them as the blade flames came close to his skin. His armor was useless here, though, now he thought he didn't need it, as long as he could evade the obsidian ire. Moving forward with the sword, he thrust it at Gergo who evaded the strike by phasing through the chair to his left. Another strike, another illusion, and he hurled himself, striking every which way, evading the flame that threatened to erase his existence from history. No telling exactly what it did, what the long-term effects of these flames might impart from that.

"Gergo," he panted, thrusting another blade at him. "Put an end to this, now! It's not too late."

"The battle is already won," Gergo said, evading the strike, and large black spears designed to be set up with barristers formed in the air. "You come here, and you're alone. I gave you your chance."

"And you never gave Carmielle a chance," he said, thrusting again. The spear impaled him, and the sword came free as he was propped up on the ground. He felt his muscles shredded and blood escaped his lips. Eyes gaped open as he looked at the king, his body growing cold as his blood leaked from his wound, spilling onto the ground like rain. He coughed, trying to get some breath, but his lungs seemed compressed.

"I gave her all the time in the world to fix our mistakes," he said, pacing back and forth with a scowl. "To give me a consistent heir, but no. She denied me and left me only Kora who doesn't stay in the forest for very long. I'm old though I might not look like it. Arenia might not look it either, but nevertheless, this is the path Carmielle compelled me to walk."

"That can't be—" he coughed, and blood dripped down his chin. "True. She's good. She's good if we aren't. She'd never abandon us."

Who was he trying to convince? He mentally came prepared with the expectation that he was to leave the forest, and all the elves now, as they would doubtless try to escape their cruel fate. Such a dismal state of affairs he found himself in, and even now, dying, albeit slowly, hope seemed a little too unrealistic. He was just poised there as the king walked to him, a sword in his hand, and the blade pointed at his heart, poking at it. *Just finish it.*

"Can't you see?" Gergo shook his head. "It would have been better for everyone had you taken the gifts, and those few who would have rejected it just simply perished and go silently into the night as their souls flew away. Why did you resist? Now, I fear you must die. The Rangers' Guild ran its course, and we're thankful for all your years of service, but we don't need you anymore."

"No," he coughed. "Carmielle needs this forest. It belongs to her."

"No," the blade pierced his skin. "It doesn't. Now, go to sleep."

"It will not be he who falls asleep tonight," came a voice from the shadows. Teyerien's vision was fading, but he could see a blurred vision of Gergo cautiously backing away from him, eyes investigating the room. A warm hand touched his shoulder, and the spear which held him there disappeared, and he collapsed into the arms of a person, whom he didn't recognize. "Gergo, what happened to you?"

"What happened to me?" Gergo said. "Carmielle left this forest, Marelo, you can feel it can't you?"

"I didn't ask what happened to her, I asked what happened to you," Marelo replied. His hand touched Teyerien, and he felt rejuvenated as his muscles stitched themselves together. "Teyerien, you must go. Go with your brothers and lead them out of this forest."

"Who are—" he coughed, feeling his strength returning. "You?"

"I'm the prophet," he answered. "I'd love to answer your questions, but I have a teacher to contend with, now go! Carmielle healed your wounds and aches, you can make it out of the forest but do not delay!"

Teyerien wasted no moment. He didn't know the prophet, but one did not claim that status lightly, and with his elven strides he fled from the royal tree, hearing nothing short of high-pitched creaking of wood, fires cackling, the emission of spells being cast with reckless abandon, but he wasn't going to be caught unawares. Not like this, after all, he earned the right to live to fight another day, and alas, one half of the oath was broken, while the other remained. Just, perhaps not the half he intended to keep.

CHAPTER 11

The Dawn of Forest Black

Teyerien ran as the light from the sun faded to dark and the grasshoppers didn't chirp. The owls didn't hoot. The wisps stopped shining and all that remained for him to remember his way was a little light in the distance, torches shining through the silhouette of trees and caravans, and countless humanoids littered the landscape ahead of them, running at a breakneck pace, and several archers at the rear, advancing slowly behind the caravan. His feet crashed into the ground, hard, as he pushed off it, and moved into the tree line, weaving through the bush.

"Identify yourself or I'll impale you into a grutting tree!" Supesien's harsh voice echoed through the trees.

"It's me!" Teyerien said, panting through the trees until his face shone through the light of a nearby torch.

"You're alive!" Manuille exclaimed, running to him, observing the break in his armor. "What happened?"

"You did it? Did you actually kill the King?" Supesien put both hands on his shoulders as he pushed her aside.

"No," Teyerien panted, looking into his brother's eyes. There was a darkness about them, a subtle hatred inside those orbs that wanted nothing more than to enact vengeance on the dark elves for invading and stealing their home. That's what Supesien likely believed, and since they had no evidence, no firm evidence that provided a basis for Teyerien's hypothesis, it was as good a reason as any to suspect the natural decay of the mortal's flawed bodies and spirits. "I was saved and spared by the prophet of Carmielle."

"What did he say?" he jerked his shoulders. "Teyerien, speak. What did the prophet say?"

"He healed me," he said. "I'd have certainly died, but we need to keep going, or else they might catch up with us."

"How much further now?" Eahemien said.

"Just ten more miles, just ten, until we've reached the natural brush of the forest's end," Supesien said. "Look, let's not tarry much longer. Teyerien, can ye run?"

"Yes," he said. "I've still got some stamina left in me. Let's get out of here."

Teyerien let Supesien have control of the caravan. The last thing he wanted to do was lead. Anything to keep him occupied was more than welcome. He didn't want to hear bows stretching. No metal clanking. No screaming. No cries or grunting. No sounds of bodies falling from dangerous heights to the ground. Just silence, that was what he needed after this long ordeal of failure. Yun never should have trusted him. But what could or would he have done differently? He wasn't so sure.

A sudden dread came over him, and it felt like a piece of wood was impaled in his chest again. Looking down, nothing. Just an enormous emotional weight as they approached the forest wall of Kinasa, departing the land he swore to protect, but failed. But perhaps the people in the land would be safe, and needed no more protection from the Guild, and effectively, this Guild had been disbanded. Looking back as he passed through the forest floor, he noticed the green leaves turning black, and his foot felt a sharp pain in it. Tripping, he rolled onto the ground as his blood painted the way on the ground to this road towards Malitu, and he looked at the trees as the blades of grass were literal blades in the ground. And his blood kept them satisfied, as the trees, the birch, the oak, the pine turned black. A leaf fell at his feet, striking the ground like a comet, and he turned immediately to run behind Supesien.

"I don't understand what's happening," Teyerien said. "The forest—"

"It's dead," Supesien said, wiping a tear from his eye as he wept. "It's dead. The forest is grutting dead."

"Dorio?" Eahemien called from one of the wagons. "Dorio, it's Dorio. Where the Hell have you been?"

"Atori!" Teyerien saw the paladin covered in blood, and Atori was dead in his arms. So soon, he'd tried to return to Kinasa to bury her, most likely. "Dorio, speak! Where is Solistus and Xelanai?"

"I don't know," the paladin spoke gravely. "What happened to the forest?"

"Carmielle abandoned us," he said. "You, come with us, we'll bury her somewhere suitable, but away from here. I just—I can't right now."

"But she needs to be buried in Kinasa!" Dorio shrieked. "It's my fault. I'll see it done."

"The blades of grass will cut right through yer boots," Teyerien replied. "No, our custom is to bury in Kinasa, but Kinasa is no more." Teyerien gritted his teeth and pointed at him. "Perhaps if She hadn't gone out to find you, then she would have advised me right! Dorio, add her death to the list of debts you owe!"

BLENHEIM

Gordir

ordir looked at the road from atop the wagon leaning back, reins of the horses firmly in his hands. His wife next to him, inclining her chestnut-colored hair on his shoulder. His two children, Murine and Sarine, snored carelessly in the back with their rations and waterskins as the horses kept clopping forward, the wooden wheels creaking on the well tilled highway leading them north. The crickets were singing, a woodpecker striking a nearby oak tree, and some other birds chirped as he continued riding through this diverse fauna.

He was rather excited, though. Corela, a temple city, seemed far enough away, where he would see some family. Coming from the farmland of Zinasa's Crenshin, he didn't come to Kinasa very often, least of all with his high-born family and his wife who was a distant niece of King Crillion. But here he was, nearly dozing off, and his head rested atop Zarin's gorgeous head. He married well, even if her family didn't much care for him.

Clicking his tongue, he paid little attention to any shadows moving along the road. This was a rather peaceful part of Kinasa. Well, Kinasa was never known for violence or bandits *within* its borders. Most travelers could expect to get from one end of the forest stretching hundreds of miles in all four directions without incident.

"Papa," Murine groaned in the back. "Are we there yet?"

"No." Gordir smirked, tapping his son's head. "Not yet. Still a long ways away now. Go back to sleep."

"But I'm hungry," he said.

"Don't eat too early," Gordir replied. "It isn't good for you. Go back to bed for just a little while longer. I'll stop at the next clearing and we can make breakfast."

"Okay!" Murine exclaimed, and he snored almost immediately.

"Dear," Zarin said, yawning, a hand covering her mouth as her eyes fluttered open. "We really should find someplace to stop. You're tired."

"I know." He kissed the top of her head. "I'll rest with breakfast."

"See that you do." She patted his shoulder. "I'll take the reins when you sleep. It'll be fine."

Seeing a clearing, he steered the horses into it. He covered his gaping mouth, and Zarin got the children up as he started a fire, grabbing sticks and dried up leaves. A metal slab was placed above it, heating up, and then they put some eggs on it for cooking. He procured some logs on which they could all sit amiably.

With a fork and stick, he cooked the eggs. His children were still rubbing the sleep with their eyes when they sat with plates.

"Can you tell us about Auntie Mar?" Sarine asked, a hand covering her face.

"You've never met her," Gordir said, tiredly. "Trust me when I say she has the voice of a siren. Much less dangerous, of course. She is a kind person, much like your mother."

"Oh," Zarin cooed. "Please, Gordir, sing me more praise, will you?"

"I'm afraid if I did, the birds would stop chirping." He smirked, serving his children first. "After all, you know, that when I sing it moves people and creatures. Usually in the opposite direction."

His children broke out in laughter, and he served a portion to his wife, who took it with gnarled lips. Shaking her head, he couldn't help but wonder if he offended her in some manner. No, there was no wondering about it. He certainly overstepped something, which ought not to have been stepped upon. Before he could open his mouth to apologize, she put her fingers to his lips to shush him.

"Gordir." She frowned. "What am I going to do with you? All I want is some praise, is that too much to ask?"

"No." He took the fingers from his lips. "This is what happens when I don't get too much sleep."

"Of course," she shrilled. "And who's fault is that?"

"Mine," he admitted, looking to his eggs.

"Honestly. . ." She brought her voice to a whisper as the children kept eating their breakfast. "Try to be respectful to us when we meet your sister, eh? I don't want to have to explain in detail my disgrace for marrying you."

"Oh." He put his hand to his chest. "That hurt."

"Well, so will this." She flicked his forehead.

"I hate it when you do that!" he jeered.

"Well, be better." She smiled. "Now—"

She was interrupted by neighing. Gordir jerked his head immediately to the horse, heart pounding as a sound echoed through the forest as both horses jerked their bodies, hoping, trying to be released.

Several bolts struck the horse's neck, and it collapsed. Gordir turned from the direction of the attack and more shadows moved behind the trees. More noise and the other horse fell. His children screamed, hiding behind a rock.

"Run!" He seized a rock and hurled it hard against a tree.

His children and his wife scurried behind the wagon. More bolts flew, and Sarine was struck, bone snapping as she fell to the ground. A high-pitched scream echoed through the forest as he darted past her, pulling her up with firm grasp. He hoisted her up as he sprinted. Zarin grabbed Murine, and they ran at a breakneck pace.

"I swear, Gordir, who did you rip off this time? And when will you stop?"

"I haven't done that in decades! Damnit. Murine, cover your ears!" he growled with the strides he took to place the pursuers far behind him, but nevertheless, it didn't stop the bolts from flying, nearly hitting his own ankles.

"Papa!" Sarine whined. "The horses. Bel and Far. They're—"

"Dead," he said. "Now, quiet now as—"

His foot hooked a rope, and he tripped. Twisting his body, he landed on his back, Sarine atop him as she shrieked. A grunt escaped those lips as he looked, a weighted net was hurled from the trees.

Footsteps followed, and he heard his son screaming his head off, and Zarin was calmly trying to soothe him. They were all caught in the net. Peering through it, he pushed on it, but the weight was too heavy for even him to lift. *My family.*

Several shrouded people stood over them. One carrying no small amounts of weighted chains, and barbs. Part of the net was lifted, and his wife and son were dragged out, shackled immediately as they were tied to a tree securely, both whimpering with great dread. He observed the ground as he could, and he found a rock, taking it with the palm of his hand, he concealed it. The net lifted, and he bolted upright, taking the elf who did by the collar and smashed his face in with the rock. Another tried to restrain him, but he pushed him on the ground, his daughter shrieked.

Warm blood coated his face. In a rage, he screamed. One rock hurled, and someone grappled him, flipping him on the ground. He heard a snap, and he knew. He'd had it done before. His shoulder popped out.

Ignoring it, he tripped the elf who tried to grapple with him and leaned onto him before caving his skull in with the rock.

"That's enough," a female's voice said. "Now, put the gruttin' rock down!"

He turned.

"Papa!" his children cried in unison.

"Sarine!" Zarin finally wailed.

Sarine was held up on a limping leg, a knife to her throat and tears streaming down her face. Her body shook as the knife was firm, pressing against the flesh, and a shadow loomed over the blade as the indent pressed into it. But not hard enough to draw blood. Not yet. The elf glared at him, seeing her dead comrades on the ground, and a snarl upon her lips.

"Drop. The. Rock!" she said. "Or I'll spill her blood on the ground, water the trees with it. Is that what you want?"

"Don't hurt her!" he shouted, standing.

She jerked Sarine at the sudden movement. The break at the ankle swiveled, and she shrieked. No doubt, the pain was unbearable for her. His heart jolted as he took a hand out; the bloody rock shook. He knew not where these elves came from. This land simply wasn't known for its bandits. Did it change?

"I said drop the rock!" She rotated her head to the shadows. "Drop the rock, or I'll kill all of 'em! Now! One. Two. Th—"

"Wait," he said, putting the rock down. "Don't hurt them."

"There," she sneered. "See, that wasn't so hard now was it? Hurry, shackle him!"

Hands grabbed him, and his wrists and ankles were tied to with iron clasps, weighed so he couldn't move so regularly. The elf who threatened his daughter tied her with the iron clasps, and they put them together in a line. Honestly, tying Sarine wasn't necessary. She couldn't run if she wanted to. And the poor girl certainly wanted nothing more than to run and never enter this forest again.

Gordir was firmly pinned against an oak tree as the group of shrouded individuals walked down along the line, speaking with one another in a dialect he knew not.

"I'm liking the male," the female who seemed to be leading this group said. "Strong, built like an ox. Perhaps fetch a nice price in the games."

"Nah," said another. "He's too strong. We should at least make him play our little game and cast bets on him in our name. After all, it's only fair since he killed some of our own."

"Yeah," another replied. "The disrespect."

The female chuckled, pointing to Sarine. "Take a look here, see what goes on with this ankle. Can it be mended?"

A shrouded man took Sarine's ankle. She shrieked leaning into the page. Searching through his tools, more blood seeped on the ground. Gnarled his lips, he gazed at the woman, and shook his head.

"Nah, the bolt came in, shattered, which turned the bone in 'ere to dust," he said. "She definitely don't walk the same."

"Well, she's grutting useless," the female said, walking over, and she cut Sarine's throat open. Blood poured out, and the body convulsed as if seizing

"No!" Zarin shrieked. "No! Why would you do that? She's just a child!"

"You!" Gordir growled, trying to break free from the chains.

"Oi!" said a male elf. "Don't go about doin' that! Have some respect for the chains you twat!"

"I'll kill you!"

"While the father is screaming incoherently, can we even use the boy?" she caressed her chin.

"No," another female elf said. "We can't use him. Too weak, and not strong enough for anything we'd use him for. It would be more costly to keep 'im around."

"Well. . ." She shook her head. "Two down, then, one more."

"Don't grutting touch him!" he spat. "Don't you touch him."

"Oh?" she said, walking to him. "I'm not going to touch him; I'm going to kill him. It's as simple as that really."

"Don't do it," he pleaded. "I'll do whatever you want. Just don't kill anyone here! Please. Please. I'm begging you."

She touched his cheek and smiled. There was a certainly mother-like quality about those eyes that made this all the more unsettling. Hairs standing on ends, and fear gripping his heart, he fought the possibility that he'd lose his entire family in a single night. His hands trembled, weighted, and tied.

"It's okay," she said. "It's okay. Look, this isn't personal at all. You shouldn't think about it like that. And it's just a little trade, when you think about it," he gasped as she continued to speak. "You just killed some of my friends, I'll kill some of yours. It's only fair."

"Do—don't do this," he stammered.

"I've changed my mind," she said, glowering at him, and she touched his abdomen. "I'm reasonable. I won't kill him."

Gordir let out a sigh of relief. She turned her head and pointed at an elf with neatly combed air. "Lithwe, you do it!"

"What?" he shrieked. "But you said—"

"Good friend," she sneered back at him. "I said *I* wouldn't kill him. I said nothing of anyone else. Besides, even if you did decide to consider, or take into consideration the nature of the world we're in, I'm just lying to you."

"Damn you." He looked to his son, and struggled with the chains again. No avail as the elf slit his son's throat and his wife wailed.

"Breed more girls next time," she suggested. "That was our arrangement after all."

"Gordir, what did she say!"

"I don't know who this is!" he shouted. "I'm going to cut you open. I'll do it. And make him watch!"

"I don't have enough time for bickering now." She sighed. "I've wasted enough time. Gordir was it? Well, I'm going to have fun playing with you." She walked away from him, and turned to his wife, chained, and shuddered as she touched her cheek. "We need to make sure we can recoup our investment. Miss, are you fertile?"

"What does that have to do with anything?" his wife spat.

"For starters..." She wiped the spit from her eyes. "You can be a servant slave girl like the rest of them, but such a physique like yours simply would be wasted on menial tasks. A specimen like yourself only comes around so often, and they produce great offspring when paired with the right seed."

"I'll not answer," she snarled.

"Well," the woman snarled. "We have ways of finding out, don't we, Lithwe?"

"Yes." The male elf winked at his wife. "There's time plenty enough for that."

"See it done," she ordered. "These two in the wagons! On to Blenheim we go!"

Blenheim? That was much further north than he intended to go, and certainly was much higher than his sister's abode. Oh, Carmielle, he just hoped she was okay. He was used to misery, and his wife, as he was shackled and put into a carriage which concealed the contents inside from the outside view, he was entrapped in it. Zarin was placed in another carriage, and the horses neighed as he, their commodity, were shipped off to Blenheim.

CHAPTER 2

Torment

Gordir woke up, eyes blurry as he stared at the ceiling, and he turned to his left. An uncomfortable stone slab was what he laid his back on, and a pillow, which was as comfortable as a rock. Gritting his teeth as he bent his back forward to sit up, he swayed his legs to the side of the cold floor. His lips were chapped, and the bars kept him locked inside. There were people and railings on the other side of it.

To the left of his bed was a steaming pile of Djit: his Djit to be precise in this cramped cell. And its stench was foul. He didn't know how many djits he'd taken since he'd been here. At least once a day, and flies were buzzing, maggots were crawling through it. At least someone was enjoying his captivity.

He rubbed the sleep from his eyes, walking closer to the cage. The rusty bars were rough to the touch as he got a better view and listened. Iron straps of chains rattling on the stone ground, roars of various creatures. Some he could determine: lions, coyotes, wolves, and hyenas, and there was another one, much louder but no such critter he recognized. Grimacing, he looked to the other side of the hole in the ground before him. Two sets of rails, more cages with people inside it. Elves, men, dwarves, orcs, goblins; whoever these traffickers were, they didn't discriminate.

He heard the sound of feet from his left. Two heavily armored men dragged a body. *Zarin!* Her hair was a mangled mess, ringlets raining down. Her body was bruised and cut and beaten. She seemed almost lifeless as she looked onwards, and her skin was laid bare for all to see. She panted, and her head tilted with a sudden jerk, and he saw the mess on her face. He gasped, but she didn't speak.

"Zarin! Zarin! No," he said. "No. Answer me!"

An iron clad fist struck the bar.

"Oi!" he snapped. "She's trying to sleep, ye know. Let her rest."

"Good little elf don't know what good for 'im," said the other. "Shut up and let her rest. Rest is all ye ever need, now. Don't let it go slip away."

"I'll—"

"You've been shoutin' ye we'e gonna kill us for months now," said the first. "Well, we's alive, and so a'e ye? What yer waitin' for?"

"He's waitin' fer a sign, he is," the other said. "Trapped in a cage. I'm surprised they not let him out yet."

"Hey, you two," came a sly voice, more well-spoken. "Get her chained back up now. Don't dawdle, and don't grutt around with the merchandise!"

"Sir," they said, and continued to drag Zarin up some stairs and into a room behind a large glass window, with others.

Chained next to them they were all bare. Their bosoms and other parts of their bodies were laid out on display as men dressed richly looked upon them.

Gordir bit his lip, anguished with anger, and the ire he felt towards those who controlled this place, and those who funded it through their illegal market. If he could, he'd have burned this place to the ground with everyone in it. Consequences be damned.

More steps came by his cell, and the elf who killed his son let out a sigh and leaned against the railing casually. Taking out a pipe as he panted just a tad, he looked over the railing. Gordir's anger burned against him, and everything *he* stood for. This elf would die. He would see to it personally. The how? Well, he had to plan that, and had to be released from his cage. But that wouldn't be easy, not with his strength waning. Lithwe crumpled up herbs in his pipe and lit them aflame before putting it in his mouth.

"You know somethin'," he said. "After all this time, I still didn't get your wife's name."

"Grutt off!" Gordir spat. "I'll find my way out of this cage, and I'll kill you!"

"My, my." He grinned, looking back at him. "Aren't we the feisty one this mornin'? What's it been now, Gordir? Two months?"

"I can't tell the time here," he snarled. "I've no way of knowing."

"Right, right," Lithwe said casually. "There's no sun out here. Just the stack of Djit over there. You really should do something about that, ye know? This is a respectable establishment."

"I don't have cleaning supplies or where to put it," he said. "Unless ye'd rather me just huck it across the hole, at yer pissant guards and—"

"Guards?" he tilted his head. "Or, Gordir, ye must have a little more respect than that. These aren't just your run-of-the-mill bandits here. You can't trust an operation of this size to the likes of them, no, of course not."

"Gah! You pissant!" Gordir said.

Lithwe scowled. "You know, I've been nothing but nice to you. It's Miura who can be a huge bitch." He shook his head, puffing out smoke through his nose. "My sister always did have more of a sadistic streak than I did. Come on, there's no need for—"

"Grutt you!" Gordir spat at him.

"Come on." Lithwe wiped the spit from his eyes. "We're all friends here. We just need to see past our little differences."

"You're no friend of mine," Gordir growled. "What friend—"

"You produced children, that means one thing," Lithwe sneered, puffing out more smoke. "And well, I happened to be copulating with her for the last two months. Now, sadly, no bump in the belly. We shared something special, you and I."

Gordir gritted his teeth, and his hands clenched into fists at his side. He punched the bar repeatedly. Banged on it till his knuckles bled.

The bastard.

He'd kill him. Lithwe raped his wife, admitted it, and used it as some real reason to establish any sense of brotherly bond in a world, in a place that didn't make sense.

Kinasa. Exactly how far have you fallen?

There was no telling the depths of depravity it ended up in. There were parts of the law which Kinasa was known to uphold, but nothing about the last two months of his miserable life was upholding that perception.

"Easy, now," Lithwe spoke rather warmly still. "Wouldn't want you to get bruised up too easily now." He whistled. Metal clanked closer. "You said you wanted to kill something right?"

"I'm going to kill you, and everyone inside th—"

"Of course you do," Lithwe sneered. "I think you've been in here long enough, now, how's your sword arm?"

"Sword?"

"Yes." He chuckled as heavily armored soldiers came in with keys rattling in front of his face. "Well, time to release some of that pent up anger, and then you'll understand how things work properly around here. We thrive on order, and you can really only have that when everyone's in agreement. Hell, you're gonna love this, I'm gonna give you a sword too! Just makes the murder a little easier, a bit more pleasant I'm sure you'd agree. Not as barbaric as a rock. Afterall, we're civilized here."

The doors opened, and the guards came in, restrained him to the ground and tied his wrists together with ropes. Chains he was embraced with, and like a dog, leashed as Lithwe pulled him from the restraints and led him several stairs downward. Faintly, he heard the roars and screams grow louder, some of which were so visceral, it sounded like someone just had their chest cut open. An interlude between the horrific sounds there were, and yet, there seemed to be applause. Was there a crowd? Was he being led to a stadium of sorts?

He came to a large iron clad door. Lithwe smiled as he went to it and opened a side door beneath it. Gordir, disoriented, was thrust into the room, and there was a wide array of weapons. The guards came in and pulled the chains off him, undoing the shackles, and they gave him a sword before exiting the room promptly. His face turned to Lithwe, who was behind the door, one hand about to close it.

"Down that tunnel there." He pointed with that grin on his face. "Is the exit. Go in there and have fun with the killing spree. It's all good fun. Do us all a favor and make it entertaining. I've got a lot of gold riding on you, and perhaps, if you're a little good, I'll reward you with a pleasant little treat. Good luck!" He slammed the door, creaking shut.

He followed the directions down the tunnel. No armor, no shields, just weapons, but he could only carry one, and this sword was just a broad sword, but it was weighty, perhaps crafted by the dense steel of the dwarves. He walked down the corridor, his hands touching the walls as his body departed from the light, and into total darkness. He came to a door, and his hand pushed against it, locked, but there was a grate, and he slid it open to look outside.

This was a stadium with a long brown hide, and atop them, the crowd filled with so many seats. Gargantuan tunnels coming every which way, and there were numerous people making bets with their own coins over the contestants, not that Gordir under normal circumstances would have volunteered himself for entry. Lots of cheering, and it appeared that there were several doors, identical save for differing sizes, the larger ones he imagined was where the lions were.

Would he kill a lion? Or would he kill someone like him, caught and enslaved to be put on as a spectacle for some twisted entertainment? No. He wouldn't give them the satisfaction of a good entertaining fight.

"Well now," said a high-pitched charismatic voice. "Ladies and gentlemen, I implore you to consider just one more round. One more round, will you? For this fight is going to be very jarring, when you consider the stakes involved. Will you side with the enraged barbarian? An elf with no shortage of a temper, bathing in his own Djit for months now and appeared none too concerned with personal cleanliness! Family wrought and pulled from an equally grim place a league south of here. Gordir, his name, and with his name comes no shortage of tragedy. Will he survive the round and move on to the next for tomorrow?"

The door slid open, and a bright light blinded him. He walked forward, hands covering his eyes, nearly stumbling forward, but the sword remained firm in his hand as he searched his surroundings.

This stadium was sufficiently bare. And there wasn't much in the way of obstacles.

How in Carmielle's precious name did Lithwe expect him to make this fight entertaining? He wasn't a barbarian. He was a farmer! Well, after he gave up his status as the king's personal guard, why? To be with Zarin!

The phrase, "Meaningless, meaningless, meaningless, everything is meaningless," was becoming a little too realistic and appropriate for his circumstances than he'd have liked to admit.

The crowd shouted his name. Blushing at the attention he never wanted, he took his fighting stance as he prepared for the other doors to open, and for the announcer, who stood high on a stone platform in the center, with no discernible way up or down. He wondered how he might have gotten up there. Perhaps the ground itself was a maze of mechanisms that moved, capable of shifting the terrain. That could prove problematic.

"Or will you side with the lovely little girl?"

The words felt like a hammer to his heart as he remembered Sarine. He couldn't save her. The guilt would haunt him for the rest of his days, as a daddy who simply couldn't protect his children. Even he, of all people, was unable to protect the lives of those so young and vulnerable. How could any story speak highly of him?

"Pulled all the way from Kenderhell, a dismal place. The citizens starve there as they await help from the king who would not help them. We offered her food and water in exchange for this. That and some trafficking of her parents. May they rest in pieces. Her name is Mar."

More cheering.

The other door opened. A little girl came out. Tunic and trousers were nothing but rags as her back faced him, dragging a sword much too heavy for her scrawny figure. How old was she? Humans aged differently, but not like this. She couldn't have seen more than thirteen summers.

She grunted and cried, whining like a little child, and the people shouted, "Mar. Mar. Mar."

"Mar," the announcer said. "You are the underdog here. Do play your part well. And with that introduction, I bid you place your bets! You'll be not displeased with this state of affairs! Remember to purchase the finest mead your lips ever did taste!"

Gordir looked closely at the girl. Her frame was small, and while it was apparent she couldn't wield the sword she was given, the expression on her face spoke volumes. Terror. Isolation.

What was there for her? In which case, the world being so cruel as he was once sheltered to think, what left? Misery? Would she continue fighting in these games?

Or was this just thrown together so Lithwe could torment his soul further?

Gordir felt a pain strike his heart as he remembered the knife slitting his daughter's throat. The people who brought them here treated others unlike them with the same contempt. He gritted his teeth as the bell rang, and the girl inched closer to him, the sword dragging in the ground. Scowling, his hand gripped the pommel of his sword.

She threw her shoulders, and the blade lifted off the ground. Shaking in her grasp, he pivoted with ease, avoiding an attack on him. A cry of frustration left her lips as the sword struck the ground, and she backed away from Gordir, who made no attempt to move against her.

Shaking his head, he heard laughter from the seats of the stadium. Turning to them, he saw several making what he imagined to be snide remarks. He swore under his breath, and she looked at him again.

"You'll have to do better than that, Mar." The announcer chuckled. "After all, Gordir won't stay tame for long. He is a barbarian after all."

"Please mister," Mar stammered. "I don't—I don't wanna die. I don't wanna die!"

No one ever did. But what remained of her after this? Say she killed Gordir, or at least seriously maimed him, what would that do for her? Lead the way for more misery, whether it be another game with someone with the will that was beyond Gordir's comprehension at the moment. She had no future here. There was nothing he could do any differently that led to Mar having some semblance of a happy ending to her horrible life.

For the victims of trafficking, those select few who escaped were never the same, and were only ever happy while eating hallucinogenic mushrooms.

She struck at him again as a tear escaped his eye. He parried with ease, and she staggered backwards. The tip of the sword struck clumsily to the ground. She stood as sturdy as she could, and prepared another pointless, feeble strike. More cheers in the back. These bastards. These grutting lunatics!

I'll kill them all.

"Oh, the barbarian's toying with the little girl now," the announcer jeered. "Come on and finish it then. Ye haven't got all day, now have you?"

"I'm sorry," he whimpered.

"Mister, stop!" she cried.

He walked right to her. She threw another strike at his head. He ducked. Her body turned too far, and he heard a snap. Her scream pierced his ears as his blade entered her back, blood dripping on the ground as the little child let go of her grasp on the hilt of the sword and it clattered. Gritting his teeth as he came to the realization that he murdered a child, allowing it to sink it, he shrieked loudly like the barbarian they called him. Not out of some battle cry, or a wail of victory.

"And we have our victor," the announcer cheered.

The people stood up and gave him a range of applause.

"Gordir the Barbarian, you get to move forward. Congratulations!"

But did he want to move forward? He didn't.

His hands shook as guards came and pulled him off the stage without warning. They shackled him intently. They brought him a room where there was running water and forced him under. The liquid was cool as it touched him, but running over the water wasn't cleaning away his guilt. They cleaned the blood off with clothes. R

Removing his tunic and trousers, they threw him back in the cell, naked and bare. He gritted his teeth in anger. They locked the door behind them.

"Come on, Gordir," Lithwe's voice said, and there he was leaning against the rail with a grin upon his face. "It's all in good fun. You had fun, right?"

"What sick twisted demon from the Abyss did you get your pact from? Who finds enjoyment in this?" Gordir threw himself against the cell, his face between two bars. "You're—"

"Well, by the round of applause you've earned, I think you know. Besides. . ." Lithwe put one hand out nonchalantly. "We don't really need a god to be cruel to others, now do we? We do that well enough ourselves without interference from the divine or the accursed. Though, we'll never say no to a little help."

"I'm going to cut out your innards," he screamed.

"Based on my understanding, you've been shouting those same lines for the last two months." He sighed. "You had your chance to cut out some innards, and you elected just stabbing her would do." Lithwe clicked his tongue. "Well, all of us are very much alive, and thanks to you not killing us due to your noble lineage. Yes, yes, we know who you are, who your wife is."

"Don't you dare touch—" he began.

"I'm afraid it's late for that." He laughed. "While ye were busy trying to avoid killing poor little Mar," he bent forward. "I was a little preoccupied to enjoy your performance by attempting to put a baby inside her. After all, we can't just let royal breeding sows go to waste. Their offspring fetch us pretty prices."

"Lithwe," he growled.

"Oh." A sharp pressure was pressed against his heart.

Looking down, Lithwe had struck him gently with the sharp tip of a rapier."

I seem to remember promising a reward for you if you were good, didn't I?" He whistled, and the sound of clanking approached. "Get on your bed now. This doesn't have to hurt anymore."

The doors were opened by heavily armored guards, and while he was still nude, he was beaten. Metal hands punched his limbs, and shins, and he screamed as the pain was like fire touching his body. The metal was cold, and he could smell the Djit. That was the only thing pleasant right now, and his head struck the slab, warm blood caressing down his face.

While on the ground, he was kicked repeatedly, and he heard a crack in his ribs. His body shaken as the kicking stopped. His eyes gaped open as his torso touched the cold floor.

"I told you this didn't have to hurt," Lithwe's voice came, and the sound of boots approached him.

Gordir gritted his teeth as he felt warm bare flesh touch his back, gasping.

"No," he cried. "No. No. No!"

"Yes," Lithwe said, tongue licking the blood off the side of his face. "Yes. Yes. Yes."

CHAPTER 3

Blenheim

The five elves walked down the path with their horses carrying a variety of equipment. The birds chirped and sang in the afternoon, the leaves shielding their path from the sun. Yun's hand touched the reins of her horse, Litho, and she pet his cheek as they continued to walk forward. There was some silence, of which she was thankful, and now being on the road, there wasn't much pain left in her abdomen from being cut open. Not paying attention to the days as they traveled, she couldn't remember how long ago it was since that was.

Staring over, Lorana and Yurilo were getting along quite well. She was still nervous with the prospect of traveling with someone from the Assassins' Guild. However long it was since his separation, there was always the risk they were working for someone behind the curtains that would make their journey all the more hazardous, whether anyone wanted that or not. Yara was scanning the trees for danger.

Good. Be vigilant at all times. Who knew when someone might try to attack them? Kinasa was a safe haven for elves, the likelihood of them running into trouble was very low. Though not zero. Those pesky roots in the ground always had a way of trying to sprain an ankle.

Anaergienne was silent. His common attire wasn't going to bring attention to him. That was good. For his sake. Though she found it in her to be kinder and sympathetic, knowing that his exile wasn't his fault. However, there were things he could have done that would have made the transition smoother, even if he had to leave overnight, which is exactly what he did. Some might recognize his face, but this far down south, further away from the land of Cadrasar, they wouldn't know what he looked like.

"Anaergienne." She waved him over. "Come here."

"Why?" He turned his head. "So, you can slap me again?"

"Anaergienne, you galook!" She frowned. "If I wanted to slap you, I'd come over there and do it."

"Fine," he said, not breaking his pace, he walked over to her.

"Now that I think about it. . ." She touched her chin, looking at the leaves in the trees. "It would save me some extra effort if you came to me so I could slap you whenever I felt the need to."

"Did you often slap him?" Lorana asked, tilting her head. "I find that to be quite barbaric. Carmielle wouldn't approve."

"Well. . ." Yun touched her chin. "Anaergienne always does things that deserve a good slap. It's not like it's one and done either." She noticed a thin smile on his face. "It's a consistent pattern of behavior."

"If you treated him kindly," Lorana offered. "He might be a little more receptive to this pilgrimage we have going on. Corela, it's not far off, now, is it? It's been at least a century since I've been this far south."

"Well, if I needed your opinion," Yun hissed. "I'd have asked."

"Yun," Anaergienne said.

"Shut up." She slapped him. Admittedly, there was no reason for it.

"Forget I said anything." He rubbed the wound. "Now, was there a point to this?"

"The silence was discomforting, so I removed it." She smirked. "Besides, we're getting close to Blenheim now."

"Where did ye say ye two were off to?" Yara finally said, addressing the wizard.

"We need to solicit help from Anaergienne." Lorana tucked her braid into her hood. "After his confession to find the previous capital."

"Oh, yes," Yun sighed. "That nonsense."

"There is nothing nonsensical about the old ruins," Lorana snarled. "There is lots of information to be found there, and hidden treasures which Kora has taken an interest to."

"If it's important." Yun shook her head. "She'd have gone there herself. She knows where it is."

"Yes," Lorana said. "But you and I can agree that she rarely does much herself that doesn't involve her leaving Kinasa for any length of time."

"This is true," Yun admitted, bowing her head low. "Things would be different, much different if she just took the kingdom. But she doesn't."

"What's wrong," Anaergienne asked.

"Oh—oh," she stammered. "It's nothing."

Turning her head away from him, she noticed Yara's eyes shifting towards her. An uncomfortable movement, and it was clear now that Yara had taken an interest in her old love life. How deep that interest went, however, she couldn't right discern.

Infatuation wasn't exactly something out of the ordinary for rangers, especially when they went long periods without seeing loved ones. Looking up at the path, the silence came back, and Anaergienne stepped away. But she wanted him not to, but she kept all gestures to indicate that desire hidden.

"So…" Lorana stretched the word. "Where's our next rest stop? I want to sleep in a real bed."

"Well," Yara spoke, eyes squinting to peer in the distance. "Can you hear that? Sounds like a festival."

"We're not here for some festivities, Yara," Yun said. "We're here for a confession."

"I know that." She jerked her head. "But surely it isn't all so urgent we can't afford a little distraction."

"Oh, Carmielle." Yun glared at her pupil. "Now, if anyone needs to confess, it's you! Don't think I don't know what ye've been doin' behind my back!"

"What?" She chuckled. "It was one time."

"More like every time I have my back turned. It's like I'm putting up with children," she spoke lowly as her attention was fixated on Yurilo.

He was the silent type, and he spoke in hushed whispers only Lorana got to hear, unless he attempted to speak to Yara, which was rare. In fact, she almost forgot what his voice sounded like. But there wasn't much diversity he brought to their fellowship, just a little bit of this and a little bit of that, eyes focused, carefully searching the trees for danger.

Yara backed away from the lead to talk to Lorana, and they both chatted amiably with one another like they'd known each other for years.

She did take a quick listen though, to the sounds of the festival. Seeing a large tent set up in the distance of green and white. Wisps danced on the road, illumining the path and the village, it appeared, or a small city forward. Blenheim. The sounds of laughter, shouting, and announcers came into her ears. She couldn't smell anything yet, for she wasn't close enough. But she assumed there was no shortage of baked goods which she could enjoy.

She turned to Anaergienne again, and remembered he and Lorana shared a mutual friend, of whom was a baker. A terrible fate befell her, and every once in a while, she listened to Anaergienne talking to Lorana about Quarala. She was a kind spirited human being, one curious about the elves to even risk coming into the lands of Kinasa.

Few humans who weren't adventurers rarely did that. Yun couldn't help but wonder exactly what Quarala did to earn Lorana's fancy for she shouldn't have been around for too long. *If you know, you know, I guess.* But even after fifty years, her feelings towards Anaergienne never waned, and she wouldn't let the fire be snuffed out. No, it needed to be rekindled.

But how was she to do that? Save a couple of baked goods? Surely there must be something else she could do that wasn't nearly as romantic.

"Well. . ." Yun smiled. "Lorana, you might get your wish for a bed tonight after all."

"Thank Carmielle." She traded the smile back. "A nice comfortable bed, some covers, and a nice hearty meal. Rations should be for the road."

"They are," Yun said, as if that was not a generally understood fact. "No one should eat those for the sake of eating."

"No?" Anaergienne asked, pulling out some of his rations and eating it. It was a little bar of oats mixed with some honey and nuts. A sweet delicacy, but one should ration them out. Hence the name. "I find them quite tasty."

"Yes." Yun rolled her eyes. "Yummy, yummy for the tummy, but not self-sustaining of all the nutrients we need, yes? You of all people here ought to know that!"

"I sense another slap incoming," Yurilo finally spoke. "Anaergienne, I dare say, you might do yourself in before we get to your confession. If I didn't know any better, I'd say you liked having Yun slap you."

Anaergienne, is this true? Is this all I must do?

"What?" He blushed, waving his hands as if a stench was wafting up his nose. "Preposterous."

"Me-thinks you like pain." Yurilo snickered. "And Yun appears to like inflicting it on you very specifically. A match made in the heavens. A union perhaps Carmielle might approve of. A sadist and a masochist, what's not to love."

"What?" Yun and Anaergienne exclaimed like two siblings.

"Now, Yurilo." Lorana glared. "We mustn't be spouting off heresies. As much as I love dissecting a good heresy, that simply isn't something I've the time for right now."

"Look at you." Yara pointed and laughed. "We've a heretic, and someone knowledgeable about heresies!"

"Indeed," Lorana hissed. "I'm very knowledgeable about all sorts of heresies."

"One might think twice about traveling in your company," Yara replied.

"We didn't know, and we didn't really have much choice in the matter," Yun replied. "We're getting close. Let's put this talk of heretics behind us, yeah?"

"No," Yara said. "We're going to the temple. We can't be spouting off heresies in their midst. You know that!"

"Well, then they confess just like everyone else," Yun said. "After all, that's what this one is going for. You should consider it too."

"I don't know what you're talking about." Yara crossed her arms over her breasts. "I've had my fun, and I still have it."

"I don't know what this is about," Anaergienne hissed. "But this probably is a conversation meant for your ears alone."

"Anaergienne." Yun scowled. "Shall I slap you again?"

"Yun." *Please say yes.* "No."

"Fine." She bowed her head, disappointed, and they neared the town of Blenheim.

Nearing the town, they crossed through the dirt road, still shielded with the covering of trees, and many-colored leaves littered the road.

Residential trees were planted five hundred feet apart from one another, and the large roots implanted themselves firmly in the soil, still moist on this particularly dry morning. The branches interwove themselves, spiraling like the strands of a rope to one another. Elves danced gleefully on the thick branches, and there were tents set up upon them. Little children played, running through the dirt, and laughed as they played with the nearby wolves, foxes, squirrels, and chipmunks. As they walked in, Yun noticed the clothing here was very different from what she was used to in the north.

Light leather, not the thick hide she wore, just light, like the inside of an animal was wrapped around some of them, little strands hanging from the sleeves and trouser legs. Boots too had these strands, plain, and beige they were.

Other families, who seemed a bit more formal and reserved, wore extravagant robes, both male and female as the ends of their robs glided with careful steps, just hovering over the dirt. These robes had elegant threading on the entrance of the sleeves, and the belt, which too was made from silk. The clothes seemed light and comfortable enough as little families walked from tree to tree, some dancing in a fit of glee. Squeals of excitement escaped many lips, and there was a loud rhythmic drum playing in the distance, and some high-pitched singing.

"Well," Lorana said. "Time we best stock up on some supplies, yes?"

"Why yes," Yurilo replied. "Don't tarry for too long, yeah? I must—"

"What's got you so worked up?" Yara noticed his eyes narrowed. "You were calm a moment ago."

"I recognize someone." He brought his voice down real low. "Best I hide in the shadows." He turned to Lorana. "Be quick, please. We probably should leave 'ere tomorrow before too long."

Without an answer, he stepped back behind the shadow of a tree and disappeared. Yun clicked her tongue as he considered the strange behavior, of such a degree, he seemed to have changed his personality when walking here, but then, if he was concerned enough to hide, perhaps that was enough for her to have her guard up. She turned to Yara.

"Keep an eye on her." He pointed to her. "Make sure she comes back. Anaergienne and I will search for an inn."

They went their separate ways while Anaergienne and Yun walked through the crowds, entering the bustle of this festival. Winter was coming soon. The first flakes of the snow marked another season, or it would in a few short weeks perhaps. The festival or Icelidin. An elvish festival to mark the end of the fall into winter, and to prepare for the cold season.

Farmers would start producing as many fruits and vegetables as they could before the soil would become impossible to work with, and those wanting to have one last fun night before the dead of winter. This festival, which she understood Blenheim to currently celebrate, was marked by bright colors, music of the bards and the storytellers, weaving high tales of legends slaying giant snow beasts, mythical creatures, she knew, from a world and people long lost.

Children seemed to have a fascination with these creatures, as she noticed a bard had their undivided attention while he danced on the stage, weaving his tale and strumming to the sound of his lute, and plucked away occasional notes to play a melody.

She ignored the sight, and a scent of sweet honey filled her nose, and she looked west, some smoke rising. Much chatter passed by with the kicking of dirt with careless steps as those around her seemed to try for their pre-lunch and wanted to get their tummies filled with something sweet.

"Anaergienne, care for a sweet roll? You like those, didn't you?"

"I can't taste anything," he replied.

"Sweet rolls," she urged. "Come on, it's your favorite."

"Yun." He frowned. "Let's just get to the inn—wait!"

"You galook!" She took his wrist as she pulled him through the crowd. "Honestly, what am I going to do with you?"

"We need to look for an inn!" he shrieked. "Not sweet rolls!"

"The inn can wait!" she snapped, slapping him in the face.

"Ow! Yun, I said—"

"I know what you said," she hissed. "But you're not behaving! Good grief. You're like a child."

"Why would you slap a child?" he protested as she continued to push and weave through the line to get to the tent with the sweet rolls.

"Two sweet rolls please!" she said, before turning to him. "I'm not slapping a child, I'm slapping you!"

"Fine." He said, and the baker presented them with sweet rolls. Yun paid the baker.

"Now, we can find that inn," she said.

"You're too much," he said, biting into it as they walked back through the forest of faces.

"And, how is it?" She bit into hers, and it was sweeter than the ones in Kerina.

"It's sweet," he said softly. "Almost like home."

"Well. . ." She smiled at him, but he didn't trade the smile. "You're home."

"I don't understand." He said. "I've been gone for all this time, and you seem to think that wasn't so short a distance. As if it was just a dream."

"It was just a nightmare." She replied. "Sure, things won't ever truly be the same, but it doesn't mean I don't want things to go back to the way they were. Things were simpler back then, until you started meddling with the affairs of humans. But that's then, this is now."

"It's been fifty years!" he said.

"Don't remind me," she said. "We can still pick up where we left off, unless. . ." She bit into her roll as she stared down. "Unless Quarala truly did take your heart."

"No." He turned his head from her. She saw a blush color his cheeks. "I've told you; it wasn't anything like that. Not at all."

"So, don't tell me you've fallen for her lover then?" she replied, remembering the lengthy tale he spun of how he knew Quarala to Lorana as they spoke often in secret.

"Lorana?" he said. "No, hard to get a sense of privacy with Yurilo skulking around anyhow—"

"Ooooh—" She blushed, a finger to her lips. "There was something—"

"No, don't put words in my mouth, you always do that!" She noticed the way his lips twisted. He used to do that when he tried to hide a smile.

"Oh, but you love it, now don't you?" she sneered. "You said it yourself, too, before I beat the dung pie out of you, or did you not mean that?"

"Mean what?"

A child bumped into him, and he staggered to one knee, and the burly kid took the sweet roll and ran with it.

"Oh, Carmielle, he stole my sweet roll!"

A smile curled upon Yun's lips, and a blush. She pointed at Anaergienne before she threw her head back in laughter. Chuckling, her stomach started to hurt, still unaccustomed to it, she put a hand on her belly as she leaned forward, a free hand offered her half-eaten portion to Anaergienne. He looked at it suspiciously but shook his head. She grinned, and she propped herself up against a small tree, looking onward towards amore heavy chatter.

"Anyway, what I meant was. . ." she trailed off with a smirk. "Before someone stole your sweet roll—"

"What?" an elf said, wielding a spear. "Someone stole your sweet roll? Pathetic."

"Oh." He grimaced. "Piss off."

"Foul mouth this one got," he said.

"Oh, trust me, when it comes to foul language, no one is more filthy than me," Yun replied. "Just children being children, no cause for alarm, I assure you. Be on your way."

"Who are ye—"

"Ranger's Guild," she said.

"I beg your pardon."

"Just leave, this was a private conversation." She scowled as the guard walked off. "Now, where were we?"

"I know not," he admitted. "You've been interrupted twice now. Almost like we shouldn't be having this conversation or rekindle what was once burning."

"We can still have this conversation." Yun said, walking closer to the tree with a sign of a bed carved meticulously on it. "Did you mean what you said though? Did a day pass by when you didn't think about me?"

"Yes," he said. "I just—I just didn't know how to explain what happened, and after a certain point, it seemed pointless to write a letter. So, I tried to avoid any contact with elves during those fifty years."

"Well, you can't escape us now," she sneered. "Come, let's get to this inn, make sure everyone has a place to sleep tonight. My belly could use a break from sleepin' on the roots."

"You need to take better care of your back," he suggested.

"And you need to take better care of your friends. You lost the last two."

"You're cold!" he snapped.

"Have to be. Won't last in this world if ye aren't."

CHAPTER 4

Pilgrimage

Lorana was at the market stand which had this wonderful herbalist attending, with vines interwoven into her thick brown hair for decorum. Fake leaves, she assumed, the bother, filled with multicolored, and some were from a cherry blossom tree. Those weren't even in season, but if they were fake, she supposed it would be okay. Given the deplorable nature of her supplies, the amount of times she had to prepare on such short notice, and her heart still aching with the notice of Quarala's death, it still wasn't easy for her to accept.

Carmielle gives. She also takes away. It's up to the mortal to decide the reason. Perhaps it wasn't meant to be? Perhaps there was some grand scheme at play which required Quarala to die. Perhaps it was punishment for a transgression she didn't know she committed? Often with the most uncertain answers, this is more likely the case. But what was it?

Oh, Carmielle, my heart aches, but if you could satisfy me with a little discernment, I'd appreciate it.

"What brings us here, specifically?" Yara asked.

That's right, temporarily, Yara was her protector as Yurilo disappeared with little notice as to why, and why his concern was so great. Perhaps with a little ease of the night, he could relay some of the secret notion as to why his awareness was heightened. Though the thought troubled her, she ignored it as she addressed Yara with a smile, a weak one, but a smile nonetheless.

"If you're referring to Anaergienne, I'm surprised you don't know," she answered. "But I can't speak much on that anyway."

"I'm interested more on your journey," Yara said, leaning in closely. "It's not often I find myself in the company of a damsel."

"Oh, for shame." She pushed gently on Yara's collar to allow some space between them. "Intimacy, the last time I found myself here, it was me doing the pursuing. We all know how that ended up. Careful, Yara, my love interests have a habit of dying. But anyway. . ." She turned to the herbalist. "I need one pound of cordyceps, chaga, maitake, and shiitake, and six grains of ginkgo, ginseng, yarrow, rosemary, and nightshade."

"Nightshade? Are you planning on poisoning someone?" Yara asked.

"Oh, Carmielle, Yara!" she snapped but couldn't hold back a smile. "You can't just ask people that. What I do with Nightshade in the privacy of my own tree is up to me."

"Your journey then." Yara smiled as she twirled her ponytail with a finger when the herbalist departed from the stand to prepare the herbs.

"I find it unbelievable you weren't paying attention at all," Lorana said.

"Too busy, but now that I have your attention without Yurilo eavesdropping on us, you now have my attention, undivided," she smirked.

Lorana heard the sound of wood on wood as the herbs were being mashed together, ground finely like dust, the way she normally used these herbs with their salves. It was more costly making them herself rather than purchasing them directly.

There would be rations too, she needed to pick up to make them last further down the road as they traveled to Corela. But the sudden ask and mention of Yurilo's absence was a cause for concern, and her eyes narrowed. Why wouldn't she be compelled to speak to her before? Lorana had to admit a fit of lust had taken her, but she had her emotions in check, cautiously aware of the dangers of too much trust.

Cynical, perhaps a little, but even this was paranoid for her. She didn't want to wake up dead in the morning. Silly Lorana, she wouldn't wake up dead. She'd be dead.

"Why did you home in on that detail?" Lorana said.

"You must find me suspicious," Yara jeered. "Good, you'll live longer."

"It is most wise for you to continue this conversation in the inn," a voice said.

They both twisted, a human-like figure behind them, cloaked. Turning the hood to the side, the familiar gaze of Yurilo was behind it, eyes searching for familiar faces. Biting his lips, frustrated at the two, clearly, for he greeted them with gnarled lips.

Lorana was pleased to see him and didn't question his attire. Perhaps he felt this conversation of this flirtatious ranger would end no place good. Admittedly, if that was correct, he wasn't wrong. Bedding wayward wizards were one thing, bedding flirtatious rangers who can kill without a second thought was something entirely different.

"Here ye a'e," the herbalist said.

Lorana shifted to trade some coins for the pouches of herbs and mushrooms. She offered a smile with her head turned. Yurilo disappeared again, and she and Yara made their way through the crowds of people. There was a festival going on, but Lorana didn't feel the need to stop and celebrate the season's change. There was a sudden wind chill; she brought her shoulders together as Yara started talking to herself.

CHAPTER 5

Masked intentions

"Could you not have found a more suitable place?" Lorana asked. The bread was rustic, hard on the teeth, if a little salty for her preference. Clearly, Quarala wouldn't approve. Anaergienne of course, wouldn't really care all that much, for the blasted elf claimed he couldn't taste it anyway. The inn smelled of horse piss, and the ale in front of her was the most foul thing. She couldn't tell which version of piss was worse, the one in the air, or the one in her cup. Despite the decorum of a very guttural voiced singer, the flavor of the food and drink, the two rangers weren't bothered by it. Yara had already disappeared with a servant girl? She thought that's who it was. Carmielle! Why did she get stuck with companions who were constantly at it? One might have thought they evolved from rabbits.

"Just like the dripping bucket?" Yun exhaled with a great smile on her face. "A little bit of home."

"Why is everything so foul?" Lorana coughed. "The food is deplorable, can ye even call it food?"

"I must say," Yurilo said, pushing his barely eaten plate away from him, sniveling his nose. "Spicy, that I can deal with, but you Rangers have the most deplorable of tastes."

"We all can't come from Grento, now can we?" Anaergienne quipped.

"No, and the liquor there is fine, nothing special," he said. "But how the hell can you grutt up mead?"

"Yes," Yun said, hand to her chin as she looked to the ceiling. "Even I must admit the liquor could be much better."

"Sheesh." Lorana shook her head, yawning. "Suffice it to say, I'm looking forward to my bed. You did get us in separate rooms, did you not?"

"Why, of course, I did." Yun said. A chair creaked. "Ah, you're back."

"Yes," she shrieked, sitting down, panting with sweat beading down her head. The tunic was untied towards her bosom. She peered down at the table at the uneaten meal from Yurilo. "Ye gonna finish that?"

"Carmielle!" Lorana put her hand on her head, surrounded by lunatics.

Of the three rangers, Anaergienne seemed by far the normal one. Yun was abrasive, rude, didn't have a care in the world, it seemed, for today, save for subtly fawning over him. And Yara, oh, she might as well have been just as frustrated as a mercenary going to and from village to village bedding any wench she could find.

"Go right ahead." Yurilo was all too eager to give up his food.

"Thank you kindly." She reached her hand over the table and grabbed his food and ate with her hands like some barbarian. Putting the piece of chicken in her mouth without regard: she chewed it.

"What's that smell?" Yurilo sniffed the air. "Is that. . . is that you, Yara?"

"What?" she said, and Lorana suddenly knew the stench of which he spoke.

"Oh, trees, no." He waved his hands in front of his nose. "It's none of my business whatever it was that you did, but you really ought to have taken a bath before coming back down here. And you're touching the plate. Lorana, get away from her. She's infected!"

"Infected with pure bliss." Yara smiled, unashamed.

"Oh, that's foul." Lorana covered her nose, creaking her chair closer to Yurilo, away from Yara.

"So," Yun said. "Yurilo, I feel like now is an appropriate time, don't you think, to tell me about why you disappeared from our presence."

"I recognized someone," he said, bringing his voice down low, and everyone brought their ears closer to the table. "Someone from the Assassins' Guild, an elf."

"Just how many elves joined that Guild?" Anaergienne asked. "I used to know, but it wasn't many."

"Couldn't say, really." Yurilo leaned forward.

"You'd know that if things hadn't gotten out of hand like they have," Lorana reminded him. "But that isn't the case here. Odds are, if they noticed Yurilo, that would put a hindrance on our plans."

"That doesn't have anything to do with this pilgrimage," Anaergienne reminded. "They'd likely leave us alone."

"Not me," Yurilo whispered. "Which might have nothing to do with you, but everything to do with Lorana here."

"She's not in the Guild." Yun tucked some hair behind her ears. "That shouldn't—"

"No, if something happens to Yurilo, that throws a rock into my roots. I can't have that," Lorana explained. "That would make my journey to the old capital that more treacherous. It's best he lay himself on the ground while he's here."

"So…" Anaergienne shook his head. "Who is your former associate?"

"Some prick," Yurilo said. "Lithwe, is his name. A deplorable fellow who got roped into the guild about a century ago with his sister. I can't remember her name. Him, however? I never forget a prick."

"Why?" Yara finished eating. "He owe you gold or something?"

"If it was that simple." Yurilo replied. "It was an accident, but I poisoned his youngest sister. There were two sisters, not one. Forgive me for missing that detail."

"Well, no helping that now." Anaergienne sighed. "And this isn't even our business, ye shouldn't be disclosin' that!"

"You asked," Yurilo said, and he leaned forward, chin propped up as he stared into the rangers' eyes. "I am intrigued. You and I come from similar paths, but Anaergienne, what exactly drove you away from Kinasa?"

"I was exiled."

"So, a great hunter who achieved almost legendary fame and fortune could simply be ordered away, and he'd bark like a dog," Yurilo hissed. "Is that what you're telling me?"

"Yurilo, this isn't the time and place for this." Lorana rolled her eyes.

"No, but there are a number of things that don't quite add up, like why he hasn't tried to kill me yet," Yurilo said. "Anaergienne, the blood thirsty ranger, a demon, a dragon from Hell. A name to be feared in all of Alkathos, and yet, just a simple hunter in the north? Why?"

"Why what?" Anaergienne sighed, leaning back to his chair, fingers interwoven across his chest.

"Why didn't you challenge the exile, you know you could have," Yurilo said. "I wasn't even in Kinasa at the time, but I caught wind of it, that's when I knew Sipus wouldn't wait idly by and let the Rangers Guild off on such light-handed behavior."

"There wasn't anything light handed about his departure." Yun slammed her fist on the table. Tankards atop it rattled with their liquid swooshing inside. "We suffered because of it, and then, well, mistakes were made."

"Yes, one too many mistakes, and people died, or suffered to be beyond recovery," Yara inserted herself. "Like Dorio. He'll never be the same."

"That's my fault," Anaergienne said.

"And you let this all happen," Yurilo said. "All I want to know is why? Why didn't you push back on the crown? What's a hundred measly guards to you? Master of his craft, and a Guild master, no less."

"Because the amount of people who died as a result of those actions would have been staggering, and dare I say, it might even cause the whole forest to burn to the ground, killing everything and everyone inside it, and simultaneously, violate both oaths I swore," he said. "This way, I could violate neither. Is that satisfactory, to you, Yurilo?"

"Why do you even care?" Yara snapped. "You're not one of us, ye—"

"Enough, Yara." Yun took a deep breath. "Yes, we don't like assassins very much, but this one here was kind enough to alert us of the presence of one. It's best we let this go. He stirred a pot we don't need stirred, and we don't need to fan the flames."

"No." Lorana leaned back in her chair and put her hood up as a breeze entered the room from the windows. "We've had enough discourse for one night. Honestly, I almost wish we didn't stop. You three degenerates are crazy. Why did I let Kora talk me into this?"

"Who knows—oh, what's this now?" Yun turned her head to the servant girl who came.

"Hu—hello." She bowed to Yara. "May I interest you in an ale?"

"Sure," she replied. "Get me somethin' bitter."

The servant girl scurried off with the request. She noticed the girl's stammer, the scurrying feet as she wove through the crowds of people, the tavern being as busy as it was with all the candles lit. The sticky floors echoed in her ears. She took a draft of the horse piss and stomachs it to wash down that bread. Honestly, both were almost equally terrible. Shaking her head, awaiting the girl, Lorana thought to say something.

"Why in Carmielle's green forest would you want a bitter drink? This is akin to your Dripping Bucket! Everything tastes like piss." Yurilo shook his head.

"Piss. Piss. Piss. Carmielle." Yara put a hand on her bosom. "You're so vulgar."

"Says the ranger who just bedded some random person a few short minutes ago," he commented. "Even Grento elves aren't nearly as promiscuous as you."

"You just don't know how to find them." Yara winked.

"Oh gods—"

"You heretic!" Lorana pointed at Anaergienne before he could finish his thought.

"I'm trying to help you!" Anaergienne snapped. "Yun, aren't you supposed to keep a lid on this? I don't know what transpired over the last fifty years, but last I knew, holistic approaches to bedding was not something we were going to accept."

"You're not the guild—"

"Keep it down!" Yurilo hissed.

"Here ye a'e," the girl said.

As she brought the tankard of ale over to Yara, who looked at it like a thirsty dog, she slipped a parchment on the table. She bowed before turning, fleeing swiftly from the table. Lorana was perplexed as she reached over to grab the parchment of paper and brought it to her eyes before she could search its contents. She could tell Yun was barreling her gaze into her.

"Did you ask for the transaction?" Yun asked. "We weren't quite done."

"Oh," Yara cooed and then slammed her tankard on the table. "Now, that's the stuff."

"You're unhinged!" Yurilo shook his head disapprovingly.

"No," Lorana answered Yun's question. "I didn't ask. But we should ask and discuss this letter. Perhaps Yara isn't too drunk to handle business."

"Business?" Anaergienne's eyebrow raised.

"Come here." Lorana pointed at him, and all the elves leaned forward to listen. "I think something might be running amiss. This note, from the servant, is not a transaction request."

She slipped the parchment to the three rangers, and Yun took it, carefully reading it. Cupping it with her hands every time someone walked behind her, as if aware someone might want to pry on their private business. Couldn't blame anyone really, everyone always wanted to know what the Rangers' Guild was up to, especially if they were inside Kinasa.

"What have we here?" a voice said, and an elf pulled up a chair where Yurilo was just sitting.

This elf was finely dressed with golden inscriptions on his robe. Yurilo disappeared again, this time without a thought. Lorana wondered where he hid this time. Yun deftly hid the note in her pocket.

"A wizard, by the looks of it, and three rangers, but wasn't this seat previously occupied? Where'd your other friend run off to?"

"Oh heavens, no," Lorana said. "He might have had something particularly bitter and had to relieve himself, I'm sure."

"Of course." He smiled warmly.

"I'm sorry, who are you?" Anaergienne squinted his eyes.

"Oh." He laughed nervously. "Manners. My name..." He stood from his chair and bowed. "Is Lithwe, and I co-own this establishment."

"Your food and drink taste like horse piss," Yara said. "According to our resident wizard. Why she knows what horse piss tastes like, I don't know and I'm too afraid to ask."

Lorana looked up to him, and he gave her a bright smile. Someone scheming something, of course, had to be. She wondered, no, it had to be. Lithwe wasn't exactly a common name. This had to be the one Yurilo mentioned as a face of familiarity.

An Assassin.

What were they doing here operating a tavern, no less? Something was going to run awry here, but what? What were the assassins doing operating in Kinasa, that was strictly forbidden, and the Rangers' Guild always kept a tight leash on the borders. Owning the establishment, no wonder the girl subtly asked for help. Did he see the note? What would happen to her if he found out? This world was filled with consistently inconsistently cruel people, but the Assassins were all cruel, and competent.

"I'm sorry you don't like it, but we like our things a bit on the bitter end," he explained. "Perhaps a little bitter for most people's palates."

"Yes." She wiped her lips. "Perhaps too bitter for my taste."

"Sorry we can't help that," he replied. "What business, might I ask, brings a wizard and a trio of rangers through our town?"

"A confession," Yun replied, hand covering her mouth.

"Indeed?" Lithwe shrilled. "Well, we all love a good confession. What mistakes has whom made?"

"None of your business," Anaergienne said. "Lithwe, I appreciate your coming over here to make us feel welcome in a tavern filled with horse piss, but we must really get going. Isn't that right, Yara?"

"Right," she said, red blush to her face as she slurred her words.

"Well, I'll send the transaction request over then." Lithwe bowed. "I do hope you trust your stay here for the night before you go off whenever you do."

"Of course." Lorana traded a smile, as ingenuine as she cared to make it. "Thanks."

She watched him walk away, nearly disappearing into the crowd of scuffling dancers. Appearing again by the bar with the servant who provided them their meal, he traded words with her. Frowning, she shivered like he was about to hit her, and he did have a raised hand as if to sap her, but he refrained, handing her a piece of parchment, and she hurried with it through the crowd towards them. A door behind the counter opened, and Lithwe disappeared behind as it closed shut. Gnarling her lips, Yurilo took his seat again.

"You need to give us warning when you disappear like that," Anaergienne replied. "We can lie for you, but we need to know what you plan on doing."

"There wasn't time," he whispered, putting his hood up. "That is him."

"What are Assassins doing here?" Yara hissed.

"Something is going on." Yun took out the note. "She asked for help."

"Not much we can really do," Yurilo said. "We don't have a lot of information."

"We can ask her," Lorana offered.

"No, you can't!" Anaergienne rolled his eyes. "That will put her in a more precarious situation than she already finds herself, besides, someone might be listening to us. Lithwe didn't just come here by chance. Was he triggered by the note? Or Yurilo's presence? We don't know."

"Hello." The servant girl came and gave them the transaction request. Yun immediately paid her and sent her on her way.

"There might be a cellar." Lorana looked in the direction of the servant girl who slyly disappeared into the crowd. "Should be investigated."

"I appreciate your concern," Yun said. "But we haven't the time to perform an investigation of this magnitude."

"What do you mean? Just a night," Lorana suggested. "Surely, we can delay sleep for that?"

"Lorana," Yurilo spoke softly. "It is unwise to get involved with anything of this magnitude related to the Assassin's Guild. It asks way too many questions, and we might be walking into a trap."

"Why a trap?"

"I'm sure he saw me," Yurilo said, eyes carefully searching the room for familiar faces.

"We really should do something," Yara said. "Not me, I'm too drunk."

"Well, Lithwe would know who I am," Anaergienne said. "I'm too known."

"But you are the type of person who would just walk into the cellar," Yun said. "But you can't open locked doors."

Everyone turned to Yurilo as he took a sip of his horse piss. His eyes searched the sudden attention placed on his shoulders as if he had some magical solution. Lorana knew, though, he could pick locks and open and locate doors most of them would have missed in an urban setting. Caverns, perhaps these rangers would be better for that sort of thing. But that's not where they found themselves in.

"Don't stare at me like that, you lunatics," he hissed, baring his teeth. "You'll give out my location."

Lorana put her hand on top of his palms, and he glanced at her. Looking into his eyes, she considered what good they could do, and the call for Carmielle was one to help others in need, regardless of the situation.

If elves were enslaving other elves, all the more reason to put a stop to this, and what better place, than a tavern where everything tasted like piss. Quarala, she could never have brought her to a place like this. So uncivilized. Gnarling her lips, she considered the implications this might have on their relationship, considering it was meant to be strictly business, but now, this crossed the line with what he agreed to do for her.

Of course, he could be inclined just to say no.

"Yurilo," she said. "Will you?"

"Fine," he sighed after a period of silence.

"I'll join you," Anaergienne replied. "We'll leave in a few hours, but first, let's take a nap. Who knows what's down there."

"How deft are you? Weren't you recently wounded?"

"Nearly died as a matter of fact. I'm sure we'll be fine," was his reply.

The Cellar

Yurilo listened to the door of his room. Anaergienne sat behind him, his sword on his side, patiently waiting for him to give the go ahead. Yurilo heard several footsteps in the distance, and the activity from downstairs was becoming less bothersome. But they were still there.

The room was lit by a lone candle, and he thought to blow it out, but no, that would alert the Assassins who were looking for Anaergienne, for some damnable reason he couldn't comprehend that they were sleeping. What better place to kill a Ranger than in his sleep? He'd slit enough throats to know.

After all, there was only a sliver of a chance an Assassin could beat a Ranger from the Guild in a fair fight. That was why dirtier was always preferable.

"What can you hear?" Anaergienne asked. "We've been up here for hours. Surely, they can't be drinkin' themselves to death down there."

"If you knew anything about Grento, there are some taverns where the wenches don't sleep, the keeper has an extra hand for cleaning," Yurilo replied. "But there's always a brief reprieve for the staff. Now, you remember where that cellar door was, right?"

"Of course," Anaergienne said, stretching his joints. "Right behind the bar. Easy enough to get to, definitely locked."

"Sure," Yurilo shrilled, ears pressing against the door. "Of course, why wouldn't that be locked?"

The sounds of doors and moans were heard in the other rooms. Clearly, a level of debauchery he knew some people wouldn't approve of. But that was simple enough, and loud enough to permit even this galook's heavy boots to go unnoticed. He looked to the Ranger, traded a smile. "Well, now's as good a time as any now. Let's go, find out what's what."

"All right." Anaergienne bowed. "After you."

"Just try not to stick me with an arrow, will ya?" Yurilo opened the door silently into a dark hall. His hands glided on the walls as the screams of wailing continued to push the boundaries. Males and females screaming ecstatically.

Biting his lips, he touched the railing and carefully took himself downstairs. Apart from the squeals, everything was silent downstairs, and upstairs. The night was late, and the candles and torches were all out. No alcohol, no rotting food, no sweat, and no creaking or scraping of food, or chairs to hear. Just silence.

As he passed the threshold into the common area of the tavern, the tables were polished and the chairs standing atop them. The floors were cleaned, spotless even. The bar was empty, and the crickets sang from outside, and the fireflies roaming around at night illumined his sight so he could see.

When he glanced carefully toward the bar, there was nothing of concern, no moving shadows, nor anything resembling a trap he recognized. He let out a brief sigh before stepping forward. The wood didn't creak underneath his weight as he gaited toward the bar, gently walked over to the side, and lifted the barrier up gently, and Anaergienne crawled right after him.

He took his hands to the door, and tried turning the knob, on the off chance it was open. It wasn't. He heard a low growl from Anaergienne when he fumbled for his tools. A lock pick, and he shimmied it through the hole where the key was, moving the mechanisms inside. Moving the metal levers inside it, the lock lifted, and the door swung open.

Hissing silently, he reached for the knob before it slammed against the wall on the other side. He stepped through the darkened corridor, and Anaergienne closed the door behind them, and the two of them were settled finely in the opaque chamber.

"Careful," Yurilo breathed. Taking his first steps, he walked on the floor, noting there were stones that were raised and depressed into the ground. "Weighted stones. Step where I step. You can manage, yeah?"

"Of course, I can," Anaergienne breathed, sniffing the air. "You smell that?"

"Liquor?" Yurilo sniffed.

"No," Anaergienne said again. "Iron. There's iron in the air. Lead the way, Yurilo, keep aware of traps. There's blood in the air we breathe. Lots of it."

He nodded, not sure if Anaergienne could see him in the obscurity. Inching forward, they inhaled silently, and his steps glided along the weighted stones on the ground without touching them. His hand reached out, caressing a moist wooden wall, and he used it to guide his way, ears ever listening with each breath and step he took. No steps down the halls, but his heart raced. Centuries of doing this kind of work, but to do so against Assassins was always asking for trouble. He felt his palms sweat as he noticed an orange hue of a light coming towards him.

"Anaergienne," he whispered. "You see that?"

"Yes," he breathed back. "Let me take care of it."

"Aye."

Yurilo stopped moving and Anaergienne's body moved past him. The elf ranger moved towards the light. A human-like figure in armored clothes came by, nearly called for help before dropping the torch. Anaergienne took a hunting knife and cut into the man's gullet before a sound could be heard and deftly grabbed the body before it clunked to the ground, dragging him into the dark avoiding the pressurized stones which would spell disaster on everyone involved.

Yurilo felt a hand touch his shoulder again. "Let's keep goin' eh? Just figure out what's going on, how big this operation is, and such. And get out."

"Sounds like a fantastic idea," Yurilo said, relieved as he stepped into the corridor where there was some light.

He allowed himself to be seen in the light of the corridor as the two passed by. Anaergienne offered no words, but his sword was drawn, prepared for battle. Yurilo had his dagger out; it was not ideal should a full out brawl summon itself in his face, but it was better than nothing.

He wondered, as he passed each step, looking for traps and hidden doors, or if any of the engravings written on the stones of these walls would tell him there was a hidden entryway somewhere, but why was he doing this for Lorana? It wasn't included within his contract and his agreement with her, and certainly it didn't involve something he needed to be involved with. Sipus, and Lithwe, least of all, cruel heartless bastards.

After walking down this corridor, slanting deeper into the ground, he heard the sound of muffled speaking. He stopped, and put his ear to the door, hearing Anaergienne's steps behind him, hand leaning against it. He listened to the tone of the speaking, but couldn't make out the words, but they were coming from this end of the hall, and only the voice he recognized, Lithwe, and Sipus. They were both here? Why? And why is this corridor made from stone here? How big is this hole in the ground?

"What is it?" Anaergienne asked. "I could have had time to make my tea."

"Sipus and Lithwe are behind this wall," he said, turning his head along it. "Where is the entrance?"

"Don't worry about the entrance now," Anaergienne said. "We need to find out how big this is. If Sipus is here, and it can only spell disaster. We need to know how large this is."

"Are you not bothered by the stones being here," he whispered. "This is Kinasa, stones just don't grow underground!"

"Of course, they don't," Anaergienne said. "Which again, is why we're here. The Guild is definitely gonna wanna know about this."

Yurilo shook his head, not wanting to go any deeper into this pit, but he did. For Lorana at her request. Why was he doing this? Even now, he couldn't reconcile the why, but he did. Taking down the steps until the corridor opened up into a large dome.

Torches moved along the walls. There were chains and barbs holding prisoners up, sleeping. They continued to walk this path, the stone underneath, and the railings rusted. Males and females hung together, some dead, just dangling on chains above some horse hounds barking for a fresh piece of meat. Sickened, he pressed on, moving towards a crevice which had a barrier behind it, and a door to the side.

Six women hung there, barbed links to their wrists and ankles. Pools of blood rested at their feet, soaking in the decay, and some groaned for release. Hair wiry as they were uncleaned for some time, and the chains kept them up somewhat, but it was clear, these women had it, bare naked for all to see. Wounds, cuts, whips and bruises decorated their bodies like canvasses.

Some were panting, others had their mouths nearly cut open. Some cried, screaming for help. When he got a look at her eyes when she turned to him, the elf had both of them carved out, blood dripping from the eye sockets. A sickness fell upon him, and he covered his mouth as he vomited to the side.

He heard Anaergienne's boots approach past him, and walked to the door, opening the iron entry before stepping inside. Boots coated, he raised his sword and cut the first one's head off. The second one, he pulled the hair back and slit her throat. The other four he cut down mercilessly without delay, unarmed they were, and Yurilo could only stare in horror as the elf cut them to pieces. This was the ruthlessness he'd heard about. Killing others without question, armed or unarmed. Anaergienne left the room, the sex slaves dead inside, and the portal shut behind him.

Anaergienne panted, an angry scowl upon his lips. His hand firmly gripped the sword in his grasp before returning it to its sheath, blood splattered on his tunic, trousers and boots. Baring his teeth, a rage swelled within him, Yurilo could tell that much, and perhaps, he thought, just maybe the most terrifying thing he'd ever done was leave the Assassins' Guild, but to cross Anaergienne in a bad mood, he'd take Sipus on any day, not so much Anaergienne. Not even in the best of conditions.

"Let's go," he spoke harshly. "Let's find out what's going on here."

"Yes," Yurilo replied. "Keep that temper under control will you?"

"I'm going to find who is responsible," Anaergienne said. "I'll make it hurt as much as I can, twist the knife in their ribs, and pry the bones out."

"Gods," Yurilo said as he walked along the path of the railing. "Keep that under control, I already told you, It's Lithwe and Sipus. They're behind it. Though, Sipus is never in one place for very long. You can massacre Lithwe tomorrow morning."

"Don't think I won't do it," Anaergienne hissed. "I'll gut the bastard!"

"Anaergienne." Yurilo turned sharply, pointing a firm finger at him. *What am I doing? He could kill me.* "We don't know how many people are down here, or what not yet. If you just sta't hackin' people away, it'll get us nowhere, and we'd be dead before we got back to the tavern. What's more, Yara, Yun, and Lorana for all we'd know would have their throats cut open before they knew it. I don't want that. Do you?"

"Of course not," he whispered calmly.

"Then control your emotions," Yurilo said.

Who was he to talk about controlling emotions. He rarely had any. He walked down the corridor, hand on the railing as he looked at the sleeping cell mates. Poor miserable fools, caught in someone's game, but to what end.

Traffickers almost exclusively hunted females, but why the males? What purpose did they serve here? He wondered, continuing down the path, silently evading to the shadows whenever a guard came by, and Anaergienne followed, also hidden away.

They continued silently until they stood above a railing. Roars of lions and hyenas were inside an arena, tens of thousands of specta-tors were chanting, nearly wanted Yurilo to cut his ears off with the noise. Glancing down, he saw a little boy with a sword much too big to handle, and it shook in his grasp as the lions were released from large doors. The little boy shrieked, running as the blade clattered on the ground. The lions pounced on the boy, ripping him limb from limb and the blood splattered all over the ground. Yurilo noticed Anaergienne touch the railing with a clenched fist and gritting teeth. His hand touched his shoulder.

"What is it?" said the ranger.

"We should go," Yurilo said. "I think we know just how big this place is. I don't know how or why it's as big as it is, but it can hold an arena. And thousands, tens of thousands are here. Which means, this operation is very big."

"Let's get back to Yun," he said. *Yes, his little friend there. Probably his best friend.* "They'll want to know."

"Contestants of death games," Yurilo said, catching himself gritting his own teeth. "Could be useful."

"Hmm?" Anaergienne said.

"Never mind. Let's get out of here before they discover the body in the cellar," Yurilo answered. "Ye should probably get that body out of there too, find some place to bury him."

CHAPTER 7

Deliberations

There was a knock on the door. Yun bolted upright, the bed covers pulled off, and her white nightgown flowed with the sudden jerking of her body. Panting, she grabbed her knife from the nightstand as Lorana woke up, dreamily wiping the sleep from her eyes. When she approached the door it knocked again, the light from the fireflies came in the room with the activity. Opening the door, a very exhausted Yara collapsed in her shoulders, in the nude. Lorana shrieked before covering her eyes with her pillow.

"Carmielle," Yun said, hoisting Yara up, panting and sweating as she dragged her to her bed. "You really need to get your sleeping around under control. If anyone needs to confess, it's definitely you."

"I was—"

"I don't want to hear it." Yun pointed a stern finger at her face. "Now, go to bed, and don't leave. Never know what could happen in a place like this. No more alcohol until we get to Corela now."

"But—"

"I couldn't drink it even if I wanted to," Lorana said. "Way too bitter for me."

"But—"

"No time for that," Yun warned. "Or I'll take your rations for the week away."

"Can I go back to bed now?" Lorana whined. The wizards and their beauty sleep.

"Yes—"

"But I must tell," Yara squealed.

"No, no one's interested," Yun snapped. "Go back to bed, put your—put your night gown on, for Carmielle's sakes now. What is this? A bard? I swear, traveling with you becomes more like a chore each and every day. It's more stressful than getting shot in the shin with a crossbow bolt."

"Why is the door open?" Anaergienne's voice came out from the other side of the door and he and Yurilo walked in. She gaped her eyes open when she saw the blood on his tunic.

"What did you do?"

They shut the door behind them.

"I murdered someone, buried the body," he said. "Now—"

"What is going on below?" Yara asked.

"Carmielle, Yara!" Anaergienne snapped. "Have some decency! Put something on and leave something to the imagination, would ya?"

"No," she protested.

"If I have to spend another—"

"No more time for bickering!" Yurilo said. "If I never have to travel with rangers again, it would be too soon. Now, what's going below? The most advanced and complex, intricate form of trafficking I've ever seen!"

"What?" Yun shook her head, unable to believe it. "How? This is just a village. How big are we talking?"

"There's a gladiator pit down there, large doors for larger animals," Yurilo explained. "Probably for some death games, spectators, tens of thousands at least down there. Stone pathways—"

"Stone? This is Kinasa. Where the hell'd they get stone from? Korilya?" Yara interjected.

"Probably," Anaergienne answered. "Though to think of mining something like that here would take dwarven smiths and architects unnoticed."

"There were sex slaves too," Yurilo said, pointing to Anaergienne. "That this one saw fit to just execute for no reason."

"What life would they have had, even if we freed them? Years would go by, and they'd have nightmares, and that wouldn't heal. They'd probably cut their own throats if given a knife anyway."

"There are wizards for that sort of thing," Yara groaned, finally covering her breasts with a pillow.

"Is there a wizard among us who can do that?" Anaergienne asked. "Lorana?"

"No," she hesitated, but answered. "There are certain things only magic can do, and I don't know all things. That's beyond me. I can do with medicinal herbs, but those won't affect conditions of the mind."

"There we have it," he grumbled. "It was a mercy killing."

"They're going to find out," Yun snarled. "I don't want to delay our trip, but we might not have much choice now. If this operation is as big as you say it is, we need help."

"Homing pigeons won't work," Yara said. "It's not like they won't grab our messages to intercept them."

"No." Yun knew the logistical fallacy of the carrier pigeon. There was no way to alert the Guild of their location now. The murder of the prostitutes below, and whatever foul thing Anaergienne did recklessly fouled all their plans up. There was going to be blood, but when? It was only a matter of time, and Lithwe had already met them. There was little way to escape quietly.

"There are," Anaergienne began. "Fighters down there. I don't know how efficient they are, but they are numerous. I'm sure if I can free them, they'll aid us in removing Lithwe and the Assassins from this place, and we can send them back from where they came."

"But the labyrinth underneath," Yurilo warned. "Likely extends beyond all the nations of Alkathos. There is no telling how large it is."

"But you and I saw that there were tens of thousands of spectators." Anaergienne raised his hand. "Which means they have lots and lots of money, dwarves, elves, humans, they were all there, we saw the diversity. Sure, it reaches past our borders, but if they came here, that means Blenheim is the center of their operations. If we cave even this part of it, we'd likely remove the threat entirely from our lands, perhaps even the rest of Alkathos."

"And how do you propose we do that," Yurilo asked.

"Ale and flame," Anaergienne said. "If nothing else, there's plenty of those two to go around to cause a collapse."

"No." Yun shook her head, her tone harsh. "That is reckless. You can't predict how big the explosion will go and get caught innocent dwellers within that. It's too reckless. I won't repeat Sterilus."

"We won't," Anaergienne replied.

Yun noticed Yurilo scratching his chin.

"Besides, the dwellers are caught into it whether we do this or not. It's only a matter of time before they need to replenish their stock of fighters, and who else will they turn to?"

"You're right," Lorana hissed. "But I don't like this, not one bit. Carmielle wouldn't approve of our actions here."

"No," Anaergienne said. "She wouldn't. And then I'll have another thing to confess. But we can't let this go unchecked and unchallenged. We will do it. We will break the Guild of Assassins."

"All right." Yara burped. "But how will you do it?"

"Yurilo is a charismatic individual when he wants to be." Anaergienne smirked.

"Well, that's a grutting lie," Yurilo swore.

"No, no," Lorana said. "He's right. You certainly can be."

"No, I'm not." Yurilo frowned.

"So, this is what we do, and Lorana, it's going to get dangerous, so, Yara, why don't you be her bodyguard tomorrow. She'll need it," Anaergienne said. "Yurilo will create a distraction tomorrow at breakfast. I'd say the good old tavern brawl should suffice. That should do just nicely, all the while, I'll sneak or break through that door, head down the corridors and hastily retrieve our help."

"That will never work," Yurilo said. "You don't know what's down there."

"We do," Anaergienne said. "And it isn't anything I can't handle."

"You've not been in a proper fight in fifty years," Yun said, remembering his recent experience. "I should do it."

"It doesn't matter which one of us does it," Anaergienne said. "But I do have experience setting snares in no small amount of time. That would work better for this I should think."

"So, tavern brawl at breakfast, eh?" Yurilo said. "Well, I can't exactly feign being drunk that early, but suppose I could try that."

"And how do you propose you're going to start that? Everyone's tired or hung over to start fighting each other," Yara said.

"Quite simple, I'll steal from their pockets," Yurilo replied.

"How will that help?" Lorana asked.

"Simple, I'll get caught."

CHAPTER 8

Bloody Breakfast

Lorana got as good enough sleep as she could, anxious, and filled with fear and trembling with her fingers wrapped tightly around her staff, sitting at their table. Despite the early hour, there were plenty of people here, and servants bringing out breakfast plates of toast, milk, eggs, and bacon, and the scent of burning meat filled her nose, and it was the only thing soothing about today.

The Rangers wore all their gear, and so was Yurilo, though, cloaked so no one of importance would recognize him. Searching the room, she noticed there were more soldiers running amuck, most likely from the labyrinth below this tavern, high alert now with the disturbance that was a few dead slaves beneath their feet.

Anaergienne scarfed his food quickly, as did the rangers, but once completed, he leaned into Yurilo, hand on his cloak as he pulled him closer to him. "Are you ready?"

"As ready as ever," Yurilo said, putting down his cup of milk, licking his lips. "Just don't miss your moment, eh?"

"I would never." Anaergienne smiled, and Yurilo allowed a thin grin the crawl its way upon his lips.

Yurilo stood from his seat, and Lorana watched his movements. Slyly, he walked through between each table, sneakily out in the open with a knife, and deftly cut open coin purses and permitted the currency to clatter gently in his hands as he moved on to the next. He made friends, it seemed, talking away with others with that charisma he said he didn't have, and she felt easy, waiting for the distraction, and her attention returned to Anaergienne, who kept an eye on the cellar door.

"Lorana," Yun said.

"Yes, Yun," she replied. "What is it? Speak quickly, for my nerves are on end."

"Exactly, I can tell. Why don't you go outside for some fresh air, and prepare our horses," she replied. "If things go the way we want it to, it's going to get chaotic real quick." Lorana nodded, and stood from her seat after finishing her eggs, and walked towards the door. "Yara, follow after her, will you."

"Give you two some time for rekindling romance, eh?" Yara sneered.

"What?" Yun blushed, then immediately scowled after. "Piss off. We haven't the time for romance right now."

"Maybe tomorrow," Anaergienne replied, and there was a softness in Yun's glare. So, even her rough edges could be smoothed.

"Oi? Where's my money? Who took my money!?" a squeamish cry came from across the room. Lorana swiveled in her seat and saw a tall man was rummaging through his pack when he found his coin purse was empty, a scowl on his lips, and he grabbed a knife. "A filthy pickpocket, where are ya? I'll gut ye like the gruttin' pig ye a'e!"

She turned her gaze towards Yurilo, who was behind another man, a knife already cutting the coin purse of what looked like a very dangerous woman, a barbarian, perhaps. Large burly arms, and thick hair tied into braids like the more savage elves further south and secluded in Kinasa. Yurilo pivoted around and bowed at the man, and all eyes were upon him, and he smiled brightly at them as if he was a bard on a grand stage.

"Hey!" The man pointed his finger at him. "You, give me my money back!"

"Sir," Yurilo replied as all eyes were on him. "As you can tell, my coin purse is quite full, and I've plenty to share, but have you a way to identify your personal property?"

Everyone in the tavern started shuffling through their things. Yurilo was quite busy, and his coin purse was inflated with coins, and the patrons of this tavern were not going to be happy about it, and the indifferent stares became glares of condemnation and large amounts of anger.

Especially since Yurilo just confessed to everyone he stole from them. *Such audacity,* she thought as she neared the threshold of the door out of the tavern, before it would grow violent.

"I can't quite return what's yours because I don't know which ones belong to you without being fair to everyone else," Yurilo replied. "I'm afraid there's nothing to be done except for me to keep my winnings."

A man rushed over to tackle him. Yurilo swiveled his body, jumped and he was nowhere near anyone now. He ducked; a chair was thrown over his head. He sneered, a hand on his dagger, ready to draw, and his boot stamped firmly on the man that was now on the ground. "Oh, too slow! You'll have to do better than that!"

The tavern was like a circus. Constant shouting and swearing at him, and many were drawing weapons as they approached him. She glanced, and Lithwe came out from the cellar, and seeing the commotion, his eyes gaped, and he left the cellar door open. Anaergienne swiftly departed from the table, and snuck behind the bar and shut the door behind him. This seemed to work the way they intended, but Lithwe shouted, banding the hilt of a knife on an iron pan, and the shouting stopped.

"What's going on?" he shouted over the crowd.

"This lunatic stole from us," a patron said. "Look at his coin purse! Who carries that much!"

Lithwe squinted at him. "Yurilo, you son of a bitch! What are you doing here?"

"Lithwe." Yurilo's arms opened wide as if to greet an old friend. "Nice to see you, old friend. Now—"

"I ain't yer friend," Lithwe snapped, a knife pointed at him. "What is the meaning of this? Why are you here?"

"Funny story, really." Yurilo laughed nervously. "I was just minding my own business, eating my breakfast, you know how we elves like our eggs. When the coins in everyone's purses were talking to me, asking me to free them from their prison. Who was I to deny them their liberty? So, I only did what any reasonable person would do at a cry for help, and unchain their bonds, so I did."

"Wha?" Lithwe seemed bewildered. Who in their right mind would think to compare the coins to slaves meant to be freed? Lorana knew Yurilo was not someone who often thought about money, or needed much of it, but with a little switch in his personality, one might think he was from the Thieves' Guild, rather than the Assassins'.

"Give them back, now. I'll deal with you later."

"I was just telling this fine gentleman," Yurilo replied, scratching his chin and he coughed. "I have no way to identify whose coins belonged to who. It wouldn't be right to return his money to someone else, now would it? It's only fair I keep these. It's the only fair solution that works for all people involved. Surely, you agree, old friend?"

"No wonder everyone hated you." Lithwe glowered. "Damn you."

"Well, we're cut from the cloth of Assassins' Guild, now aren't we?"

"Gods no!" Lithwe scowled, and there was silence in the room. The innkeeper looked around cautiously, and half brought their voices to a dull roar. "I apologize about these interruptions. You can have your meals on the house."

"How generous," Yurilo sneered.

"Yurilo," Lithwe growled. "You're on ice, I'll kill you."

"I think these lovely people have a right to know who or what cooked their meals today," Yurilo bowed, smiling at the other assassin from his guild. "Now, why don't you enlighten us."

"I'm not affiliated with the Guild," he clearly lied.

"No? Then why are there dead slave girls in the cellar?"

The people inside the tavern didn't like that one, and they all glared at the innkeeper.

"Do you even have proof?" Lithwe frowned. "Those are some wild accusations."

"Then, I daresay, I must have been dreaming. Corridors of stone, and cages with men, dwarves, and elves, bloodied, sex slaves chained to the walls, most of which are half dead," Yurilo said. "Well, those whom I didn't free their souls from last night."

"Speak!" a warrior growled, hand on his axe as he glared at the innkeeper.

Yurilo searched the tavern. Everyone was good and riled up, and Anaergienne was gone. Now, he just needed to make sure no one went down into the cellar, not yet. The guards around shifted uncomfortably, metal clanging through the air as their iron clasped hands touched the pommels of their swords, ready to fight this morning. A very bloody breakfast is what this was.

Rather, what it was going to be. *Lorana.* He looked to the table where he once was sitting, and she and Yara were gone. Yun still drank her milk, but he could tell those pupils were scanning the room, preparing herself for a brawl that was going to go real sour real quick.

"No, there are no stone corridors," Lithwe said. "Where would I get stone? Korilya is leagues away! There are no slaves in the cellar, do you think I would partake in such barbarism? No. We're civilized here."

"Prove it!" the warrior swore.

"Are you going to believe me?" Lithwe pointed a sturdy finger. "Or the grutting elf who stole all your money?"

"You got me there," Yurilo waved his finger, but didn't let his smile fade. "All right, everyone, here is the deal."

"Yurilo," Lithwe snarled again. "I should have killed you when I had the chance."

"You and I are beyond niceties now, never liked each other, friend," Yurilo said. "Everyone, I have your attention now, Lithwe and I worked together a century back now, in the Assassins' Guild. Unlike him, I no longer associate myself with the Guild, nor do I work for them in any capacity. In fact, they even have a kill order on me, a fancy four thousand Grentonian coins. I was out here last night, when a girl slipped us a note. A bird and I investigated, and we discovered what really happened beneath these floorboards. If you want your money back, I'll gladly give it back to ya. After the violence of course."

"You wouldn't!" Lithwe snapped.

"You and I both know I would. Afterall, what use for money do I have?" Yurilo replied. "I removed those chains from me long ago."

"Answer me, are there slaves down there?" the warrior shrieked.

"No!" Lithwe jerked his head.

"Prove it, open the cellar, we'll find out!"

"Guards!" Lithwe said. "Restrain them."

"Proof right there," Yurilo said, a sword swinging by him. He parried the blade and thrust it in the soldier's throat, twisting it and the gurgling blood spat in his face. "What kind of innkeeper keeps guards like these?"

"Burn down the place!" the warrior called. "Give these slave drivers a taste of their own medicine. Start a fire. We'll burn them alive!"

Lithwe scurried behind the bar to the door. An arrow pierced a servant girl in front of him, pushing him on the ground. A warrior rushed past the chaos as guards and adventurers fought one another for dominance. Lithwe impaled the warrior with a rapier, and pushed him down, spraying the blood before bludgeoning the man's face with a pan, blood painting his fine tunic.

"What's going on?" another voice cried out.

"Miura!" Lithwe called. "Get some help from the cellar door, now!"

"Who started this?" Miura asked.

"It was grutting Yurilo!"

"So, he is here!" she shrilled.

"A good old comrade reunion." Yurilo grunted as he tripped a guard, and jumped on him, slitting his throat. "Just like old times, eh?"

Miura bolted for the cellar door.

"Yun!" he shouted.

More arrows were loosed into the wall.

CHAPTER 9

The Beaten Down Warrior

Gordir woke in a fit of his own Djit. He heard the guards clamoring up and down the corridors with haste. Metal clanked along the halls, and his vision blurry, he wiped it clean. Clenching his teeth, he crawled to the bowl by the bars that kept him inside and took the warm water to his lips. Refreshing, chaffed, his body weak, and humiliated.

His hands shook as he saw Lithwe bolting up and down the stairs, the elf who raped him and his wife repeatedly like they were nothing but toys. He wanted to wring his filthy little neck, but there was something going on. He looked up to where his wife and the other sex slaves were, dismembered. His heart raced as the guards talked among themselves around the butchery. Hissing, and panting, he was going to find who put them here, and kill them. Find who killed his wife and kill whoever it was. If it was the last thing he did.

Guards kept running up and down the corridor, screaming for someone to find an intruder. There was something or someone here last night, it seemed, who killed all the slaves above.

But was that all they did? He had to wonder what purpose they had to do just that? Or was the intruder among them?

He didn't know, all the more reason to find the culprit and murder them dead, and then they'd wish they were never born. He'd make certain of that, with all the iron in his blood, he would gut them open. But first thing's first, he had to get out of his prison, but there wasn't a way out that he could see, and he imagined with the commotion, the contests below which he had been winning, would be rescheduled. He took to his seat, pulled some blankets over his cold body as he waited for his moment.

It wasn't long now before the commotion ended, and the guards stopped patrolling this part of the prisons. There was some rattling of cages, and men, dwarves, and elves were pleading to be let loose. Hell, there even was an orc and goblin on the other side, gnawing on the iron bars like animals. The guards now couldn't be seen, and with his ears on the wall, he couldn't hear any words coming from the lips of his captors.

Clicking his tongue, he reached through the bars of the cage, and looked up. Someone was cleaning the mess up, but no slave, a warrior, it seemed with a mop and bucket, removing the carcasses, and the body parts into a bucket.

There was a commotion, another one, far away. Sounded like metal clanging above, and shouting, incoherently. Looking down, guards came, heavily armored again with swords drawn. Shouting orders to kill the intruder.

The same one? He looked up, and an elf ranger was above, and he threw himself at the man cleaning up the mess and hurled him over the railing. The man screamed. A sword the elf drew as he descended upon the path to confront the soldiers.

With an elf-like fury, he struck the steel, clanging clearly with the reverberations, hard. Warriors were pushed back as the elf made swift work with deft strikes, and hurled them off the side, and one other, before the elf was impaled with a blade, but it didn't seem to bother him, as the elf decapitated the culprit, and ripped the blade out from him.

"Get us out of here!" a dwarf called with a rustic beard. "Get us out."

"I've come to purchase your services, but I must ask you to fight once more," said the elf, as he approached Gordir's cage. "You there, will you fight?"

"Fight what this time?" Gordir sighed, unsure if this elf was responsible for the death of his wife.

"I think the most appropriate adversary is none other than your captors, wouldn't you agree?" the elf said. "Names, Anaergienne. What's yours?"

"Gordir," he replied.

"Now, a cage is no place for an elf, let's get ye out of here, yeah?" Anaergienne pulled out a ring of keys, unlocked the door, and it swung open. "Grab a sword and meet me up there. There's an inn, and what not. I doubt my friends are making any improvements on the place. The ale tastes like horse piss, as one of my friends described it. Much like the Dripping Bucket."

"Before I do anything," Gordir said as Anaergienne peered to the other cage. "The sex slaves. Do you know who killed them?"

"Yes," he removed the dwarf from the cage.

"Who did it?"

"Me," Anaergienne replied, gravely turning to him. "Look, Gordir, I've seen this Djit a number of times, and it never ends well, especially if you can't get the good and proper help ye need. Ends in suicide most of the time, or else, start inhaling mushrooms hoping to keep the nightmares away, or in less severe cases, one might just succumb to alcohol poisoning."

"Zarine was among them!" Gordir pushed on him as the dwarf grabbed a blade and started running up the path where the elf came from, screaming loudly. "My wife. You murdered my wife—"

"And when you all escaped from here after we did what we did? What life would there be to have?" Anaergienne pushed back on him. "She would wake up with the nightmares of being raped, again and again, and again. She wouldn't be able to handle it, and either consume herself in toxins till she died, or slit her own throat! She would essentially be a walking corpse. There's nothing you could do about that, nothing I could do to save her from that Hell. Is that what you want?"

"Even so," Gordir said. "What gives you the right—"

"No one has rights. They're just an illusion." Anaergienne frowned. "Now, for grutt's sake, just get a sword, and start charging up there like the dwarf did. The more help we get the better. Now, if you'll excuse me, I have people to save, and halls to collapse."

Gordir gritted his teeth, fists clenched at his side. The elf walked away from him, freeing one cage after another, and the people freed all too enthusiastically grabbed weapons from the ground and started running up with reckless abandon. This elf, Anaergienne didn't seem too disturbed with the prospect of letting out a few orcs and goblins who sprinted upwards, running past him. It seemed they all knew and understood what and who was responsible for their calamity, and that suffering brought them all under a symbolless banner. He wanted to kill this elf, but for the time being, his rage would subside for him, but burn against Lithwe, and he would cut him to pieces.

A loud roar interrupted his train of thought. The cages burst open, and the remaining prisoners fled. Anaergienne stumbled, grabbed hold of the railing and he grunted as the bar pressed against his chest. Shaking his head, the elf turned downwards, the loud warm breath of a beast he didn't know caressed him and made his ragged tunic whistle behind him.

"What—" He grabbed a sword. "—is that?"

"A dragon." Anaergienne chuckled. "Of course. Well, I suppose I don't need to ruin good ale to collapse this operation."

"What do you mean?"

"You," Anaergienne sneered at him. "Have a romantic date with Lithwe, do you not? Kill him. He's up there. I, on the other hand, will kill this dragon and collapse all these tunnels with it."

"A dragon!" Gordir shrilled. "You can't be serious. You can't kill a dragon."

"Oh, contrary," his eyes lit up with excitement. "I absolutely can. It's been an age, but I've done it before, and with Carmielle, I can do it again."

"Who are you?" Gordir asked.

Thoughtfully considering the actions, and the words which left Anaergienne's lips, and the mannerisms of both subtle humor, and gritty seriousness, Gordir thought Anaergienne was insane. He must be insane to even think of taking a dragon by himself, but Gordir was no fool. One elf or several hundred could not stand against the fabled might of a dragon. Few in number they were these days, and he knew, one simply didn't just attempt to kill a dragon. You outsmarted it, and hoped to trap it in a cave, and it would just starve. But no, that didn't seem to be the idea Anaergienne had.

It didn't matter. Anaergienne was right, he needed his vengeance. No noble deeds would prevail this night, and he hurried up through the corridors of this so-called tavern of hospitality of Blenheim. He would have his revenge, kill Lithwe, and make him feel the blade in his gullet. For all the horrid, traumatic things he did to him. It was the least he could do to attempt to return the favor. Perhaps he could kill Miura and make him watch. Yes, that would be fitting, after all, it was she who murdered his children in front of him.

CHAPTER 10

Freedom

Yurilo flipped over a table. The loud ruckus of metal clanging rang in his ears repeatedly in the inn, the noise magnified by the acoustics of the building. The guards, adventurers, and assassins moved against one another. Yun was in the corner, grunting as she led a group of soldiers out of the tavern. His heart pounded as a series of knives struck the table he used for cover, and he glanced behind it, seeing a very angry Lithwe, and Miura unable to open the cellar door with the arrows pinning the locked mechanisms shut. They shrieked in terror before Lithwe scowled at him.

Yurilo's gaze was obscured as an armor guard charged at him like a mad barbarian. The wood creaked, and he turned the table into the soldier, the table split apart with the sword, and a shield came for his face. Ducking, he put his hand on the ground before twisting back on his feet, taking his rapier out, he pierced through the man's armor, and kicked him off the blade. The man, in a dying thrust, struck at him, and he felt a metal gauntlet strike his cranium.

As he shook his head, another guard came out at him with a club. He ducked, and took a gander at the scene, and he was alone in here, blood dripped on the floor through the floorboards, and the dead bodies were numerous. But here he was, alone, and not with Lorana, or any of the others, since Anaergienne was doing what only he knew how to do, and Yun just left him! She just grutting left him!

The club swung again, slicing through the air. He ducked and kicked the man hard in the gut. The rapier pierced his side, and

Lithwe was behind him, rapier poised to strike. He parried the blade, stepping backwards, foot slipped on the flesh of a severed limb, but he retained his composure as the other assassin sister scowled, nearing to his left flank.

He took a step back, disengaging from the fight, and vaulted out the window. Grimacing, he slipped on the dirt, and pulled himself up to his feet with the loud clamor of fighting, and women and children screaming as the immediate area where the tavern and festival was, was now a flesh pit of violence.

A rustle of leaves to his left. He turned, a soldier, less armed than everyone else swung a sword at him with great haste. Yurilo jumped back, twisting his head as the point of the blade cut his cheek. He hissed, sliding in the dirt, and placed his hand on the wound, and warm blood coated his fingers. He looked again at the soldier who came barreling down at him, and still hadn't been able to confirm if Lorana was safe with Yara.

Hopefully, these rangers were good at their word, for that was the only thing he had left to assume she was safe so he could deal with this man, who swung his sword wildly with great dexterity. His eyes kept watchful of what was behind him, but he stepped carefully, parrying anything that came too close.

The steel came near, and the tavern door opened. Lithwe cut down an adventurer who happened by, before shoving himself into the fray, and pushed Yurilo away from the man, but before he did, he took a careful note at the emblem on the man's shoulder, a golden sword. He was from the Warrior's Guild.

Thank you, Lithwe, though you didn't mean it, you just saved my life! He staggered further into the fight which no one asked for, but Lithwe kept coming after him, and thankfully, a small group of fighting adventurers took on the man from the guild. The noise echoed in his ears as he parried a blade for his heart, and Lithwe's weapon got caught in a nearby adventurer.

Yurilo reached for his pocket and pulled out throwing stars. He threw them with a flick of his wrist. Miura separated him from Lithwe, deflecting the stars from their target with deft strikes of a knife before hurling herself at him. He twisted his body and threw her into the crowd with a scream.

As he panted, his eyes scanned for Lorana briefly, unable to see in the fray. That could be good news, assuming she wasn't already dead and trampled on. He twisted his body again, but caught between two fighters, Lithwe's rapier made contact, piercing the skin by his abdomen. He coughed and punched him in the face. The rapier was removed from his body, and he twisted another strike at him, which was parried.

"You son of a bitch!" Lithwe swore. "Why would you do this?"

"Why? You mean why would I get in the way of human traffickers from enslaving elves and all other races because their boss told them to? Oh, I don't know. I thought it would be funny," Yurilo replied, ignoring the pain. "What say you then? That you sold even your own kin."

"Ignoring that," Lithwe struck at him, and Yurilo twisted, the rapier stuck in another body.

He kicked Lithwe and that's when he heard creaking wood. Glancing behind him, the door to the tavern splintered with several exhausted people pouring out of it. One man drew himself to the man from the warriors guild, tackled him to the ground before slicing his throat. Standing, he raised his sword in the air, blood smearing his rustic beard as these prisoners joined the fray.

"FREEDOM!" the man cried. "FREEDOM!"

"FREEDOM!" the prisoners shouted.

"Damnit!" Lithwe disengaged with Yurilo.

"Thanks, Anaergienne," he put his hand on his wound, and sheathed his rapier. "And never a moment too soon, eh?"

The distraction was exactly what he needed. Deftly, he wove himself through the crowd of fighting people slyly to avoid further confrontation. Getting hit in the head with anything wasn't ideal, so he moved, still following the trail of blood, taking note of the faces dead on the ground. As he passed, none of them were Lorana's, and for that, he was thankful as he got to the other side of the chaos, he couldn't find Yun, but he found Yara all alone, with a number of dead assassins at her feet. Grimacing, he dashed towards her, drew a rapier, and stabbed a soldier in the back before he confronted her.

"Lorana!" he grunted. "Where is she?"

"We were separated," Yara admitted, drawing her bow, and loosed an arrow into a slave driver. "Bastards!"

"You were supposed to protect her!" Yurilo said. "Where was—"

"Well, in battle things never go the way you expect or want them to," Yara growled, loosing another arrow.

"Where was the last place you saw her," he snarled.

"Oh, I don't know," she said sarcastically. "Maybe when your whole speech about slaves being underneath the floorboards to stir this violence. We were supposed to be gone first! Nice speech by the way."

Yurilo ignored the awkward praise. "I'm going to look for Lorana."

"You're leaving me?" she shrilled, loosing another arrow. "Here I thought you were one of the good assassins."

"Good and assassin should never be in the same sentence," he pointed a stern finger at her. "And if you didn't leave me in the tavern all by myself, Yun too, I might be inclined to help you. You aren't my priority!"

"Grutt!" she swore, drawing her sword to cut down a guard.

"'Grutt' is right," Yurilo swore, walking away towards a nearby tree. "Bitch."

CHAPTER 11

Dragon's Head

Yurilo sat on a branch high above the chaos that formed beneath him. The fighting was still strong with little sign of stopping, save for several armored guards wearing those patches getting organized, and pushing on the adventurers, who were grossly undisciplined by comparison. Shields were raised up, and spears held up, stabbing at the adventurers, until one by one they fell. Slave drivers with their chains came up with rabid wolves, howling as they stirred into the disgruntled mess, biting and gnawing at everyone they could get their hungry jaws on. Searching the mess for Lorana, he couldn't find her, but he saw Yun and Yara together trying to push guards away from the tavern as best they could.

Watching the two cut with their swords was much like watching a ballet. Deft strikes, blood spraying in the air, twisting, and pivoting of the feet like they'd done this a thousand times. Of course, they have, and that was apparent. They took their swordplay very seriously, and no one could ever take that away from them. But where was Lorana? His nerves got the better of him, but he noticed Lithwe and Miura getting an attachment of soldiers who were bringing chains and wheeled cages around the bend, and that's when he noticed Lorana's green cloak by the table, and the horses neighing.

He jumped down from the tree, rolled on the ground, darting back towards the other part of the village. The wind whistled through his hair and a hand rested on his pommel. He gritted his teeth, sliding through the soil as he made his way quickly to Lorana.

He felt a grip on his ankle, and he tripped, sliding, his face eating dirt. He rolled, seeing Miura with her whip and dagger scowling at him. Oh, what did he ever see in her? She was more of a bitch than Yara ever could be. He jumped up, drew his rapier.

"Lithwe!" she called. "Get yer ass over here. I've got him. We need to kill him now!"

"No," Yurilo said. "Do we need such violence between old friends?"

"No," Lithwe approached, rapier in hand. "For old friends, no. No violence required, but you aren't our friend, traitor. So, violence is highly recommended."

"And besides," Miura gritted her teeth. "If you didn't start all this, this wouldn't be necessary."

"No?" Yurilo tilted his head. "No matter, it was worth a try. Lorana! Run far away from here! Many of these slave drivers are mere humans. They can't outrun you!"

A whip from Miura, he turned, evading the leather snake. Lithwe thrust his rapier, and he pivoted, taking his hand, he pushed the blade away, and thrust his knife, scratching the elf's cheek, blood drawn.

Just like his, though, the strike on his own cheek was undoubtedly deeper. Hissing, the whip came, and Miura closed her distance on him, the dagger near his chest, he twisted his body, elbowing her in the face, pushing her into Lithwe, and he thrust again. The rattling of chains continued. His blade was parried by another sword; a warrior with the emblem punched him in the face, and he collapsed to the ground.

The warrior kicked his rapier away and tied him with rope and leather straps for good measure. Hissing, the assassins moved away from him, and he wondered why they didn't just finish killing him. But with his blurred vision, he saw a cage which he was being marched into, and several of the prisoners were re-shackled, if not dead, their bodies littering the ground. He panted as he was thrust into the cage, and a large lock placed on it, with several chains. The room was cramped, with several other slaves in here, begging to be released.

He touched his head as he made his way to the bars of the cage, and he searched for that cloak. Unable to find it, he sighed, and leaned back into the cage. He didn't recognize any of the slaves in here, and Yun and Yara weren't in any of the cages he saw as the violence ended. Though he still heard metal clanging, albeit in a distance. Lines of slaves were marched, and those who refused to comply with the demands to be shackled again, were tackled to the ground, for the sake of freedom, and cut open.

He heard Lithwe's boots coming over this way. It was a mess, Yurilo had to admit, to be caught in a cage, but with all the slaves free, and many dead, perhaps with the little glimpse of freedom they got to know, maybe it was worth it. Even if the freedom obtained was little more than a turn in the hourglass.

Perhaps there was more to this than he realized, but he couldn't think about that, except for his promise to Lorana to keep her safe during his journey, but now, that seemed so trivial to think about it. Considering he was about to die.

"Yurilo," Lithwe growled. "You fool. You bastard, and all the words and curses in the tongues of humans, elves, and orcs, and the blasted dwarves, there isn't one suitable for one filled with your treachery."

"An Assassin of the Guild." He said, sitting on the uncomfortable iron plate. "Treachery is all we know. You should forgive me for trying to leave that part of me behind."

"You could have made something for yourself, you know," Lithwe said. "Could have become our Guild Master, but you squandered your talents."

"It's a little-known fact that position was in fact offered to me," Yurilo sneered. "Had I taken it, would things be different? No, I don't think that would have changed anything in the grand scheme of things. I'd just be the same person I was, the one I hated, and that's no way to live life, am I right? At least now, the choices I made are a little more bearable to my soul. Can you say the same?"

"Yes," Lithwe said. "Because I killed my heart a century ago. As did my sister, hers. You should have done the same, and like ye said, nothing would have changed."

"In the grand scheme of things, nothing ever changes things that the machine already set in motion," Yurilo replied. "But our perspective and our minds and hearts and souls change with the passing of time. I killed my heart, but something that day revived it. I'm not entirely sure what I owe to such revival, such redemption is beyond me." He waved his hand. "But you've got a job to do, people to kill, to enslave, males, females, and children and little puppies to feed to dogs or rape. Good to know you've not changed after all this time. Even if I always found you deplorable."

"Such harsh words for someone who consistently called us your friend," Lithwe said. "But you're with the ranger lot, and a wizard, apparently. No matter, we'll find the wizard—"

"Of that," Yurilo smiled. "I've no doubt. Catch her unawares, I'm sure you'll find no prey easier, however, she is a wizard, and damnable good one at that. She's filled with resources that—"

There was a loud roar, and the ground shook. His hand grabbed hold of the bar as the slaves inside the cage he shared were unsettled and looked to the ground. Yurilo stood, and another reptilian roar entered the ground, and the shaking of the earth increased. Lithwe tripped on the ground, and pushed himself away from the cage, and Yurilo listened closely as the roars of ferocity turned into squeals of dying. Several cries for uncertainty, and the hands inside the cages stretched out, crying for release.

Yurilo looked at one of them, eyes gaped open, sweat beading down his face. Hands trembling, and the voices hoarse as their cries scratched their throats. Terror, he knew, but of what? What did they know was down there that he didn't? He saw the cages, the cells, the large doors, but surely, not something that these contestants down there would be contended to and expect to die every single time. It wasn't like it was a dragon down there. He knew they were extinct or close to it. They were so rare to see, if they did exist, they might as well as not exist, but the ferocity of a dragon was legendary.

The guards were ready, spears, and shields raised up. Assassins were working together, ignoring all fighting, grabbing chains, and some wizards among them chanted, with enchanting circles scattered throughout the village. Large, weighted nets were raised in the tree, and a ballista was rolled in, several in fact, poised at the tavern. Looking at it, a roar, a final one, a high-pitched squeal like a dying pig scratched against his ears, his hand closed them.

The ground creaked, and the foundations of the earth gave way. The wood wrenched and shattered like an exploding barrel. Another roar, and a spurt of an ungodly amount of blood rained down from the hole that was the tavern. Trees fell to the ground. A green wing, a snout with sharp teeth, a red illuminated eye, fading now as the beast collapsed to the ground.

Several cuts at its cheeks, and on his neck. The wing fluttered, but the flaps of the wings couldn't lift it, and a long tongue hung out of his mouth. The neck was partially cut open, and the flesh hung out with a bleeding esophagus. The side of the hide of the beast. Blood shimmered in the light.

The guards cowered beneath the gaze of the dead dragon. Metal clamored as their joints trembled. The weighted nets weren't thrown yet, and the magic circles didn't activate whatever spell it seemed the wizards were trying to cast to contain the dragon.

Yes, this is what it was, and there was an elf in one of the cages shouting something Yurilo couldn't comprehend. But the shock of his heart looked upwards, despite the distant murmuring of one another, and he thought, Lorana must be kept safe, from whatever this was. Yet, it was dead, despite the jaw moving, still attempting to breathe, to hang onto what life it had left.

Anaergienne, whose clothes were in tatters while he was covered in blood, jumped on the snout of the beast and impaled its head with his sword, twisting the blade until the dragon screeched once more, and the warm breath, saliva and blood painted the cages and the slaves, inside.

Yurilo felt disgusted with the matter all over his fae and clothes, he was going to need a strong bath after this. Hissing, he looked closely at Anaergienne, who now faced everyone in equal stupor, but he smiled, baring his teeth for all to see as he panted. He seemed happy. Or so it appeared to Yurilo, after all, in what state of ecstatic joy could one find reason to smile so widely?

"My name is Anaergienne," he announced. "Leave the keys, and depart from this place, or I will kill you. Don't think I can't. Numbers mean nothing to one who dare slay a dragon."

There was silence, and no one moved.

"How," said the elf in the cage. "How did you kill the dragon? That's a fool's errand?"

"So is fighting to the death so someone else can make a coin of your labor," Anaergienne replied. "And here we are. Leave the keys to the cages and leave immediately. There will be no further trafficking here."

"Who are you—" an assassin began to say before he was struck in the head with an arrow.

Yurilo leaned closer to the barrier of the cage, and beheld Yun and Yara, on which they stood a mound of bodies, and their faces and cuirasses covered in blood. The crying from the dwellers ceased, and the assassins, and the Warriors fled through the trees, leaving everything behind. Anaergienne hopped down after procuring some keys and freed everyone from the cages.

"You got caught in here," Anaergienne noted. "Eh? What gives, Yurilo, you weren't supposed to get caught."

"And you were supposed to collapse the tunnels," Yurilo said.

"Well," Anaergienne opened the cage, and he hugged him. Yurilo recoiled at the touch. "I should figure that the entire body of a dragon should suffice as coverage, and should be in the way of further attempts, at least here. Hey can do that elsewhere for all I care."

"I see," Yurilo panted. "Then, we've got a journey to—Lorana!"

"Lorana," Yara said. "Did ye not find her? You left me for her, didn't you?"

"Anaergienne!" an elf came running.

"Yes, Gordir," Anaergienne turned to face them. "You—you actually did it. You killed a dragon."

"I even dragged the evidence up here to prove it," Anaergienne replied. "But you still doubt me. These are my companions, Gordir, pleased to meet you and I—"

Yun approached, nodding to Yurilo as she dashed away. He understood she meant to track Lorana down and bring her to safety.

"I'm sorry for what I did to your wife. That was Yun, this is Yara and Yurilo. Lorana will be back shortly, I hope."

"Wife? What?" Yara's jaw dropped. "Anaergienne, what did you do?"

"Something noteworthy of confession," he replied grimly. "And I regret it, but I'd do it again. Sometimes, Gordir, holding onto hope is a good thing, it gets you through tomorrow, but there is a time where one must accept reality, and hope need not apply. I've lived long enough to know that hope, in some cases, is just postponed disappointment."

"You took her from me—"

"She was already gone," he said, eyes glazed over. "I'm sorry. Truly, I am."

"Anaergienne, when Lorana gets back, we really should be going," Yurilo said.

"We can't leave things the way they are," Yara said. "This place is a mess."

"It wasn't our fault," Anaergienne replied. "But you're right, we can't leave things the way they are."

"But we have our own responsibilities now," Yurilo replied. "Don't we?"

"Yes," Yara sighed. "Let's get this done, and then we can get back, patch things up uninterrupted. Perhaps send a homing pigeon out."

"Just one more night," Anaergienne suggested. "This would have taken a toll, and you," he pointed to Yurilo's wound. "Got stabbed yourself. You could do with a little rest."

"The people are free now," Gordir said. "With a little guidance, they can rebuild this village, but I must be going, myself."

"Oh?" Anaergienne tilted his head.

"Yes, I must return home now, and see my sister. She's going to want to see me and hear of her family. I must also report this all back to Zinasa,"

"Oh, a high elf!" Yara exclaimed. "Eh? Been awhile since I recall one of you roaming through our forest."

"We can all share in our stories together, but perhaps some food, help carry off the dead, and bury them if they're of the village. Burn the rest," Anaergienne said. "They deserve no proper burial, and we'll feast and drink, and tomorrow we all go south. Gordir, you're welcome to come. We're on our way to the temple."

"That's on the way to my sisters," he said.

"I'd be pleased if you came with. After all, more is the merrier." Anaergienne bowed.

Yurilo wasn't pleased with the idea, but he helped. By nightfall, Lorana arrived, and so did Yun. The rangers assisted with the removal of the dead, delegating tasks to dwellers to achieve the goal of cleanup, mopping up the blood, and trying to salvage what they could from the inn.

Pieces of the dragon were cut out, and put onto flames, and inside pots for the late-night feast of the evening, and they all took a nice long bath in the lake nearby, removing the muck and grime from them. Feeling refreshed the following day, they continued their journey to Corela, with Gordir among them.

DARK ELF'S SNARE

A Darkling's Seduction

Sheris

The city gates revealed themselves, parting a mist wall as the guards opened the iron shutters, creaking for those ahead of Erdan's sight. His hood soaked, hair tucked inside with the downpour, and he contemplated, as the wagon rolled forward with Glentor and his goods, wheels creaking through the dirt. Chatters, he heard, still muffled by the rain in the puddles.

Past the gates, Sheris, inside was a place he'd not seen in recent memory, but the memory of an elf was outlasting, especially those of Zinasa, who trained their mind over their bodies. Though, Erdan never neglected his own, especially with his occupation, but now, listening to Glentor talk with the city guard, he chose to not hear the words, but his eyes scanned the people coming and going from across the way in this torrent.

City folk were cloaked as they went to and from, with little casing over themselves, some magic green auras protected them from the rain as they carried sacks of flour and other goods. There was no sound of music, no laughter here, or was there the sound of gleeful children or balls being passed through streets.

The houses and buildings here were of a variety of make, speaking of its great diversity, fine stone work of the dwarves, and they carved into rocks, transporting them into great forges, one of which had their fire lit in the distance; there was a local item shop, from which, he could smell the delectable herbs and spices inside, the building of carved mahogany wood, and branches stretched forward with its sign, the letters on which, even his elven eyes couldn't decipher, and some stone and wood used in tandem with one another for the localized houses, and the portable shops for which, additional out of city merchants set up their shops by the city square, where there was a large fountain, and three marble statues standing in the water.

As the wagon rolled forward and Glentor signed the papers for their entry and the state of their current affairs, Erdan's mind wandered as he considered the path ahead of him, and that which he left behind. His thoughts meandered aimlessly to Glenroy, his friend who stayed behind in Malitu to search for Anaergienne. The woman on the road, the black knight even, forces of nature to contend with that which could easily kill any one of them.

What trouble did his cousin get himself into? No telling, especially this far on the journey, and for now, he could relax, seeing there was nothing further that he could do about his cousin's mishap without hearing word from Malitu.

"Erdan." Glentor raised his head up as the pony trotted towards the square. "I'm gonna need yer help puttin' things together, now."

"Yes," he gasped. "Of course."

"On second thought…" Glentor arrived at the city square. "I think I should be okay by myself for a wee moment, but perhaps…" He reached for his coin purse. "Get yerself to the inn, purchase for me space for the pony, and some rooms for the inn. Make sure to secure a room for two-months' time."

"Understood." Erdan nodded, catching the coin purse in the air. He hopped off the wagon and sprinted through the rain, moving north of the city, where the main road was, leading further north into the lands that were by all accounts, no mortals' land, for it was well known to be contested between Grento and Cadrasar, a bloody mess it was, more than anything else by all known recollections. He walked to the farmhand, standing underneath the stables, and the wood dripped with the rain into puddles. Horses ate from their pales, but a sharp smile the boy had, but even amidst that smile, a show of discontent hid behind those eyes.

"Oi." Erdan waved at him.

"What business now," the boy replied. "Does an elf have in my stables? What use have ye for a horse anyway?"

"Sometimes for the sport." Erdan smiled, stretching a hand out. They shook hands. "Or in my case, to transport goods."

"You transport? You're a ranger, are you not? Dreadful Guild!"

"I assure you…" Erdan gave a light bow after retracting his hand. "I am a ranger, but a hired hand. I've no affiliation with the Rangers' Guild, you understand. I'm not even from Kinasa."

"Ah, one o' you high elves then." The farmhand bowed. "My apologies. We rarely get *elf* visitors, except when they try to tell us what to do, and what God or Goddess to worship. We've no love for that kind here."

"Well…" Erdan brushed off the racist comment. "Forgive me, then, I don't care to keep up with current events as far as things go, but I'm here on business, and my employer has imparted to me the responsibility, you understand, to secure some stable room for two-months for one pony. I can pay in advance."

"Who is your employer?" the boy asked.

"Glentor is his name," Erdan answered, crossing his arms. "A halfling from Paxis, we'll only be here for that long."

"I see, I see." He nodded.

"If it is at all reasonable, we can purchase the room up front or take it week by week," Erdan replied.

"By all means." He put his hand out. "Now, with all things to be considered now, let's go week by week. Wouldn't want the little halfling to starve during those two months, eh? I'll keep the space in good faith, but the moment ye miss a payment on each seventh-day, I remove the pony."

"Understood." Erdan nodded.

"All right," he said. "That will be seventy Shironian coins."

"All right." Erdan pulled out the coin purse, and counted seventy Shironian coins. He'd organized the purse inside to not be confused with Grentonian coins, and Crestien coins. "My name is Erdan," he said. "Pleasure."

"Nice to meet ya." The boy took the coins and pocketed them. "Pleasure also. Nice to meet an elf with no ties to that wretched Guild.

Hard to take them seriously most times. Name's Verdik. Erdan, I presume I can expect the pony in the mornin' or shall I wait after?"

"Glentor's settin' up shop now, and I must secure room at the inn. I'll help him afterwards. Once that is all set and secured, I'll return with the pony. I'd say I should return within three hours."

"Try not to be too late now," he said. "Sometimes crazy people come from the road at night."

"Crazy?"

"Nothing to really worry about, I think," Verdik replied, putting his hat on. "They just come off screaming for help about some witch or demon. Honestly, we've got to worry about some bandits, orcs, goblins, the occasional crazed dwarf and such."

"Seems few things rarely change," Erdan commented. "Forgive my abrupt departure, friend, but I must be going. I'll see you soon."

"But of course," Verdik replied.

Erdan took himself, drenched still, water dripping from his cloak with each passing moment into the puddles, rippled with each drop. The inn was brightly lit, the shutters closed, save for a little hole in the wall which was meant to remain open at all times of the day. For what purpose, he could only guess. A view unhindered by those around the city square.

It was just a stone's throw away from the rest of the traveling merchants, still arranging their carts and tents, struggling and swearing as the elements were not kind to them. He pushed the polished wood door open and was met with the scent of perfume, offensive in more conservative parts of the world.

Women walked back and forth between the tables. Vixens. They wore scanty clothes, some showing too much bosom for his personal taste, and the makeup was done perfectly, as if these women made plenty of effort to attract the ideal male or mistress to their beds.

This was a fine inn, lots of food to go around, the fresh baked bread in the ovens burning so hot, he could hear the cackling flame from inside the kitchen. He took himself towards the barkeep, a heavy man, burping behind mutton chops.

"Oi," the keep said. "An elf. What can I do—"

"Let me stop you right there." Erdan waved his hand dismissively. "I've no affiliation with the Rangers Guild." He withdrew his hood, and pointed to his chest where the emblem would be if he was of that Guild. "See, nothing. I need two rooms for two months. One for a halfling—nice and cozy he likes—and one for me. Doesn't really matter how cozy mine is."

"Well…" He leaned forward. "Might I have two rooms available for those requirements. How will ye pay for the rooms?"

"Simple." Erdan pulled out Glentor's coin purse. "We pay each week, on the seventh day first thing in the morning. I pay for seven days right now. I've Shironian coins to fit the bill. How much?"

"One-hundred forty coins," he said. "Comes with breakfast."

"Honestly," Erdan sighed at the idea of counting so many out, but he poured the coins on the table, and they clattered on the top, and he felt eyes gazing towards him. "With the cost of so many materials, one ought to have thought about consolidating things a little more."

"How do you mean?" the barkeeper asked.

"Oh." Erdan counted the rest out and pushed them to the bar keeper. "Nothing too fancy, but perhaps a way of exchanging coins that wasn't so cumbersome to count out for anything beyond a hundred. For example, a coin that would be worth ten, instead of just one and exchange them accordingly."

"Perhaps you fancy yerself an economist," he replied.

"No." Erdan shook his head as he was handed a pair of keys and some parchment with the directions to get to the respective rooms. "I just like things simple. Life is complicated enough, wouldn't you agree? Perhaps some fool would be a bother to someone else should there be methods of making some complex things simpler."

"Perhaps," the innkeeper said. "But until some genius finds a way to implement those things, we keep things as they are. No one figured out the implementation."

"Not around here anyway," Erdan replied, for he knew Zinasa had a system in place.

The Standard Zinasian coin, a Korilyan gem, a Kinasian token, Shironian coins, Crestien coins and Grentonian coins all had varying degrees of value. Rarely were Zinasian coins exchanged for the amount of value they held, and each additional token was worth less than the last. There was no need to consider cultural and inter-regional exchange rates, for it was all worked into the economy. Of course, a Zinasian coin would have to be converted to an appropriate currency before someone could purchase goods with it.

There was a loud ruckus outside.

"Excuse me." Erdan put the keys into his pocket, and rushed outside, pushing a drunk man on the ground on his way out the door.

Throwing his hood up, his eyes scanned the perimeter of the square, several merchant stands were broken into, and pushed aside. One merchant was nursing a broken arm behind the chaos of running merchants.

Guards pushed their way through the city with poised weapons, ready to strike. Erdan's hand rested on his pommel as he searched for Glentor's stand, partially set up. Several vials were on the ground, and the halfling scurried about, a cloaked figure was upon him with a rapier, hand reaching for the chest. Guards sprinted, but not before Erdan's foot pushed off the ground.

His sword drawn, slicing through the air. The thief turned around, cloth around his face and his ears. He couldn't tell where this person came from, but he parried with such ease.

The close blade pierced his shoulder, and Erdan jerked his body, tensing his muscles within, keeping the sword impaled in him, before throwing down with great strength his own blade at the hilt. The sword clanged against the cross guard, forcing the thief to abandon it, and he turned and sprinted the other way.

Grunting, he took the rapier out, and drew his bow, nocked an arrow, pulled the string taut, and loosed. The arrow flew through the rain, impaling the thief in the back, and he fell to the ground. Guards rushed towards the thief, and Erdan sheathed his blade and helped the halfling up to his feet. He gritted his teeth with the strain on his muscles, and placed his hand on his shoulder, blood dripping through his cloak.

"You're not hurt, are you?" Erdan hissed.

"No." The halfling drew his cloak over himself, picking up the small box from the ground before placing it on his merchant's stand before securing it closed behind several locks. "Just startled, is all. Did you do everything I asked?"

"Aye," Erdan replied. "Pony is all set, I need to fasten her to the stable."

"Yes," Glentor said. "She's ready. The key to my room?"

"But of course." Erdan retrieved the key from his pouch before handing it to him. "I'll stable the pony."

"Of course." Glentor nodded. "Ye should probably get that looked at before tomorrow."

"You there." An armored guard approached him. "What ye doin' out here this late at night? With bow and sword, ye shouldn't—"

"Well…" Erdan smirked. "As you can see, I was saving this halfling's wealth from being stolen."

"I need to see ya documents," he said.

"Mine or Glentor's? We checked in with the gate."

"Yours. Are you his bodyguard?" he asked.

"Yes." Erdan rolled his eyes. "As you can see, it is very wet outside. If you come with me to the inn right there, I'll show you my papers, and we'll get this done and over with. I've got things I need to do."

"Hurry on then." The guard scowled behind that beard.

"Erdan," Glentor said. "I'll take care of the pony. We can call this a night."

"Of course." Erdan nodded, motioning the guards to follow him, and they passed through the threshold. He pulled off his backpack and pulled out a file with some papers with it and handed his papers to them, who investigated it.

"Where's your companion? It says a company of three—you, the halfling I presume, and a Glenroy?"

"We were separated," Erdan sighed. "A long story, but he's in Malitu for the time being until such time his current errand affords him the opportunity to join us. Hopefully he's on his way with a mighty fast horse."

"Sorry to bother you." The guard handed him his documents.

"Very well, if you need me for anything else," Erdan hissed, putting pressure on his wound. "You know where to find me, and please *hesitate* to ask. Especially tonight, I've a wound to nurse." He gnarled his lips. "Never mind. I'll let this wound nurse itself back to health. Not worth a trip to the ward."

He waved the guards away. An eye peered through the rain as they departed the inn, and he took himself a seat to one of the tables in the corner. Many people were still drinking as if there wasn't just a robbery attempt, or perhaps this was too common an occurrence to warrant concern, or perhaps everyone was simply too drunk to notice.

Anyway, he waited for the tavern girl to arrive, and he placed an order of ale with her. She hurried away to retrieve it. He leaned back, removed his hood, and scanned the tavern more intently before his ale arrived.

Sheris was devoid of elves, it seemed, or rather, they took better company than the common riffraff of people coming into this inn. Funny, his mind already started equating rich merchants to common citizenry, and without cause to do so. He'd only been here for a few hours.

A woman sat down in front of him, a mug of ale it smelled like in her hand, and she leaned forward, a blush in her cheeks and brown ringlets of hair framed her face. Eye shadow over her lids, and a scar on her lower chin up to the lips. A wry smile she had, baring white teeth, and the scent of heavy ale departed her lips as the odor confronted his nose. A ring there was, on her finger with an emerald stone on it, and no engravings. Some necklaces over her bosom, which was generously displayed for him to look at, but he averted his gaze to her eyes.

"What lures you all the way to Sheris?" she asked. "There is something pleasant about you. You belong on a fine canvass."

"My…" He leaned back as his ale was brought to him, and he pulled it from the center of the table immediately. "To what do I owe the honor and privilege of find such company?"

"Oh." She chuckled. "We rarely get elves here, and when we do, it's quite unlike them to visit this here tavern. One might say they don't like jewelry all that much."

"That's a filthy lie," Erdan replied, bringing the ale to his lips. The bitter taste drenched his tongue. "Well, that might be true for those of Kinasa, anyway. Zinasa elves love jewels, some say almost as much if not more so this age as dwarves. Seems like something fowl went amiss in the air and their soil."

"I saw you outside, you know," she swooned, leaning forward. "Such a fine job dispatching that thief the way you did. Such dexterity."

"Oh, my." Now *he* blushed. No one ever complimented how he'd killed someone before, and that thief wasn't the first one.

"Such a display of expertise, I dare say." She tilted her head, and twirled a strand of hair with her finger. "A mortal such as yourself must have been bred by good stock."

He spat the ale on the table. Was he being objectified? The insecurity swelled within him. He'd been the target of many people trying to kill him before, but never by one so direct about their desires upon him. Simply and indirect flirting, yes. But outright? No. *This must be a trap*. He wiped his lips.

"Oh, I didn't mean to be such a bother to you." She smiled, taking a draft of her ale. "But I recognize good stock when I see it."

"Is this the part where someone knocks me in the head and I get shipped off somewhere, tied, and gagged?" Erdan replied, coughing.

"Only if you're into that sort of thing, sweetie." She smiled, rapping on the table with her knuckles. "Such good stock is a terrible thing to waste, and I know something about rearing animals, hogs, cows, horses, and hares of course."

"As you can see, I'm neither of those things, and…" He felt blood rushing to his penis. "You're making me unnecessarily uncomfortable. I'm going to finish my ale and get going now."

Glentor came and pulled a seat up with a tankard all on his own. He turned to the woman, and then back at Erdan with a raised brow. His knuckles rapped on the table before bringing some ale to his lips and touched the elf's shoulder, softly gripping it.

Erdan's heart pulsed, and he felt sweat beating on his forehead. His eyes grew drowsy, wanting to put himself to sleep, even temporarily. Some rest would be good. Just rest, nothing more.

"I've had that effect on many people," she said. "But I'll be gentle. After all, we wouldn't want damaged goods."

"Erdan," Glentor said, eyebrow raised. "What or who are you talking to?"

"I'm talking to—" He stopped himself when he realized the woman wasn't there, nor the tankard where she had been. He turned around and saw nothing behind him, quickly searching the room for his would-be trafficker. He couldn't find her. "I was just talking to a woman here."

"Yeah, well." Glentor sipped his ale. "You were talkin' to a pocket o' air, is what ye were doin'. Look, I'm sure you're worried about Glenroy and Anaergienne, but worrying about them when they're wherever they are at the moment, isn't going to help you in anyway, least of all when ye start seeing things that aren't there."

"Somehow, I don't think that's how paranoia works," Erdan replied, imbibing the rest of his ale, and putting some coins on the table. "Yes, I worry for them, because that woman—her sword, and what else, the knight and wolves were unlike any I've seen."

"No?" Glentor replied. "I remember them, all too frequently in the night, but when I wake up, they're gone."

"In much the same way I wake up, and Glenroy isn't here with us." Erdan sighed. "He was wise in his years."

"And ye aren't?" Glentor rubbed his hands together, removing his cloak and hanging it on the back of his chair.

"I'm older than he," Erdan replied. "But his body aches I'm sure. He may never admit it, pride often gets in the way, or if he did, I simply forgot it, but even he can only be so nimble when such a time for violence comes, and dealing with the likes of that woman, calls for no shortage of violence, and rage in small supply."

"Be that as it may," Glentor said. "I'm sure with all other things to be considered, we'll receive word by pigeon. After all, he knows where we are, and so do people who are at Malitu who are in the know. If something happened, we'll find out about it one way or another." He let out an exasperated sigh. "Perhaps, Erdan, it's best you get yerself some sleep before tomorrow. We've business to conduct and all that. Make sure no one tries to sneak in the back while I'm not lookin'."

"Absolutely," he replied. "Make sure the tavern girl gets this, yeah? Wouldn't want to start our stay here on a rocky note."

"Yes," Glentor replied. "Yes, of course. We wouldn't want that. Fare thee well, Erdan, and get some rest and nurse that stab. It might be a good idea to go to the forge and armor tomorrow too, yeah, get that repaired? You didn't have time in Malitu or Felldur to contend with that damaged armor."

"Yes." Erdan stood, looking to the cut in his leather cuirass. That cursed *thing* did a number on his protection, including that dreadful serrated blade. "I think you're right in that regard, I'll see to it in the morning."

CHAPTER 2

The Smith

Erdan stared at the stone sign; it was hanging loose with heavy chains, and carved within it was the shape of a fire, and of course, the inscription; Guri's Forge. The scent of soot entered his nose. Burning coal and black smoke escaped these windows, inlaid with stained glass. The sound of hammer on steel echoed in his ears, and he took to the door, pushing the only wood thing about this building open.

The door shut behind him as he entered a room of gray stone. Torches were lit every ten feet in a large area behind the counter. Another dwarf, a woman with red braided hair was hammering away at a sword on the anvil. The metal was red hot as it was being bent into shape.

There was a basement door, open, and a ladder which went deeper into the ground. Steel stands rested against the walls to the left side, holding all manner of weapons, and to the right of that, a larger more intricate case held several types of heavy armor. Much of it was the make that the soldiers of this city wore. Stone canals circled around, holding molten liquid as it lit the room with it hue, warming the place, and already, he felt a sweat about him.

Looking to his immediate left was a man, largely built, but he just had a tunic, and no blade, no armor on his person. He tried to recall if he saw him at the inn and if he was just merely passing through. He guessed the man to be in his mid to late thirties, a rustic beard, but a small smile crawled upon his lips as he watched the blacksmith hammer away at the sword, hungrily.

No, perhaps it was the sword, not the dwarf that held his affection. Strange times, truly, in which one might find themselves attached to inanimate objects. No, that was a falsehood, Erdan realized, for history often tells of mortals attaching themselves to their own swords, and in some rare and serious cases, ending up fusing their souls to them.

He took himself to the counter, his cuirass in his hand. The dwarf smiled as he leaned forward, observing the beaten-up leather. Gnarling his lips, he looked heavily at it, observing the tears, and with a wide gaping mouth.

"Oh." He chuckled. "This is gonna be bad. What did you do to it?"

"I did nothing at all to it." Erdan shook his head. "I was attacked on the road."

"With what?" the merchant shrilled. "This wasn't done by a blade."

"Oh, yes it was!" Erdan shrilled. "Some lady attacked me on the road far out west. She had a serrated blade. I've never seen one of its make before. It cut through this like hot knife on butter. Trust me when I say, I nearly died!"

"A blade did that?" the man spoke from his seat. "Even I can tell from here that was no ordinary blade."

"Of course, it wasn't." He turned to the man. "Serrated. Should be nearly impossible to be of any use in combat. Didn't stop her from nearly cuttin' me open."

"Such prowess of a blade of that should render any other blade fundamentally useless," the man replied, hands touching his thighs as he stood. "I'm something of an accomplished swords person myself."

"Indeed." Erdan nodded. "Nice to meet someone with such care then, Erdan."

"Nilor," he spoke.

"Anyway," the blacksmith said. "It's gonna take some time to get this in tip top shape, good thing ye came here and not the tanner."

"Why's that?" Erdan placed his palm on the counter when he turned.

"Oh, he'd make this look nice, but aesthetics can wait when protecting your own hide is of monumental importance." He stroked his beard. "Anyway, name's Guri. I'll have this up and fixed in about two days. Just watch your back until then."

"Always do," he replied.

"Never want to find a cold knife stuck in your back wielded by the insane," Nilor replied, looking at the sword, now being doused in water.

"Insane?" Erdan jerked.

"Yes." Guri took the armor behind the counter. "There had been recent reports in the last few months about people coming up from the south, insane. Shouting and screaming for help, all the while claiming to see a ghost in these parts. Ghosts are in Cadrasar, they ne'er come this far south."

"That's worrisome." Erdan brought his tone low, remembering the shades of white that woman turned into. Her tattered rags and rotting flesh entered his mind as the vision of the ethereal substance plagued his thoughts. "Ghosts have got to be getting' bold now if they risk traversing this far from home. Makes ye think what the Rangers' Guild have been doin' lately."

"They made the mistake of too much political games in our lands." Guri sighed. "Unfortunately, I grew fond of elves, Kora, she'd been known to pass through here time and time again."

"Yes," Nilor replied. "Elves. Elves. Elves. Fucking elves! Probably best if the Rangers stay in their wee little forest and let humans take care of things north of their lands. Humans, and orcs have grown to live harmoniously with one another, you see, and we can very well handle battle here, up front, and personal."

"Save for the Warrior's Guild in Core Crest." Guri nodded. "Some of the most violent and unreasonable humans I've ever had the misfortune to come across."

"Life is constantly on the line," Erdan agreed, ignoring the racist remark from Nilor. He didn't appreciate that tone too much either. "Hard not to be rude and violent."

"Ah, 'ere ye a'e," the smith said, waving the sword back and forth. "This will get ye up and hacking and slashing away now. Don't go swinging it just yet, let it cool a wee bit first. Dwarf steel is the sturdiest ye'll find, but if it doesn't cool just right, brittle as glass. Keep it tucked away and sheathed for at least a few hours before ye go and cut off some goblin heads."

"But of course." He sheathed it immediately. "Erdan, pleasure to meet ye. I've a question if you don't mind a moment."

"Why don't you two take your business outside for a spell, give me some time to get a head start on this repair," Guri offered.

"But of course." Erdan bowed before walking out the door and down the path in the early confines of the morning with Nilor.

The birds chirped and perched themselves on the fountain to get some water before fluttering their wings off; a variety of persons came out and started setting things up for displaying their goods, and thankfully, Glentor wasn't out yet, as they walked further away from the town square, Nilor finally saw fit to open his mouth for his proposal.

"You're a ranger, yes?"

"Yes." Erdan nodded, one hand on the pommel as he searched the road for traps or shadows lurking. "But I've no affiliation with the Guild."

"I see, I see," Nilor replied. "The purpose of my asking is I'm on the hunt for a particular individual, you understand, and I've been having a hard time tryin' to track him all with all the rumors and such being past and outdated. Trying to catch a rat as it were, and I could use some help."

"I can't be bothered with a hunt at the moment, Nilor," Erdan answered, but he was curious. "I'm a hired hand right now for a merchant, and I need to be here for at least two months' time, and then I escort him back home. I'm a little preoccupied at the moment, but you've my interest."

"I see." Nilor stroked the pommel of his blade as if petting a rat's head. "It's been hard really, just trying to find someone to join me on this lone journey, such savagery of the rotten world we live in where truth and justice is just as elusive as an arrow loosed in the night."

"Might I ask why you're hunting this individual? Or if it is a hunt? I presume vengeance is on that mind of yours," Erdan asked as he passed by a stone wall. His hand brushed against it.

"This individual was responsible for some massive sewer damage which resulted in no small amounts of disease in decay from where I'm from." Nilor sighed. "It killed my parents. Buboes formed on their face, and sickness took them. It took most of that city actually."

"I see," Erdan replied. "Well, the Black Plague is a serious endeavor, and I'm sorry for your loss, but you should know that vengeance is a fool's errand, and nothing good can come of it."

"I see," Nilor said. "You just don't understand."

"I'm just repeating wisdom I learned from a friend who knew people who walked down that path," Erdan replied. "Wrath eats us on the inside, always does, and no one is quite immune to that charm."

"Charm or not, it is mortal behavior—"

"Animalistic and carnal desires get us nowhere and gives us only heartbreak in the end," Erdan snapped. "What do you think will happen if you get it? Kill this person? You'll be left with nothing else."

"Fuck," he snarled. "Fine then, if you won't help me—"

"Nilor, you're not being rational at all." Erdan failed in soothing him. "Even if I was inclined to assist you in your barbaric quest, I couldn't help you for the foreseeable future."

Nilor stormed off and Erdan watched him with a brisk pace. Erdan knew to trust Glenroy's wisdom in all this, but despite it all, he never understood why people resorted to violence. Even if someone was directly responsible for something like causing the Black Plague, from wherever Nilor was from.

Such riddled emotions produced violence, unnecessary violence, but the battle that first be won—rather, the first battle that be lost is the loss of reason and rationality, for which, apparently Nilor threw those aside, discarded in the wind never to return to his mind, and no peace dared enter his heart for the flames of hope would undoubtedly be snuffed out by the amount of rage he was certain rested in the man's soul.

In a world devoid of justice, violence bred violence. A cut for a cut, as the old saying went. That was not what vengeance ever was; it was always a cut for a maim, or if one was lucky, murdering off the object of their rage's children.

Rumors

Another day passed in his job. Already, had to put down a few pick pockets, surprisingly, Glentor had all the goods, and the people of the town knew it. In addition to it, he found one of his competitors put a hit out on him, though, wasn't very successful in getting someone serious to take on the job, and the guards put the merchant in prison, and confiscated his goods at least until Glentor removed himself from the square.

Such a dreadful business here, Erdan was beginning to think it was safer for the halfling to stop at Malitu, closer to home, and much safer in terms of who did what, and how much risk was involved in that Merchants' city was significantly reduced.

Sitting in the tavern, an ale to his lips, he listened to the chatter, and a man with a rustic beard came in with his lute towards the stage of this tavern before he strummed away. The words sang in a low guttural accent he recognized as Grentonian. He ignored the words and the melody for a time as the clatter of mugs clinking against each other filled the air, adding to the sloshing of ale, mead, and wine in those wooden cups.

The bitter ale touched his lips as he set it down, leaning back as he searched the room for danger. Always on his guard, but still, he had to admit to anyone, even himself, his certainty of awareness paled in comparison to those of the Rangers' Guild. A feat that always prevented him entry from that glorious Guild.

Glentor sat at his table across from him, a tankard in front of him and a meal of steaming hot pork, some steamed broccoli, with some leak peppers by the scent of it. Of course, the halfling would be hungry after a day of haggling and trying to not get stabbed, especially after the first week of them staying here.

They had already paid their dues to the farm hand and the barkeeper for their stay, and so far, the temporary residence had been more than hospitable to their needs, here in Sheris. Out the corner of his eye, he did see Nilor at the bar, chatting away with one of the servant girls, of course, for what purpose? He didn't seem to be like the kind of man that would just stick his prick in anything that moved. No, he must be looking for information as to someone who might join him on his quest for vengeance.

"You look distracted, Erdan." Glentor opened his mouth. Some of the fat he slurped from his chin, wiping it clean with a handkerchief.

"Sorry, a man I ran into at the smith is over yonder," Erdan replied, sipping the bitter drink. "Nothing you need to worry about. Such a bother. Glentor, don't you worry."

"I'm worried about you." Glentor sighed, and leaned forward, folding his hands as his elbows propped up on the table. "You're distracted. Perhaps you should get some more rest tonight. I'm sure I'll be fine first thing in the morning."

"You're the only merchant I've ever worked with," Erdan replied, "who seems to care for the personal, spiritual, and mental well-being of those in your employ. It's refreshing."

"Well, need you in tip top shape now should the undesirable happen, no?" Glentor asked. "But seriously, how can you take care of me if you're half asleep?"

"That is something correct you've just said," Erdan commented. "But did you hear of the rumor?"

"Rumor?" Glentor tilted his head. "I've heard no rumor."

"If the rumor is true, at all," Erdan replied, remembering some talk of some adventurers coming from down south earlier at the square when they were stocking up on supplies. "Getting' ye back home to Paxis is going to be a chore."

"What rumor?" Glentor shrilled with gaped eyes.

"I overheard a conversation, you understand," Erdan replied. "I'm not sure what to make of it, as I've no way to verify the validity, but we should assume it's true."

"Stop dodging and just tell me about this rumor!" Glentor snapped.

"I—" Erdan stammered. "I'm sorry, I've stalled and didn't mean to. Rumor claimed wood elves are departing Kinasa in droves."

"What?" Glentor asked, surprised. "That can't be. What drove them out? No. It's a rumor. It has to be."

"But do you know how many people it would take to think of a rumor and a lie that big just to even think of it?" Erdan replied. "Again, I've no way to determine its validity."

"We shouldn't worry about it," Glentor panted. "Not right now. If it's true, I'm sure there will be some sort of message going to all the north, here included."

"But suppose it's true," Erdan replied. "Then what might the cause be? What horror now resides in that forest that—"

"Erdan!" Glentor slammed his fist on the table. "We can't do anything about that, and we certainly can't be worrying about that right now. Just pray to whatever god you do believe in that whatever it is, stays there until I get back home. Listen…" He brought his tone down. "I understand you might be upset, but Kinasa isn't your home. You're not a wood elf."

"You're right," Erdan said, reaching for his coin purse. He downed the rest of his ale. "Allow me to apologize for burdening myself upon you then. It is a moment of weakness." He put some Shironian coins on the table. "Allow me to get some rest. I'll see you in the morning."

"Erdan, I'm—"

He didn't want to hear it as his chair screeched on the floor and he walked towards the stairs to the tavern's rooms. The keeper pulled him aside before he walked up the stairs, and the pathway. Startled, he turned abruptly to the scowl of the man, who held a parchment of paper in his hand, and subsequently waved it in his face.

"I ain't no courier," he said. "I don't expect mail, and I can't keep it for very long, but this is for you?"

"Me?" Erdan took the parchment, and the seal of Malitu was on it. "Thanks. I'll try not to have any other mail coming to you then, this was the only thing I was expecting anyhow. Have a good night."

Erdan bowed before bolting up the stairs, skipping every step. At the third floor, the wooden planks on which his boots trod, creaked with each pressure he placed upon it. Striding down the halls with handles lit up, and at the end of this corridor was his room.

He entered, and the door creaked shut. He walked to the window, lit a candle, and sat at the small desk where he could look outside, the chirping of grasshoppers, and a distant hooting owl entered his ears as he looked down to the parchment of paper. He unfolded it, prepared as he ever could be to dare read the contents of the letter, for the news he'd been long waiting for.

To Erdan,

Forgive the delay in my sending this. I was kept busy when I found out the intricacies of all things involved with which intertwined our meeting and subsequent departing. You asked me to alert you when Anaergienne's fate was determined, and to send Glenroy back to you when we've located your distant cousin. There is both good and foul news, and more good than foul, so I'm hoping in my communicating the good that the bad will be just a pinch to your spirit rather than a mallet to your heart.

I must alert you that Fakino has been since confirmed dead. With the help of many people, and the sacrifices of many good people beneath me, we've stopped an attack and prevented it from getting worse. We pushed her away.

She retreated to some ruins south of Glenwood, and she was slain. May her spirit rot forever, and her soul find rest with whatever Hell it disappeared to. Without a corporal body, you'll find that on your journey back, you'll not have to worry about her at all. Bandits are all we have to worry about in this part of the world, as it should be.

Anaergienne is safe, alive, and well. I recall my being cryptic with you earlier, and rightfully so, but for that I do humbly ask your forgiveness. Allow me to briefly recount what happened prior to you coming to me in Malitu with your companion.

Anaergienne went on a hunting trip, and it's presumed he stumbled upon the ruins a rousing Fakino, and he was sick. He returned to Malitu a bleeding mess, and our healer went out with him to return to Kinasa. He came up this way, and the Rangers' Guild was involved, and they killed Fakino. Anaergienne, as I understand landed the killing blow. He has since returned to Kinasa, and I do not think we'll see him again in this generation in the realm of humans.

But now I must give you bad news. Earlier in this letter I told you many good men and women died. Glenroy was one of them, unfortunately, he died in the ruins, but his body was retrieved, and I wouldn't go looking for it, as the way it was left was undignified. I do not wish anyone to see the body in the state it is, and when the flesh finally decomposes, it would be for the best, really, had nothing else happened. Since we don't know where he was from exactly, we can't exactly blindly transport his body somewhere to Grento for proper burial. We did the best we could to honor the man and have started building a memorial to him. We had a funeral for all the dead, and he shared in the blessings of our people.

This is all I have to report to you, Erdan, and I wish only good news was in this letter, but unfortunately we aren't all that lucky. I wish you the best in your travels, and may whatever god guide your path watch over you, bless you and keep you.

With Great Sincerity,
Cardur, Captain of the Guard of Malitu.

The parchment crumbled in his hand, trembling near the flame of the candle as he ignored the once serene sound of nature coming through his window. His eyes gaped open, and the fingers shook with great severity, he was unsure if he'd get his grip again as it felt like a thousand hammers struck his chest, heavy, bleeding he felt his heart was inside for the news. Glenroy, his oldest, dearest friend, dead, and improperly buried, if even with the best of intentions. He hissed at the letter, before setting it down, and staggered to his bed. He gave ragged breaths, hissing, a warm tear fell down his face before at long last, he was compelled to scream his frustration and despair away.

Chapter 4

The Dark Elf

Erdan laid in his bed, furious, sweating even in his undergarments, but with the rage swelling inside him of Glenroy's passing, as he considered all the injustices in the world, he too wanted vengeance, just like Nilor; however, the object of his rage was already quite dead, and there wasn't much more that could be permitted to quell his frustration. The sun set, the dusk had come with a blanket of the opaque, and stars and moon lit the night sky. Gritting his teeth, he could hear the noise from down stairs, though, it was rather late now, and most everyone was on their way to bed, or sleeping, or trying to copulate in one another's rooms. Oh, how he wished he'd attempted to fornicate with one of the bar maidens, perhaps he'd then have a way to vent out his frustrations of the world.

He got off his bed, put something more or less presentable on, and hurried down the stairs with his coin purse, and took a seat at the bar. The keeper was cleaning some things up before he walked over with a handkerchief, clean palms on the counter top. The bar maidens were still cleaning some tankards, and plates from the tables, and the bard was getting his lute, and walked upstairs, disappearing with a maiden himself. Some feet still danced and swiveled on the floor with drunk merchants were who none too eager to go to bed; yet.

"Ale?" the keeper said.

"Yes," the word trailed through his lips as the passing moment came by, and he put coins on the table. The keeper took them, went to the barrel and poured ale into the mug, foam at the rim before bringing it to Erdan, who eyed it thirstily. He took it in his hands, and the keeper went about his business. The foam caressed his lips as the bitter liquid coated his tongue, but it did not quell the rage, or even bring about a sense of fatigue, for his blood boiled. If only he was there, then perhaps it would be he, not Glenroy in the ground. Perhaps, but the trouble with dwelling on the past, he knew, had one fatal flaw: nothing could change it.

He sighed, feeling the stares from one of the bar maidens bringing some plates and slid them across the counter. The bar keeper took the plates and discarded them into a wooden box before taking them out the back where he couldn't see, for he had no business seeing back there, but this ale wasn't doing what he was hoping it would do, for he was still alert, vigilant even, and his despair only grew, not waned. Staring at the ripples of the cup, he took another draft, and the bar maiden sat beside him.

"What's got ye feelin' the doom and gloom? Dusk is the season of happiness, and an ale to your lips, joy should it bring," she said. "Known many a mortal had I with that look upon your riddled face."

"Misery," he growled. "Misery, death, the dead, stayed in the ground should they be."

"Lose a friend, did ye?" she asked.

"If only," he exhaled. "If only that was the only thing I lost tonight."

"I'm sorry," she replied. "Sorry times we find ourselves in sometimes. Hopefully, ye find some peace in the matter, yeah? Well, I've got some things to do, and don't be a stranger 'round here. Of course, yer welcome to one more ale after the one ye've got the'e. But might I suggest moving things about yeah? Clear the head with some walks in the nearby trail outside, out the back, I like to go when I feel a little doom and gloom."

"Thanks," he groaned, before downing the rest of his ale and handed her his cup. "I might do just that."

He stood from the bar and walked outside. The crickets sang, and owls hooted, and some ravens squawked, wings fluttering overhead as he took himself out round the back, following a dirt trail that was shielded by some trees and branches, leaves rustling in the chilly wind. Hair stood on ends with each step he took, looking down at the shadows cast from the moon, reminded him of monsters of old when he was a little boy in Zinasa, starting outside with the shining lights, the whisps, magical auras they had, but here, everything was natural with a hint of mysticism in and of itself.

His boots kicked some stones on the ground with the passing of the time, and he brushed his hair behind his ears, tucking them in a ponytail, just hanging over his tunic. Just behind the stone walls were ceramic basins filled with water, and some cups floated like wee boats with flowers and soil inside them, and some of these cups inside even had candles lit, shimmering with blue lights as the magic of Sheris provided its light. His heart, despite all this beauty, was still heavy with sadness, and he came to a small clearing at the top of the hill. Leaves coated the ground, and he sat himself by a tree, back against it. He stared downhill, looking at all the lights in front of him, and the leaves, and listened to the sound of the forest.

Taking several deep breaths, he closed his eyes, and the liquor was finally beginning to do something to him, calm his nerves, if only a little, if just to provide a moment's rest from the internal agony attempting to rip apart his heart from inside his body. He felt his heart being appeased, and the threat of wanting violence upon those who did not deserve it subsided. He let out a sigh, contemplating his rage out here in silence and solitude, and he meditated, stretching his spirit out to feel Carmielle's divine presence, praying, but not with words, just simple presence.

A stone clattered on the ground from behind this tree. He jumped, turned, immediately and backed away from it. Eyes scanning up into the branches, to the ground and all around him, he saw nothing of worry behind him. An owl threw a stone? No, that was ridiculous, something moved a stone. But what? Or who? Oh, Carmielle, he hoped it wasn't Nilor wanting to kill him. The man seemed rather unhinged since he couldn't retrieve his help, not that there was anything he could do about it, save maybe killing Glentor to free up his availability, but doing that would just make sure Erdan would abandon him completely. Not to mention that if Nilor did manage to kill Glentor, Erdan would already be dead, and he finally realized this was paranoia thinking, taking over his mind in his grief.

He pulled his hunting knife from his boot and approached the shadow of the forest. Hyper vigilant, he listened for all sounds outside what he was already listening to, shifting of the sand, boots touching the ground, even breathing as his ears might detect, but he heard nothing, and then another stone came by, a cloaked figure there was in the distance, and the stones moved. His boot came from the ground as he enclosed on his quarry, but when he got there, it was just a cloaked elf, pointed ears, and she recoiled as the hood fell off her, revealing her black hair, green eyes, and her complexion was purple, not unlike an orc. But unlike an orc, the features of her skin was smooth, perfectly clean without blemish, without wrinkles. No, she was an elf, but why was her skin like this? He couldn't fathom it, but her hands raised up, and she turned her head.

"Please, don't harm me," she said, in an accent that reminded him of the central most part of Kinasa. "I didn't mean—I didn't mean to startle you."

"What," he panted, stepping back before withdrawing his knife back into his boot. "What are you doing out here this late at night?"

"Does one require a reason to stroll through the night? The lights," she pointed down the path from which he came. "Are beautiful to watch, and the sounds of nature, to listen. Besides," she threw her hood back on. "One might say the same of you, why are you, a male, out here so late at night? Did you mean to follow me?"

"What?" he shook his head in disbelief. "No, I didn't know you were out here. But honestly, a lady as yourself could get caught unawares."

"The only one unawares," she said, crossing her arms over her chest. "Was you. I was perfectly fine until you came here in my walking space. Come here specifically so no one sees me."

"What are you scheming?" Erdan accused, eyes narrowed.

"So, I'm scheming, now," she put her hand on her chest, visibly hurt by the accusation. "Good sir, foul sir is what you are. Why would I be scheming? What purpose would it serve for me to cause trouble in this peaceful city?"

"Peaceful isn't exactly the word I'd use to describe it," Erdan said huskily.

"Any place where trade is to be had in abundance, like here and Malitu, and as far west and north as Jerto is bound to be a place for civil discourse," she said. "It's peaceful here, I find it so. And therefore, it is. But I digress with the sincerity of our conversation that we find ourselves questioning and untrusting one another, and we've no reason to, one way or another. *Male*, why are you here?"

"I asked first," he scowled.

"And a lady never talks first," she lightly bowed, eyes focused on his own. Frightened, she once was, but now, seemed to go through all matters of mannerisms as if to entertain him. Wiley, she might be, but there was something about her he couldn't quite place, the confidence of this elf made all the vixens in the tavern timid in comparison, or so he imagined. So much confidence, whoever this was even hid all things, keeping all things to the imagination, and only the imagination. "Speak, male, or our conversation ends here."

"What made you think I wanted a conversation," he said.

"What else brings you out here except solitude?" she sneered. "Everyone always wants to talk about something, even when we want to be alone, and don't have the words to say. So, speak, if you've the words or gall to."

"Fine," he said after a lengthy period of silence and gritting teeth. "I received some bad news, and liquor wasn't puttin' me to sleep, so came out here for some fresh air, a nice walk and meditation. You startled me. There," he pointed. "I answered. Your turn. Why are you out here?"

"Because I too need and want to be outside in the fresh breeze," she smirked, walking towards an oak tree, and leaned against the bark, eyes carefully observing him.

"But so late at night?"

"I uh—" she blushed and put a hand over her mouth. "When I'm seen by others, they look at me like a monster. You're the only one I've engaged with any conversation for any length of time for a while."

"People treat you worse than orcs?"

"Worse than wood elves, actually," she frowned. "Honestly, they'd much rather deal with the Rangers' Guild again than talk to me. I just go in, get herbs, sell them as potions for those who require them, and make little money. I normally sell my wares out on the road. Adventurers are more likely to ignore the color of my skin, and the unusual appearance I have. I try to avoid people when and where I can otherwise. They talk adventure and whatnot, but no conversations, at least, not with me."

"I didn't realize," Erdan frowned. "It seems you too are escaping something. At least for me, I suppose I can't get it back."

"Dearest, did you lose something?" she shrilled.

"Of course, I did," he answered, looking deep into the window to her soul, and there was a kindness to them, and the facial construction of her face was of a beauty simply indescribable. "And I can't ever get it back."

"The trouble with things," she spoke softly. "Is that we often find a way to lose them."

"Yes, but things such as things one should take great care to never lose, and I was careless," he said. "For these things can't be replaced."

"Oh? What be that, pray tell?"

"My apologies, in a moment of weakness, I find myself unburdening upon you, a stranger. I really shouldn't—"

"A stranger? Am I no longer a hostile of whom you once were going to stab? Should you find it in yourself to grieve that which is lost to a stranger? Often feelings are best told to those we don't know," she said. "For those we confide in have a way of stabbing us in the back. I've lived long enough to know."

"How many winters?"

"How, dare you, *male,* ask me my age!" she snapped, and a low hiss escaped her lips. "Forget it. I've asked you to unburden yourself, for you were going to do that anyway, and now you have the audacity to ask a prime being her age. How rude and careless. No wonder you go about losing things, important or not, the very marrow in your bones breeds carelessness."

"I'm sorry," he bowed his head, ashamed.

"Yes, you ought to be," she snarled. "I'm just out for a walk, and I get you as a little talking companion and you ask things that ought not be inquired. But I admit, perhaps I was a bit harsh on you, for asking. No one's asked me that before, and I've been caught unawares now, as to your intentions. However, If you must know how many winters I'd seen, I couldn't answer, for it seems many winters, decades even since I'd been under ground, in places I'd not seen, and would dare never return to."

"I didn't mean to pry," Erdan said, leaning against his tree.

"No one ever does," now it was her turn to sigh. "But the wooden door already splintered open. Forgive me, and my deepest regret is now I feel compelled to show you a moment of weakness, and unburden myself, and I wish you to keep these, and dare not lose them."

"But you don't trust me," Erdan replied. "You don't even know my name."

"Oh, heavens and Abyss below, forgive us for our rudeness, then, for we've been like drivel to one another," she chuckled. "Perhaps we best clear the air between us then, by the simple transaction of name exchanging. Eh?"

"How do I know you're not a witch to charm me?"

"Do I look like a witch to you?" she tilted her head, sneering.

"You're unlike any creature I've seen," and yet she was an alluring one.

"I'm just honest," she replied. "And hurt you'd call me a witch. While I do know magic, I am no witch. Your name please?"

"Erdan," he answered.

"Erdan," she smiled. "That's a fancy name, of the make of the High elves, so they claim, you must then be from Zinasa. Pleasure to meet you, as it is, even this late at night, and you might be visibly drunk. My name is Vircona."

"Vircona." He tilted his head and brought his fingers to his chin to ponder. It was difficult to pinpoint where that name might have originated from. "Lovely name."

"Yes," she said. "It is my name, and everything about me is lovely, so I should dare think so. But now that the air is thus clear, I must now unburden myself—"

"Unburden away," he waved his compliance to listen to her complaint.

"Erdan, I've always been this way, and I don't know why. Perhaps Carmielle thought herself to find a joke, and created me," she groaned. "My mother and father looked at me with disgust when I was born, and when I grew up, the little children from where I was from, a little city called Ghorhiem, a town really, and the closest landmark was the great city Rivewla out further west. The children screamed, and even when I was an adolescent, people mocked me, the color of my skin was bare for all to see, and I grew a hatred for the light of the whisps, the light of the sun even. Even these stars and flames, I don't much care for them." He saw a tear escape her eyes. "I—I wanted to be part of them, but the color of my skin forbade it, and then I was thus carried away in chains. I don't know who carried me away, but I was torn as the scent of that delicious forest escaped my nose. Decades past, and I was chained against cold stone, listening to the sharpening of blades, the same ones which attempted to mar my skin. Erdan, it was so awful."

Awful indeed, he had to admit as she told him her tale, of her past. Vircona, a beautiful creature, tortured and left alone in the dark, tortured by orc methods, far out northeast in Cadrasar. Some tunnels deep enough were cold, stuck in the ground, but the fires of the land often were randomly crafted, could cause someone to lose fingers with the ground shifting underneath for unknown reasons. He felt compassion for her, and suddenly his feelings for the loss of his friends paled, and he nearly forgot, save for the letter in his pocket. There was much less he could find himself to do, save for him listening to her escape, and perilous as it was he she evaded orcs, goblins, vampires, other undead cretins. For an adolescent who, she was incredibly adept, but he couldn't shake the feeling that she was leaving plenty out.

"I'm sorry you had to go through all that," he bowed his head. "Truly, I am."

"You were not responsible, Erdan, I cannot blame you," she bit her lip.

"Why are you looking at me so?" he asked after a brief period of silence.

"You have a—" here voice trailed off. "A pleasing look about you. The type of which that would make a woman swoon with lust, needy or not."

"Oh, I—" he blushed, the woman showcasing her bosom was one thing, but the more direct flirting and compliments he was less used to. "I don't know about that."

"Oh, don't be coy," she frowned. "After all, it's true and I seldom do lie, especially about things like this. Just look at you, cleanly shaven, and you have a chest that even the orcs might envy, and of course, your hair is neatly tied, smelling like raspberries. And strong about the shoulders, I dare say."

"I think, now, Vircona," he pushed himself off from the tree. "Now would be a good time for me to go back. As you said," he turned towards the path. "I'm quite drunk."

"Drunk, sober, it makes little difference," Vircona said, grabbing his hand. "Come on, I've told things wonderful about you, what do you find of me?"

"I personally find your mystery intoxicating," he turned to her, looking into her eyes as her other hand crept up his forearm, the warm touch compelled blood to rush to his prick. "Your eyes fill me with succor, and your accent, alluring. Your skin," she scowled. "It is the most beautiful thing of all, for you were made into an exotic creature. Any mortal, man, elf, or dwarf, would be most fortunate to be the object of your desire."

"And, Erdan," she pressed her body against his. "How would you like to be that object?"

"You're not the first to objectify me in such a manner," he breathed heavily, his heart racing. "But it's—"

"Think it not as mere objectification," she cooed. "Think of it as two people from different places, same time, and of course, both miserably, adorably broken together. Shards of steel scattered and returned to the forge mold together into one self, a blade worth its weight, and cutting through the strongest stone."

"I—"

"Be with me, Erdan," she touched his cheek, and he shied away as her face approached his, and he couldn't contain himself much longer, for she was more seductive than all the bar maidens, and those vixens who tried to make him swoon for them. "Just for tonight. I'll not ask you to wager your life away with me, no, for I've not seen you around Sheris before, not since my time here at least. I'm sure after your business here, you'll depart, and we may never see one another again. Please, be with me, just for tonight. You're the only one—"

"Vircona, I—"

"Erdan, you're the only one I've had any meaningful conversation with in an age, even when I was a child, and I'm sure, perhaps you can scarce believe my tale of my personal affliction," she reminded him, and her hand touched his belly, a nail gently scratching him. "I was never respected, but you respect me, even now. Come. It will be okay, no one is watching."

"Carmielle forbids it," he stammered. "I don't know how much of the tenants you believe but—"

"I don't love Carmielle," she frowned. "After what she did to me? What she turned me into. Can you look into my history and call that Goddess good? She made me this way, and the skin I have is a scourge upon all things living, except you! Please, Erdan."

"We just met," he leaned back to the tree. "I cannot get involved in you this way, Carmielle forbids it."

"Have you ever once on your travels taken a maiden with you to bed?"

"Yes," he spoke softly, ashamed. He was no saint by any meaning the word might have with those alive or dead, but he had his fair share of debauchery, but as much as he would like his sexual tension released, it couldn't be this way, it simply couldn't. "I can't do this, Vircona, I can't."

"But you did it before, will Carmielle forgive you if you do it for me?" she asked. "I know we just met, and we aren't lovers by any stretch of our feeble imaginations, but you make me swoon, Erdan," she gazed at his crotch. "And it seems I too am making something in you swoon. Come and we can take care of our urges together."

"Fine," he said. "But I'm not sneaking you in my room."

"Doesn't have to be in your room or mine," she pressed on his body, her lips touching his neck. "Right here, in this moment."

Her hands untied his tunic, and removed it from him, and he permitted her hands to explore his body, and she permitted him, and their clothes discarded in a fit of carnal desire led them to a night of debauchery, the likes of which Erdan never experienced, but he grew concerned with the end of the night, as no other female would ever make him feel this good ever again.

CHAPTER 5

Descent into Madness

The remaining weeks went by largely without incident. Erdan spent his nights with Vircona and woke up each morning with her before parting his ways to protect Glentor, who was trading his wares. Each day was more fruitful than the last for this halfling, and of course, for his own personal wealth, remained fixated on the coming to the close of his contract, at least, the end of his time with Vircona. Perhaps, he would make his way back here to spend the rest of his days with her. She deserved something, someone to make her feel like she was a living being, and not some walking devil roaming the lands. The constant sex, he admitted, was wonderful, and he wasn't sure, with all the ways she grew accustomed to his wants, and he with hers, would they ever find a partner like one another again with the rising and setting sun, or moon.

But this was the last day, and he simply wanted to stay here, but Glentor was already packing up. So he met Vircona out by the hill where they first met, and held hands and gazed into one another's souls. It was too perfect a thing to leave behind, and as they met each other there, he resolved himself he'd return to her, if she decided to remain his. Her skin shimmered against the contrasting flamelight she so loathed. The light in her eyes, the smile in those cheek bones, even the kiss and tongue that danced inside his mouth was divine. Sure, he'd disobeyed a tenant, but it wasn't the first, and it certainly won't be the last. Her hands grabbed his hips and pulled him close.

"Erdan, my dear Erdan," she said. "As pleasing as it was to share one another's hearts, it pains me to leave it all behind like this. We were good together, weren't we?"

"Aye, yes we were, and we still can be," he shrilled. "Come with me, and Glentor. I'll see him home, and then we can be free. Settle down somewhere, perhaps, and I'll leave this hire hand work behind me."

"Erdan." She kissed him. "As much as I would like that, it would grieve me to leave the road to go to another place, attempt to call it a home. I so adore my house, as you've seen." Yes, he'd seen it. How could he deny all her impressive art works, paints of varying color on canvasses that filled her house. Her bed too, he couldn't deny how it brought comfort to his back, the likes of which he'd not experienced in an age. "I can't just leave everything behind, but you could. You don't have to leave, you've got me now to care for both our needs, wouldn't that be something."

"Oh, Vircona, I couldn't very well leave my poor little halfling to traverse the dangerous roads all the way back to Paxis by himself, he simply wouldn't make it. The thieves at Felldur would eat him up alive, rendering this entire trip worthless." He kissed her. "Very well, I will depart with him, but I will return when he's back home."

"I dare say, there is a little hint of romance in there, now isn't it?" She smiled wryly.

"We can't have engaged in our debauchery if we weren't to risk to catch feelings." He smiled. "I love you, Vircona."

"And I you." She smirked warmly. "Let us not linger for much too longer then, the sun set, and your poor little halfling is probably wondering where you are now."

"You are right," Erdan said. "Good bye Vircona, I'll see you again."

"Oh," she said as he turned around to the path leading back to the tavern. "If you wouldn't mind, and if it isn't too much to ask, don't lay with another woman until you return back to me."

"Of course." He bowed.

***

"Erdan! Where have you been?" Glentor scowled, reins in his hand for the pony, and his wagon undoubtedly full of plenty of coins for his trip back home. He looked intently at his surroundings, many horses and wagons were being pulled as the selling season for foreigners were at a closed, and now all that was left was gems, and coins to be transported along the roads, heading towards the gates. Plenty of armored guards were afoot, and the houses were lit with candles inside them. "I'm trying to leave tonight!"

"I'm sorry," Erdan bowed when he approached the wagon, and climbed on top of it. "Had to take care of things."

"Leave it to the elf to find some romance in a place he'll not see any time soon, or ever again," Glentor growled as he ushered his pony forward towards the gate.

"I wouldn't say that," Erdan smiled as he poised himself to prepare his bow. "In fact, I fully intend to return once I get you back home safely."

"What are you saying, exactly?" Glentor frowned.

"Time might be coming, as bitter as this adventure was with us, that we part our ways," Erdan replied. "I may be putting up the bow when I get back, though of course, if you start selling your wares again here, I might be inclined to purchase something."

"You're serious," Glentor turned his shoulders to gaze at him.

"Yes," Erdan smirked.

"Well, you best be serious about 'er then," Glentor turned to face thee guard, exchanging paperwork. "I didn't want to say anything, Erdan, but I did see her. I can see she has a finger wrapped around your heart, in an *unhealthy* way."

"What are you suggesting?" he frowned.

"She might have charmed you,"

"Preposterous," Erdan replied. "For what reason would she have to do that? It's not like I can offer her much in the way of money."

"Not so much the money," Glentor said. "But if she's lonely and isolated, that's all the more reason to be concerned about being charmed, for she needs and wants something. People like that are often isolated for a reason."

"For good or ill?"

"Doesn't matter," the wagon traversed the exit of the gates of Sheris. "There's always a reason, and one ought to consider their motivations. Not everyone is so good willed as either you, me or—and yes, Glenroy. I miss him already; it's been months now."

"Yes," Erdan frowned at the reminder. "Months, and we'll not see him again."

"Perhaps we can visit the memorial they made for him on our way through," Glentor offered. "We could properly pay our respects due to him, we both owe him a lot."

"That we do," Erdan answered.

He sniffed the air.

Salt.

Odorous salt was in the air, and a violent wind brushed past them from the north. Erdan turned, heart racing, and the splintering of wood he heard, and the violent creaking of the foundations of the buildings forced them to tumble downward. Another waft of air pushed in front of them; the pony was startled, kicking its front legs in the air, wanting to find a way off the path, but the brush of the forest was too thick for pony and wagon to hop through, and the wheels got stuck in the mud by some heavy rocks. Erdan was thrown off, rolling on the ground, but his arm was scraped. Heart racing with everything else, he noticed a wall of fog rolling in on the road, separating them completely from Felldur, and the salt air pushing forward.

"Glentor, are you okay?" he rushed to the wagon, the halfling bleeding out one pointed ear, grabbed some cloth and pressed it against the wound.

"Aye, I'm fine, what's—"

"Salt water," Erdan said. "Looks like we're stayin' the night—to hell with that! What's going on with those buildings?"

"Erdan," the halfling shrilled. "We need to get out of here."

"Climb a damned tree!" Erdan snapped as he bolted back towards the gate. "Least of all, stay safe and hidden till I figure out what's going on."

"Erdan! Get this wagon moving!"

"I can't get that thing moving even if we had Glenroy here. It's stuck right now," Erdan approached the gate. The heavily armored guards quickly moved towards the screaming villagers, running for their homes. Men, women, dwarves, alike screamed, and were escorted away by the King's Guard. Panting, he saw the shattered glass, the broken twigs, and blood was already on the ground. The wind pushed past him again, whistling in his air as he grabbed hold of a small fence, before it shattered in his hands, pushed him on the ground. The scent of sea water was close. The sea wasn't anywhere near here, only fresh water. Where was this scent coming from? And why here? Why now?

Vircona!

"Everyone," a guard shouted. "If ye want to live, leave yer houses immediately and come with us. We'll take care of what it was."

"We've got it!" A wizard cried with her pointy hat, leading a band of adventurers closer to the wind.

Erdan gritted his teeth as he bolted past shattering houses, wood striking at his face, and warm blood dripped down his cheek. A small stone struck him in the leg, and he continued with a limp, eyes searching throughout anything he could see to alert him of an enemy, a wizard, a demon; not that he'd be of much use against a demon; maybe that was what Fakino was. Gritting his teeth, he made it up to the path, and moved back toward the tavern, where many adventurers were departing post haste to join in the efforts of evacuating the citizenry.

"Vircona! he called, and more wind pushed him on his feet, nearly spraining an ankle. The trees creaked and folded in on themselves. The leaves brushed off, dancing in the wind, and the water, the ceramic bowls shattered. The flames went out, and he was in darkness. He panted, rising to his feet, "Vircona!" He screamed once more, but there was nothing left. *Shit. Shit. Shit!* He rushed forward to her house and opened the door before finding the entire building had collapsed inside, and there was no sign of his beloved. A godsend, really, for if she wasn't here, she was still alive somewhere.

He dashed back towards the center of the city. Military horses were on their way to the north, and the buildings were nearly all levelled. Many adventurers lay on the ground, dead with splinters of wood impaling them, rocks and stones from the ground and the dwarf buildings crushing their bodies, and a large pool of blood surrounded his feet. Panting, he understood nothing here, save for the wind that stopped blowing.

"What the hell are you doing?" A soldier pushed him. "Either get out there and help or leave. We can't be worried about ye like this. I'll not fret if ye get hit with a flyin' fuckin' rock!"

"Gah!" A voice cried.

Erdan looked at the stone beneath him, and he quickly squatted down, and hoisted the rock up. The dwarf smith he spoke to, Guri, was his name, was there. He grunted and took a hand before he was lifted up. Staggering to his feet, he limped and grabbed a wooden shaft from the ground. The entire smith and forge was leveled. What about his wife? Was she alive or was she unfortunate? The dwarf took the ax he had, and pried apart another stone, and there she was, the red hair, and her face caved in. Guri dropped the ax, and it clattered on the ground, and he grabbed his wife by the shoulders and wept.

"There," the guard pointed. "Be good and escort that dwarf to safety. Get the body to—"

"Give the dwarf his space," Erdan pushed him back. "For all that is good here, give him space."

"He can have his fucking space in the evacuation district," the guard said. "Don't push me again before I catapult you to whatever hell is doing this."

"What is it?"

"Like I said," the guard replied. "Join us and find out!"

***

With reckless abandon, he found out. Nilor was at his side, the bard with his lute, Jeritus, he remembered, apparently very flamboyant and knew how to use a bow, and use it well, but there wasn't much out here in the north, save the mist, and fiery pillars making their way south to them, and a large bright beaming light. Guri to his other side apparently wasn't going to let his wife's death deter him from exacting vengeance so soon, but exactly, what were they up against? Violent wind? Sea water? Carmielle forbid the gods of the seas from encroaching upon the land where they didn't belong. His heart sank with the unknown, and the uncertainty that Vircona was still nowhere to be seen, or heard, or felt. He just wished she lived, and nothing more. Glentor, was right to stay wherever he was, and Erdan hoped too that he climbed a tree like he asked; not that any height of a tree would have any effect should the gods of the sea be here, and large waves and floods be on their way.

"Catapult!" A guttural growl there was on the other side of the wall. Immediately, several large rocks were vaulted in the air with the creaking of wood and rope. Flaming balls landing at the front of the north gate, rummaging through the air, and uprooting the foundations of the city, rocks splashing upwards, and berating the metal shields, ripping them apart, and the shouts of soldiers cried out. Wizards already laid their hands on the soldiers, white light illumining this darkness as he realized a wall of impressively armored orcs came screeching from the mist, organized with javelins, archers, and spears.

"Your halfling dead or what?" Nilor asked, drawing his sword.

"No," he replied. "But the same wind blew from the south also," Erdan panted, releasing an arrow into the barrage of arrows flying through the air, striking at the first wave of enemies coming for them. "We don't know where to go from here, so I've hid him in a tree."

"There are worst places to be," Nilor said, eyes narrowing on the orcs coming in close. "Ye can wield a blade to, yeah?"

"Of course," was his answer, before the orcs came to the front line, stopped by armored soldiers, and tower shields.

"If ever there was a time for the Rangers' Guild to be involved," Jeritus said. "It would be now."

"Yes, yes," Guri growled. "If a time there was, it would be now. We were blessed with them."

"Blessed?" A voice snarled.

"Enough bickering! Erdan snapped. "We've larger things to worry about now. Keep loosing those arrows, less get to the front the better!"

The orcs came and battered the shield wall, metal clanging and the arrows loosing. Jeritus was out there singing, and the sound of his voice, though highly unorthodox in a battle where his life could easily be taken, was soothing, and uplifting. The wizards cast their spells of elemental magic, and created smog, killing many orcs coming to their blind spots, and Erdan's arrows soared true, striking as many as he could with great dexterity, and Nilor walked to the front with his chainmail with Guri and started hacking away at the front, bringing much needed reprieve to the soldiers on the front.

The blood painted the ground, and the limbs severed with each limb. The singing noise was majestic as great balls of fire still struck them. Though, it seemed, as the orcs were numerous, they weren't making ground inside the city with the coordinated efforts of archers, wizards, and front-line heavy infantry. Such was the way of battle, though, Erdan knew, this couldn't be all there was, for there was the south too. But why would an enemy want to level Sheris to the ground? Much to his knowledge, there was no political strife against Sheris from any nation, save for Cadrasar, who just wanted everyone else to burn. Running out of arrows, he jumped to the front drawing his blade and he hacked and slashed and stabbed at any and every orc within his reach. The screeching pierced his ears as they gnashed their teeth at him, and he kicked them away with this well coordinated defense.

A bright line shined at his side, and he turned his gaze. Loud crash of thunder echoed in the air, and his blade was pushed, and nearly flew from his hand. The orcs too were pushed and disoriented with the light, but as it grew brighter, he beheld a silhouette of a knight, shining silver armor came out from that pillar, and the shaft of fire in the distance dissipated. Heavy clad in his armor and face hidden from view as he drew the sword, and immediately struck the shield of one of the King's guards. The steel sword cut right through the shield, rending the armor useless, and the blood sprayed. The knight came forth, hacking away at the men and women of arms, making quick work, for the deftness of this knight was beyond any of them, at least, as Erdan understood it.

"Retreat!" Called a gurgling voice, and the captain of this guard was slain, body ripped in half by the knight, and the intestines poured out.

Erdan wasted no time removing himself from the front, and Nilor was behind them. The heavy armored defense was removed, and the orcs made their way in to the city. The elf dashed faster than them all, frightened—terrified as fear gripped his heart, and he panted heavily, thinking of Glentor in the tree, and Vircona, wherever she was. Their safety was monument. It was key, but this knight would cut down even the trees with that blade. He saw Guri outside his vision coming closer, and Jeritus too, running nearly as fast as them amidst the crowd of soldiers trying to hold the knight away, with futile efforts, no less.

The constant clamoring of the orcs and their screaming came forth, entering his ears with great fear and trembling. The orc barreled their way towards them, and the shattered buildings afforded them no cover, and soon, there would be protection, and no fleeing to those who were in the evacuation district, wherever the hell that was. He turned his head briefly.

"Any plans, elf?" Jeritus said. "Now might be a great time for something."

"Why are you lookin' to me?" An orc nearly cut his head off, had it not been for Nilor, parrying the blade and striking the beast in the throat.

"You're of the Rangers' Guild, no?"

"Absolutely not!" Erdan exclaimed. "I don't have a plan for this. I'm at best a mercenary, not a tactician!"

"Some merc you are then," Jeritus said, turning to Nilor.

"I said at best," Erdan panted, a sword ready to strike again.

"Well, best get to thinkin'—"

"Erdan!" A voice shrieked.

He looked ahead. Vircona was in front of him, pointing a finger towards him, a black light there was illuming against the tip, and she wore a cloak, and in her other hand a gnarled staff. There was a necklace around her, and a traveling pack. Eyes narrowed, and she scowled, teeth bared, and her skin shone through the dark, and his three companions rushed over behind her, and a blast of black light fired past them. A loud sound of electricity struck the ground, and the orcs lit up, wreathed in black flames as their bodies burst, and only ashes remained.

Erdan turned around briefly at the sound of a wailing scream. The knight was coming, and the orc hoard approaching. A small company of adventurers, bloodied, fighters, barbarians, wizards fought against the hoard with little avail, for the limbs of the dead started moving, grabbing hold of a wizard who was healing someone, dragged her to the ground and ripped out the flesh from her throat by teeth and a bloody mouth of one of the formerly dead armored guards. Those caught aflame, rotting flesh, and those from the north rose up, orc, human, and dwarf alike set their hungry gaze upon them, and followed the white knight who clamored over.

"Vircona," Erdan grabbed her hand before running, and his small company followed him, for some reason, to the evacuation zone. "We need to get out of here."

"Kill me!" The knight said, voice muffled behind the visor of his helmet.

"Then lay down your sword, take off your armor and I'll gladly cut your fucking head off!" Nilor shouted.

"Such violence," Jeritus commented on the brash conversation, shaking his head as they continued to run.

"Sheris. Sheris," Guri said. "My city. It's gone."

"Yes, yes, yes," Nilor snapped. "We'll be too. Erdan, where ye takin' us?"

"There's an evacuation zone—"

"That's where they just came from; everyone's dead," Vircona panted as she ran.

"How?" Erdan said. "That can't be, where is this all coming from?"

"Better question," Nilor caught up to him from the clamor. "How the hell did all these damned orcs traverse the plains of Grento without being stopped?!"

"Might be coming through the mines," Guri exasperated. "They connect to Cadrasar some places."

"If you're referring to the mines coming from the north at Kell, I already leveled that three summers ago; it was left abandoned," Nilor vaulted over a fence. "A witch. Erdan, we've got a witch."

"Don't call me that, filthy male!" Vircona snarled. "I've come here for Erdan, not you, despicable drivel."

"We need a plan to leave," Jeritus said, calmly. "Please forgive for being so bold," he loosed an arrow into an orc who was mid throw of an axe. "Where can we go?"

"The tavern," Vircona said.

"It's been brought low to the ground, I saw it myself," Guri said. "One of the stones struck me."

"No, you deranged lunatic," Vircona shook her head, phasing through a stone wall. "There's a hill, and some trees there. Can't halt the soldier or whatever he is, but its hills and roots are such a chore for the undead. I can blow apart the trees, buy us some time."

"Then we can get back to the road, head south to Felldur, and I can collect my halfling," Erdan sighed. "His goods will have to wait. Undead have no use for them anyway."

They darted with post haste, and Jeritus was proving himself to be quite nimble, keeping up with the two elves, and the dwarf was a distant sprinter, apparently barreling through all the debris and not getting tripped up, and yes, they maintained their distance from the murderous, and apparently suicidal, knight as they made their way through the ruins of Sheris. Ducking and weaving, they made their way to the ruins of the tavern, wood smoldering into ashes, and corpses, limbs crushed underneath the weight, blood dripping out. The corpses, good, another distraction for the undead as they'd seek to feast upon the dead, and of course, the corpses had movable limbs did in fact start crawling out from under the debris. They sprinted up the hill, and Vircona picked up her pace, shouted an incantation that Erdan had never heard of before; in fact, it didn't seem it was the arcane language at all, a black light came from the sky, and the trees came apart, roots uprooted, and foundations were crushed and ripped up from the ground. The sound was like a cavern collapse; and there was now a cliff between them.

"Alright, now let's get your halfling yeah?" Nilor said, patting his shoulder. "Where would he be?"

"Erdan," Vircona said, embracing him. "We need to go, now."

"I agree," he withdrew his sword and hugged her. "Let's get going."

He looked over the chasm, and the orcs were shouting, some hurling axes, but to no avail for they could not reach, the metal striking the soil into the earth on which they stood. Gnarling, gnashing of the teeth, and the zombies fared no better, some mindlessly walked over the ledge, and the knight hid behind his visor as he turned his direction east, to where the road down south was. There was so much distance to cover, and now he was running out of time, and he started sprinting through what remained of the trees and stumbles, splintering wood and smoldering flames, and the rest of the party followed through the ruinous disaster, and he remembered, as he got closer to the road, where hopefully Glentor was hiding in a tree, he remembered the foggy wall coming from the south. He prayed silently to Carmielle that they weren't surrounded.

Crossing into the natural vestibule, he looked up to the trees, the pony, and the wall which was undoubtedly still there. He gazed upwards and saw the halfling's little feet waving as he sat on a branch. He let out a sigh of relief as the halfling looked at him. The pony was still there, and the wagon, and all the currency and goods he was supposed to be protecting; it all remained. Erdan opened his arms as he poised himself to catch.

"Glentor, get down now, we've got to go," he shrieked. "Now, come, I've got you."

"And the cart?"

"We don't have time for that right now," Erdan shook his head. "Nearest place of refuge is Felldur, and everyone in this city is dead. Dead, I say!"

The halfling dropped from the branch. Vircona cast a spell, and Glentor was let down on his feet safely, and Erdan swiftly picked him up in his arms, and stared right into the fog wall, whatever foul thing did this might still be in there, a refuge, a portal to some other Hell, or a demon might be in there, and the party stared into it, all nervous, and with fear trembling as they heard the clamor of metal and steel and shrieking of orcs behind them.

"Hurry, we need to get out of here!" Erdan shrieked as they turned to the wall and started running.

"Kill me now!" the warrior shrieked.

"Oh, Dorio, stop being so melodramatic, and just do as I asked," a voice parted the mist, and a beautiful maiden with a cloak appeared behind the wall of fog. A staff she held in her hand, and she appeared to be looking at all of them with a studying gaze, and gnarled lips. "A human, a halfling, a dwarf, an elf, and a—a purple elf?" Vircona gritted her teeth at that. "Odd, I've never seen your like before, or of such a company of such unlikely people. All the prime races of Alkathos have you in this little adventuring troupe, eh? How poetic. Unfortunately, I've never had a taste for poetry."

"You're behind this," Erdan said, clearly surrounded, and his eyes searched the forest for a way they might bypass both this witch, the undead, the orcs, and the seemingly immortal knight. Considering his circumstances, he doubted he would live to see tomorrow, and Glentor, probably too would die if he didn't flee for his life first. "Who are you?"

"I don't make it a habit of talking to dead people," she leaned forward, sneering. He had to admit, he found her enthralling himself, but he couldn't allow his emotions to cloud his judgement.

"Vircona, if you can, can you kill her?" Erdan asked.

"Gladly," she growled.

"Nilor, and Guri, you take the knight," Erdan said. "Don't let the blade touch you, armor doesn't work as we've seen, Jeritus, you're with me," he put the halfling down and drew his sword. "Glentor, you run through the forest, and don't dare come back!"

"But—"

"RUN!" Erdan snapped. "Don't let my death, or Glenroy's be for naught. Now go!"

"Guri," Nilor said, drawing his sword as he charged at the warrior, named Dorio. "You help them."

"This is no time for glory hounding," Jeritus called, loosing a few arrows, and Erdan jumped into the fray of orcs and battered them with his sword, slicing through the cracks of the joints of their armor, blood sprayed. "We need to work together, and his equipment is dangerous!"

"What's more dangerous than an undead sneaking behind me," Nilor struck at Dorio, who parried it with ease. "Besides, it's an entire hoard, a bard and a ranger are inefficient for that unless you've some unknown quality you've kept hidden from us?"

"No," Erdan grumbled as the scent of decayed and burning flesh entered his nose. The odor rancid, and he knew, that some of these were fresh undead, his sword hacking away into the curvature of one's spine, while others had been rotting for weeks, crawled out of the graves or even worse, been walking around without a soul for an excruciatingly long time. That was no way to go, a fate far worse than death. He gritted his teeth as he listened to the clamor, heard the crunching of the armor as the dwarf's axe impaled it, ripping them to shreds, followed by the dying wails of the orcs, soon to crawl at them. He focused on the sounds of battle behind him, and Dorio and Nilor's blade matched in unison, striking and evading with the slicing of the wind; the shrieks of magic in his ears from behind as Vircona cast her spells at the witch, the white witch of the undead, and she did so in kind. Arrows, wooden, broke, and at last the arrows ceased firing.

His heart pounded, sweat beaded on his head as he moved back, slicing the arms of the undead on the ground attempted to scratch at his boot, but little avail could he had here, for the numbers of adversaries seemed to only increase. His arm grew heavy, and an orc struck him in the face, and he was pushed back, flipping, one hand in the ground as his boot struck the chin of the orc who punched him. Salty blood coated his own lips, and he spat again, thrusting at an orc.

"How are you this strong!" the witch shrieked, and he looked back but a moment, and Vircona pushed the witch back with an impressive display of varying lights, and smoke. The witches staff shattered in her hands, and she fled without her hoard. Vircona panted, and pointed her finger, another display of black lighting struck the ground behind the hoard, and black vines of the earth pulled many of the undead into the ground, bodies and blood exploded.

"Kill the orcs," she shouted. "With her gone, she can't raise them back from the dead!"

Erdan hacked away and Guri continued striking, battering, crying out. The dwarf was in a lot of emotional pain, and some physical, but dwarves were hardy and stout creatures; they can certainly take a beating where most other races of mortals are much more susceptible, proof of that lied with him pulling a slab of stone off his body. Jeritus joined the fray with a rapier, and stabbed at it the hoard, and one by one, the orcs fell until all that remained was the party, and Dorio himself, who was striking hard at Nilor.

The ranger jumped in, deflected a fatal blow, the metal ringing, and an armored fist struck his face. The warrior pivoted his feet, striking very hard with the blunt end of the sword, the dwarf behind him, and as if he was just a rag doll, Guri flew through the air, striking a tree, and he landed firmly on the ground, unconscious. Nilor's blade struck towards the joint, but Dorio was deft, and quick underneath all that armor, ducked, and elbowed the man. Erdan moved, and his hand stretched towards the helmet, another fist struck him, and he pivoted, removing the helm.

A fair face, a scarred face, and a face of terror and tears. Pointed ears amidst that wavy hair, well groomed, even Erdan had to admit when the pommel struck his elbow, and his blade dropped, clattering on the ground. The warrior pivoted again, shifting his grip, and thrust the blade at him. Erdan bent himself back, the blade just over his belly as he flipped, his boot kicking the pommel of the blade, forcing it right in the air. Nilor tackled the elf, and ripped the sword free, but without a moment's notice, the elf rolled, hurling Nilor on the ground, and punched his face. Jeritus kicked the elf off who then retrieved his sword from the ground.

Erdan took a closer look at the strap that held his breastplate together with the pauldrons, and there was the maple leaf, the bow, and the two swords. A ranger he was not, but that was unmistakable; this elf was one of the Rangers' Guild, and he asked for death again, once more he asked, gritting his teeth as he stared menacingly at the sword in his hand which began to glow. He raised the sword up, and swung it at them, a great beam of light shined in their face, but

Vircona put herself between them, and a purple light shielded them from the blast.

Erdan's heart beat rapidly like a drum, and Jeritus and Nilor were right with him, looking at the cascade of white on purple light, the display of Vircona's prowess of magic was unmatched, and while he wasn't a practitioner of magic, he was very happy to have met her. He could see though, the light from Dorio's sword wasn't going to stop, and he was certain Vircona could only hold for so much longer in this battle of attrition. Dismayed he was, for he couldn't escape the protective bubble without being caught in a life altering injury.

Suddenly, the white light dissipated followed by a shriek. Vircona allowed the light to fade and Erdan got a clear view, and Glentor had a dagger, striking the warrior in the calf with it. Dorio dropped his sword, turned, and picked up the halfling. Erdan's heart jolted as he sprinted, but it was too late, for the halfling shrieked, tossed to the ground, coughing, and gurgling. Dorio stomped on his neck. "I'm sorry," he cried. "I'm sorry. I'm sorry!" Erdan threw his sword at the warrior, and it was deflected by the pauldron, and Dorio tripped him on the ground.

"Dorio, that is enough!" a golden light sped from the sky, striking the metal chest. Dorio fell to the ground, and nearly collapsed, standing as he parried the light. Erdan then felt his wounds being healed, and suddenly, Vircona disappeared. Guri got up, and suddenly, an elf showed up behind him, an amulet on her breast of a Royal tree. "Dorio, I can't believe you would do this."

"Ayeienne," Dorio said. "I can't, it's not—"

"Enough of this," she raised her hand and a silver light shone above her in the shape of a hand and it stretched into Dorio's heart and ripped something out of him. He cried, the sword dropped again, and he was pushed away, collapsed to the ground, weaving, and crying like a child. "Since you would create hell for others, I'll create Hell for you. Your prayers will forever be silent, now leave this place, or I will send you to the Abyss!"

Dorio gritted his teeth, grabbed his sword, and sprinted through the tree line. Erdan went to Glentor, eyes bulging out of his head, the blood dripped from the sides of his lips, but he was factually dead.

He heard groans from Guri who got up from the tree and walked forward, and they all embraced the wizard from Kinasa, all except Vircona, who was nowhere to be seen. He wondered where she went off to, but his friend was in his hands, and he wept. The soft hand of the wizard touched his shoulders.

"Dark times ahead," she said. "But let this serve as a warning to all of you, I expected to come and meet with some colleagues of mine here, but it seems they've fled or are dead. I would—not go south if I were you."

"Why?" Erdan asked.

"Simple, Kinasa has turned into a husk," she replied, a sadness in her voice. "Anything close to that might be a warzone. Even Felldur might not be a safe haven for much longer. Malitu, probably damned."

"What's happening!" Jeritus cried. "I just traveled here, and this happens. I don't know—"

"I don't have all the answers, human," she said, and proceeded to take herself through the ruins of the city. "I don't have reprieve for the weariness of my heart weighs heavier than a planet, heavier than the sun, and the warmth of it has gone cold. Leave, immediately."

"Where's Vircona?" Erdan asked when the wizard was gone.

"I'm here, my love," she reappeared behind a tree, sweating. "I'm sorry, I had to disappear, I'm not fond of elves, except you."

"Of course," he panted. "We've earned a break—"

"No break at all is what we get," Guri complained, plopping his ass on the ground. "We need a plan."

"We?" Erdan asked.

"Yes," Nilor said. "*We* need a plan. We're together now whether we like it or now, don't know where to go, don't have no place to sleep."

"I'll join you until such a time I find an audience again," Jeritus panted, leaning against a tree with arms crossed over his chest.

"I don't have anywhere to go," Guri said, lowly, head bowed. "Nothing to live for, or now to do. It took years just building that forge, and I can't be sure I've in it me again to start all over."

"I see," Nilor nodded. "I'm sorry about all that, but sometimes we've got to keep moving forward," he rotated his head to Erdan. "Erdan, you and your lady friend, where have you to go? Your employer is dead and I'm sure you're want of coin."

Erdan pointed at the wagon. "There's plenty in there for coin, and I don't think the halfling will have use of it in the next life, which ever heaven that plane is in," he leaned into Vircona's ear, who's warm face caressed his cheek. "But his family will starve, I should probably go back to Paxis, and alert his family of his passing, they'll want and need to know."

"I see, and that's in Paxis, yeah?" Nilor repeated. "Perfect, we'll all go down south, camp up in Felldur for a bit, get some rest, and then head west to Malitu, and to Paxis, make sure the halfling's family is notified."

"One thing you should know," Erdan said, considering Vircona's safety, and she deserved, no, she needed protection. Or did he just need something to protect? No matter. "Humans aren't fond of elves, wood elves, particularly; I worry about what they may do when they see Vircona."

"I can wear a cloak to hide my face," she suggested.

"But when the sun shines, there will be questions if you hide your cloak, and above all else, the Thieves' guild is right there, and that may rile their suspicions. This sounds like it is damned if you do, damned if you don't."

"In any event—"

"Vircona," Jeritus rubbed his chin. "When the wizard showed up, you disappeared. Why?"

Vircona frowned, baring her teeth at him. There was a coldness as she put herself behind Erdan, hiding from him, her hands touched his arms, grabbing tightly like a grip designed to keep steel in place when hammered. Erdan tensed at her sudden behavior before she leaned into him, her hands wrapped around his abdomen in a hug, and he felt soothed, though, he figured it was her who needed soothing, and he rested a bloody hand on her beautiful, purple fingers over his belly.

"I can't help what I am, or where I came from," she growled. "I can't, just as you can't help being a filthy little human, and we're devoid of our choice in who we become and the things we do are already decided for us before we put any action to them. Male, human, dwarf, all are despicable, but all the more distaste I treat you, I'm treated even by my own kind. Frowned, disdained, disowned, sold into slavery and to be used as nothing more than a toy for one's sexual desire."

"That still don't account for your prowess in magic," Jeritus said.

"Enough of this—"

"No, Erdan!" the bard snapped. "I saw her, white, tattered clothes, and torn flesh. That witch who was here, and Vircona here led her a dance like I've ever seen before. Do you know what matter of creature that witch is? She was a wraith. Few of them exist, and they're almost impossible to kill. And yet, she scurried off like a dog with his tail between his legs, because of Vircona, here, who is leagues of spell weaving beyond the wraith, and dare I say, probably anyone in the Wizards' Council," he pointed a stern finger. Erdan also noticed Nilor look at her hungrily, but not with carnal desire, but. . .something else. Jeritus continued. "We're going to Felldur, apparently, and that's a fortress. All I want is transparency, and you are no wood elf. What are you?"

"More questions of the sort," Vircona snarled. "I don't answer to you, pig."

"Let's just get going, and we're all irritable," Guri said lowly, already walking down the road. "It's a long road, and we've more than enough time to figure out what Vircona is before we get to Felldur. Let us not waste more time on it than we already have. Trust, Jeritus, trust, until we've reason to distrust her, she's on our side. She could simply have just run off and let the witch kills us."

"I would say that's the wisest course of action," Nilor past Erdan. "And please keep your copulation to a minimum. I know you elves, far too off swooning with desire, male or female, it matters not; almost everyone ends up in the bed of an elf, whether they wanted to or not."

"Erdan," Vircona said, and brought her lips to his ear. "I don't trust the bard; he knows too much I think. And there be cause for concern if he doesn't trust me, for he might see me burned at the stake when we arrive there. I'm trusting you, my love, don't let that happen to me."

"I would never," he looked at her and kissed as the party moved onward, and then they joined them along the long path towards Felldur, ideally without incident.

CHAPTER 6

Felldur

The road to Felldur was long, and thankfully for Erdan's feet, went without incident. He hunted for them along the way there, and they ate boar, pig, and rabbits when they set up camp every night at sundown, and the conversations was mostly lacking. His eyes never departed for too long from Jeritus, who never seemed to trust nor wanted anything at all to do with Vircona, nor he him. He noticed the dwarf, Guri, still grieving every night, crying behind some trees when he thought no one was listening, but Erdan's ears heard him, and he could very well pick up the sobbing noises of tears through each night. He couldn't blame him; he lost everything. Funny, when he thought about it, Erdan wasn't much different, he didn't think. He joined this adventure to get paid, and now that wasn't going to happen; his employer was dead, his best friend he found out was dead at Malitu, and the only saving grace was that Anaergienne was in Kinasa, which according to that powerful wizard that saved them from Dorio, was basically gone or in decay. *Anaergienne, did you have something to do with that?*

The sneaking suspicion Erdan had amidst all of this is that maybe everything was connected. Carmielle was sovereign, but why would She allow any of this to happen as quickly as it did? An entire capital fell overnight! That wasn't a small city either, and everyone, those fleeing in refuge too were now dead, dying, and he had the disgust of having to cut off all their limbs before he could retreat safely. A wraith, Fakino, apparently, yes, if Jeritus' observations had any weight on them, then a wraith was the witch, and Fakino was one too. If only Jeritus knew there was more than one wraith out there, and rare and being bold as to encroach upon the land of the living, he might think twice about and take Vircona's prowess, with how powerful as she was, with gratitude.

However, with things as they were this peculiar night, without incident, the fire cackling and the rabbits roasted, cut and portioned into some water he located at a nearby stream into a small makeshift, but sad stew, he watched Guri and Nilor muttering with themselves, as Jeritus strummed his guitar, albeit, his palms muted the sound. He rested with a log, Vircona laid her head on his chest, and arms wrapped around his abdomen, and he rested his head atop hers, feeling the warmth of her blood against his own, and such a feeling he'd been missing for months. It seemed that, at least for now, him losing his employer, and old friend was trivial. Of course, nothing could truly replace those things, well, maybe he could find another employer, but another Glenroy? Impossible.

"Erdan, my love," she said in her soft voice. "What bothers you so? You seem perplexed and disturbed amidst the darkness of the night? Does not the fire warm you?"

"No," he stammered. "It's just that, I look and consider what's around us, around you. I know you leaving things the way they were at Sheris, as cruel as it was to you, still isn't ideal."

"I'm touched," she commented at his soft words. "That you truly care about my wellbeing it seems, and with all that happened to you, I'm glad I'm your object of affection. I've never had someone care for me before, not like you."

"And it is very unlike me," he smiled thinly. "To have a care for many people as long as I have lived, save for the few I've adventured with. Sadly, they are no more, and my heart is heavy, heavier still just knowing what you must endure when we do arrive at Felldur."

"Erdan," she tilted her head upwards, and he removed his head from atop hers to gaze into her eyes. "I must endure, that's all I've ever done. It pains me that I bring sorrow to you. It will be as okay as anyone can expect it to, and should the unimaginable happen, you will protect me, no?"

"Aye," he said. "I'll protect you, at the cost of my life."

She smiled at that and stretched her neck up to kiss him softly on the lips. Her purple lips in the flame was alluring, and he returned her display of affection, and his arms wrapped around her shoulders as he felt that the world ought to flutter under the display of their love, and unlikely coupling, even he had to confess, for mostly on his account to finally pick someone to stay with to the end of his days. The words he spoke to her, he meant them with every ounce of his being, and his heart was drawn to her in a way no female, human, elf, or dwarf ever pulled on it.

"I'll have my cloak, I've my magic," she assured him. "And with those things, we can escape whatever snare is set for me. You and me. Together forever."

"Forever." He grinned. "Yes, forever. Until such a time the sword or disease take me."

"Or me," she reminded him. "But let's not think of such thoughts tonight, and let's ignore the prying eyes, and come with me, Erdan."

"Come where?"

"With me," she said. "I perceived a bed of moss not far by where we may love each other, away from prying eyes."

"Not your bed," he reminded.

"No, not mine," she sighed. "But all the better will our desire be satiated when we get to an inn, even in Felldur. Sure, some might call it unnatural, but not to me, and not to us."

***

Felldur was as bold and untouched as he remembered it, approaching the gates from the north, and the dark clouds rolled in, a torrent pouring like a thousand crying gods. Cloaked, they all were, as they approached with all their belongings, and while the clouds were dark, it was still during the day, but the sun was obscured from the dreary weather, and Erdan didn't care for it all that much. The black metal was hard, and the rain clinked on it, large puddles by the entrance, and the wooden door opened and creaked shut as the watchmen opened them for travelers. Getting around to the door, he looked into the peep hole with an old man of silver hair, a weathered face, and narrowed eyes peered through the cracks.

"What business have two men, a dwarf, and an elf, and a... a—" The man opened his eyes when he looked at Vircona. "An orc?" Erdan heard her hiss. "By gods, I know strange things are ahead, but I've never seen an orc like you before?"

"Male!" she snapped, baring her teeth. "It's been a long road ahead, and I assure you, I'm no orc, and besides, this is Felldur, no? The fortress that connects the lands of men, dwarves, and orc, what business have you questioning people of their race and business in such a matter? You're disgusting."

"Hey, hey, hey." Jeritus walked up and pushed her gently. "Let me do the talking, yeah? We don't need someone startin' a race war now," he laughed nervously, turning to the man. "Forgive my companion, she is an odd one of sorts, and I still haven't figured out exactly *what* she is. I must agree that our party composition is quite unusual this part of Alkathos, however, our mutual arrangements are temporary, you see. We all happened in Sheris and it was leveled to the ground by a horde of orcs, and undead, and some blasted witch."

"Witch you say?" The man scratched his chin.

Erdan listened quite intently as the bard worked his silver tongue and honeyed words to ease the offense Vircona caused. While she was who she was, Erdan couldn't put blame to her heart, not with the pain she was in for being treated the way she was, unable to fit in, being both wood elf, and with the complexion she had, of course wasn't accepted for who she was in Kinasa either. But looking back at the Bard, a smile on his lips and the gatekeeper as Jeritus wove his tale, telling them of the exploits and all the things that happened on the road, of course, that was the most boring part of any adventure.

"I see, I see." He nodded, looking to Vircona. "I'm sorry, miss, I meant no offense."

"See that—"

"Hey!" Jeritus snapped. "I got him to apologize, didn't I? Now, don't go startin' any trouble. I'm getting us inside!"

"But of course." She bowed. "I'm sorry to trouble you, Jeritus."

"You can save it when you buy me an ale," Jeritus said as the door opened.

"With what money?" she was indignant as they passed through.

"With Erdan's," Nilor sneered. "All the gods know he's got plenty of it now."

That was pretty close to the truth, he had to accept, when he passed through, bowing to the watchman. He took several coins, and all the coin purses from Glentor and the wagon as he could carry. There was plenty to go around to buy a hut without interest or a loan if he wanted, either in Grento, Core Crest, or Shiro, and live out the rest of his days. Okay, that wasn't exactly true, though a nice gesture. Oh, Carmielle, he'd been hanging around humans for far too long. The door creaked behind him, and he could see Felldur as he remembered it from long ago, when he last passed here, when things were more or less, going according to plan.

Erdan sniffed the air, and he remembered the scent of burning ember, but there was fresh cut grass nearby. The afternoon rain was sweet, and he saw smoke coming out from some of the stone windows, some open, and others had shutters closed. Windows of glass and wood decorated the buildings on the cobblestoned path. Black soot filled the air, and several humans, dwarves, and some orcs, though not many were roaming the streets, pushing carts, wagons, and carrying large bags of various goods as their feet splashed in the puddles between the cracks of the stones. Torches were lit outside, protected by a covering of iron above it, and the water passed over it onto either side like a roof.

Horses clopped as they carried much larger wagons, tarped with cloth and metal sheets as they delivered hay, and other goods, like clothing that ought not be wet, and some lumber, some steel and iron ingots. Bushes provided a path, neatly cut apart to be presentable, but the large thing he noticed, while still cloaked; thankfully, the color of Vircona's skin couldn't be concealed with all the light, and someone, a woman noticed, a scowl on her face as she hurried into her house and slammed the door.

"All right," Jeritus said. "I'm gonna go find an audience, and some ale, and yes, Vircona, you're buying me one round."

"Erdan, you mean," Nilor reminded.

"Oh, I don't care as long as I'm not footin' the transaction for this, besides, my lute is getting' a little wet," he frowned. "Oh well, not much I can do about that, it's raining mice."

"I'm going to go find a forge," Guri said. "If memory serves, there's an inn up two levels, has mead and ale too, be careful."

"Thieves and all," Erdan agreed, eyes searching the corridors for shadows. He certainly would be the target for such a theft, and his coin purse was heavy, and easy to cut into. He took Vircona's hands. "Let's get up to the inn, get some warmth by a fire."

"You'll be fightin' for pace by the fire in the inn," Jeritus said. "Most people are likely to have claimed a spot by now. Might needin' to push people over, or start a brawl, the likes you rangers are known for."

They followed the path through the residential district. Many houses had multiple floors and were tightly built together, some apparently seemed to share the same building, but perhaps, Erdan imagined, they were walled off as there were multiple doors, and groves to separate individual yards from one another.

There was no life, but some humans peered from their windows to gaze upon the exotic dark elf who was now in their midst, and their parents swiftly pulled them inside and slammed the shutters. He bit his lips in ire as he heard Vircona hiss back at the gesture until they departed from the residential district to the third level of the city of Felldur, where the armory was, a local pyre for where they burned witches, oh Carmielle, please no.

The stones grew steadier, and there was a stable and a steaming pile of manure entered his nose, and there was clamoring steel as guards patrolled the city, though, seemingly barren at the moment. He imagined it might change tomorrow when the weather was a bit more agreeable.

At long last, they found the tavern, surrounded by a small watering hole, and a wooden bridge with some flowers planted on the side, being drowned by the rain no doubt. The hole filled, and a small brook went down stream into a smaller pond where there was no shortage at all for places for it to go, before dripping into holey pales underneath which served as a flower pot, filled with wildflowers. The inn was tall, nearly taller than the city hall nearly several blocks down past the guard barracks overlooking the city square. A triangular roof with shingles it had, large stone walls, and shutters closed. A small stable behind it had, and there was many people inside, chatter running amuck. A small lantern lit, hanging beneath the sign which swayed. Pig's Inn.

"Well..." Jeritus stared at the sign, one hand on his hip. "Who wants to stay at a Pig's Inn? Eh?"

"Likely the common drivel of humans who don't have a choice," Vircona said.

"Bed's a bed," Nilor said, and he walked forward. "I wonder if this was the inn Guri was talkin' about?"

"He's not here with us, anyhow," Erdan replied. "We may have lost him forever, but maybe that's what he wanted most."

"Let's just get in and get some warmth," Jeritus said. "We'll find out what kind of place this is, inside, and keep your purses close."

They opened the door inside, and this was unlike any tavern he had ever seen, so ethereal, and fantastical. It had all the same things in an order for which he expected them, but so much more. Bar maidens were serving drinks on floating trays, and candles with green flames lit the window sills, while still closed, and someone was planning no small amounts of herbs and other fauna inside, that it smelled like a forest, dare say, the closest he expected to find to strolling through a garden in Kinasa. It was divine, and its scent took him to the honey to the bar of the tavern where they all sat, Vircona next to him, of course, tightly holding him close as he ordered drinks for everyone.

"Ah," Jeritus said, slamming the wood tankard on the steel bar. "That's some good ale, if I do say so, even if it does smell like shit."

"There are flowers, Jeritus," Vircona said. "Shit is exactly what it doesn't smell like."

"How you compare flowers to shit, I've no idea." Erdan shook his head, bringing sweet mead to his lips, securing his coin purse close to him, eyes still searching the tavern for individuals who might take an interest in his impressively large purse. Seeing nothing, he placed his hand atop Vircona's who smiled at him, taking in some wine of her own.

"Anyway," Nilor said. "Guri is gone for the moment, hopefully he'll catch up to us—"

"Us?" Jeritus burped. "Nilor, I've made it clear time and time again, my business with you was concluded the moment I stepped foot inside this city, and I can find an audience. As far as I'm concerned with any of you, my involvement with this party is null and void, like a bad contract," he sighed, taking another drink. "Besides, I don't very well trust this dark elf here. She's unnatural."

Vircona snarled.

"One of these days she's gonna bite yer hand off," Nilor chuckled.

"And that is all the more reason to absolve myself of this party, and get some music in my bones and sing, get a captive audience and of course, drink to my heart's content," Jeritus said. "I've no business with any of you anymore. It was temporary, just to get here, and you're off to Paxis anyway. They've no love for bards that aren't their own."

"I see, I see." Nilor nodded. "But I've my own errand."

Yes, of course he does. Erdan eyed him suspiciously as ale entered the man's lips generously. He had his own reasons for doing things, and at least, Jeritus was honest about himself, and Guri could hardly be blamed for anything, least of all not wanting to be talkative himself anyway. But Erdan knew Nilor's heart was set out for vengeance and was only coming with him in the hopes that the path of vengeance might cross, strings of fate as Carmielle willed into place. That was, he was certain, Nilor's hope anyways.

"I'm sure you do, we all have 'em." Jeritus finished his ale. "Now, if you'll excuse me, I've got a lady to woo."

"I thought you didn't have any money." Erdan reared his head.

"Oh, I do," he sneered. "Plenty of it."

"Well," Erdan sighed, looking at his now empty cup. "Perhaps it's best to get to bed, a nice comfortable little bed to sleep in."

"You two are the most perverse mortals I've ever seen," Nilor chuckled. "In the woods on a bed of moss."

"You've been sneakin' a peek!" Vircona said, her voice soft and sensuous.

"That I have, and I've been likin' what I've been seein'."

"No," Erdan waved his finger in front of him. "There will be no threesomes tonight. Especially not with you. Not with you acting all charismatic all of a sudden. No need for that, least of all not here."

"Erdan," she sneered, but touched his hand softly. "I must confess I tire of the drivel. Can we go?"

"Yes." Erdan smiled at her. "Of course."

The doors into the tavern opened with a start, the wood door nearly breaking on its hinges. The conversations inside came to an abrupt halt as the sound of clamoring metal entered his ears, and several armed guards came in, and one lightly armored, with an angular face and a rustic beard, with some parchments, protected underneath a covering. The rain seemed to have died down outside into a mere trickle, and nothing more. A man with a straw hat came in and pointed at Vircona.

"She's the one, she's the one that burned down me farm!" he shouted. "I never forget a bitch when I see one, and her skin shows it all. The whole farm I tell ye and slaughtered all me pigs and cows."

"You what?" Nilor shook his head, but a grin was on his lips.

"Good sir," she put her hand on her chest. "I don't know what you're talking about."

"Don't go tryin' to sweet talk your way out of this one, witch!" he pointed. "All of them, and you!" he pointed at Jeritus. "I saw him walk in with them, he's just as guilty."

"Me? I have nothing to do with any of them, I just simply came in," Jeritus defended himself shrewdly.

"I saw you enter with 'er," the farmer scowled, rage set in his eyes. "You let 'er in with ye, and ye deserve to burn like all witches do!"

"When would we have burned down a farm!" Erdan stood immediately. "We've only just arrived!"

"Four months ago," the farmer squealed. "Four months, and we've been unable to keep feedin' our people, kill them, I say, kill them!"

"Is this true?" the inquisitor asked, stepping forward, armored gauntlet resting on the pommel of a sword.

"If it was, we've been in Sheris all this time," Erdan said. "It couldn't possibly have been her. This is discrimination is what it is!"

"Yes, well," the guard said. "We've not enough food to go around all the time, and hence the price of goods go up, and we need to blame someone, or so this man does, and here's a scapegoat, two elves, a ranger no doubt. They get blamed for everything; we might as well blame them for this."

"I'm not even a wood elf!" Erdan snapped.

"Quiet down, and come silently," the guard spoke with cold air. "Or I will paint the streets with your blood. I've done it to less deserving folks; think how far I'll go with some fucking elves!"

"Erdan," Vircona whimpered. "Don't let them take me, please. I don't want—"

"What you want," the guard said. "is not what's important, come quietly, now, before I offer a bounty on your head, I'm sure anyone here will gladly take me up on that offer."

"Sir," Jeritus said, completely stammering over his words. "I can't attest to the burning of the farm, I've no information on that, and it's been a year since last I passed through here, but we were in Sheris, what," he turned to Erdan. "About two weeks ago, and I've been there for a season. I couldn't have been here. Erdan, I know, the elf there, has been in Sheris for two months prior to our departure from the city before it fell to the ground."

"Interesting." The guard frowned. "So, you admit, there is no one living that can corroborate whatever innocence you might have. Interesting, well, we can forgo any trial then."

"Oh dammit." Erdan palmed his forehead. "He just made it worse."

"Seize them." The guard pointed. "The two men, the two elves. Bound them and get them to the pyre. I'm sick and tired of this bullshit."

"Bulls fecal matter had nothing to do with this," Jeritus pulled out a knife, and grabbed a barmaid, and restrained her in front of him as if she was a human shield and approached. An arrow flew, impaling the woman in the head and she dropped to the floor. The guard shook his head, irate.

"I've no use for barmaids, I've no use for citizenry," he said. "You use them as a shield, I will impale them to get through you. You don't know how far my reach goes!"

"Damnit." Erdan drew his blade as a man tackled him. He elbowed the man in the head, and Nilor threw him off, stomping his neck to the ground before drawing his own sword, and the tavern became a scene of absolute violence. Shouts, women screamed as they ran for cover, wooden tables were flipped over and tankards were hurled across the room, liquid sloshing and sticking on the ground. Erdan panted heavily as he cut into a bar maid who was in the way, an innocent death on his part, blood smeared his face. Heart racing and sweat dripped down his forehead as he made his way to the guard. Vircona was behind him, and he drew the guard's ire, and they clashed together.

"Vircona, get out now!" Nilor growled. "We'll meet you outside the gates!"

"Why can't I get a moment of peace from you stark raving fucking lunatics!" Jeritus cried. "Now I'm stuck with you all!"

Erdan trusted Vircona to leave as he sparred with this guard, who was deft and swift, almost as proficient as Dorio. Oh, how he loathed the tight spaces as Nilor moved and rummaged through the debris of shattered cups and plates, splintered tankards and tables as blades of all kinds sliced into them. He grimaced as one guard came from behind him, pushing a table into him, and he nearly tripped, but he kept his blade in his hand as he staggered forward, vaulting over another table. The captain thrust his blade into a citizen, and nicked Erdan's belly. Hissing, he pivoted his foot, grabbed a tankard, and hurled it at the captain and pushed on his assault. He saw the nearby window, and Nilor and Jeritus already climbed out of it, leaving him with a mess of dead citizenry inside this tavern that he was going to sleep in, and enjoy a nice long rest with Vircona, who thankfully was no longer inside this building.

He pivoted towards the window and vaulted out of it, rolling onto the stone and put himself to his feet. Onward, down the hill of rocky stone, slippery with moisture, he bolted down, and saw Nilor and Jeritus going down another alley way closer to the center of town, the bard silent. The clamor of metal rang again in his ears, but he kept on his path, hoping to outrun them, but in the city, even his legs could only carry him so fast without crashing into something.

Where's Vircona?

He panted to the residential district, shouts and screams came from behind him, and soon, the clopping of hooves on stone as calvary arrived behind him with spears poised to thrust at him. He ducked, a spear just over head, striking a wooden wall, splintered. He shifted his weight and vaulted over the fence into a small field of chickens squawking. He sprinted through the soil of feathers loading behind him, more shouts and screaming as he pushed himself against the wall of a house, more spears, and metal further ahead. Barrels in front of him, and he climbed them swiftly as more spears were hurled in his direction. He fell on the other side, landing on his back in a puddle.

He stood, panting, hearing the spears removed from the wood on the other side of this wall, he turned and put his ear to the houses. Nothing moved around inside, and he dashed to it, vaulted into the house, candles and desk and cushions for furniture; a destitute place he found himself in. However, it wouldn't take long before the guards might make their way into the building to get to him.

He vaulted out the rear window, sliding into some dirt and sludge that made his boots soil. He put his hand on his chest, and he felt the heart inside pump rapidly. Soon, he'd have to stop. Too much excitement in so little time was gonna make his heart burst.

He found himself out of a graveyard now, the stones in the ground. More distant clamoring, but they seemed more muffled than before, and less angry. Sword now sheathed, he walked his way through the graveyard to the other side of Felldur, and took himself to another alleyway, slowly walking and listening for sounds to tell him where the rest of his party was, or at least, where Vircona was. She was more important than the rest of them. Getting out of Felldur was going to be a problem, because the gates needed to be open for them to even leave, unless of course, they could vault over the walls. No. Even he wasn't that bold.

Chains rattled in the distance. He peered his head out from the corner, sweat nearly dripping into his eyes, he wiped them clean as he observed where the chains were coming from, fearing for the worse, and Vircona was being dragged on a plateau. The captain of the guard pointed at the pyre, more wood was placed near it, and a wizard, cloaked, stood by, palms pointing towards it, and the mount of lumber placed upon a pole. The guard was none too pleased, it seemed with a scowl on his lips that would make a bear cower. Erdan gritted his teeth, and he looked to the pathway leading to the top of this plateau. He could make it in time.

"Don't even think about it," Jeritus whispered behind him, and jolted him. Turning, so too was Guri and Nilor there. "We can't take on a whole city, and now, if she—"

"I don't care," Erdan said. "They have my Vircona, I will save her."

"And how will we escape?" Nilor asked. "There's no way out of this city."

"No, perhaps not," Erdan turned to listen, looking for anything that could be of leverage. Though the battlefield would be more than apt, plenty open enough for arrows had he—no, neither he nor Jeritus had any arrows left for that kind of tactic. Think, Erdan, think!

"Look, ye all," the captain spoke as Vircona was fastened with leather strappings and chains to the pole which would be lit, others already pouring oil at the base of it. "An elf, dark skinned and all, this is no orc, and so she is unnatural even among her kind. She stands accused!" the voice bellowed. "A creature that is foul, full of nought but deception. Elves came here, they did, to rile up trouble like they always have and will do. What say you, men of Felldur, that we put an end to all this!"

Elves this, elves that. Why all this hatred? What exactly did the Rangers' Guild do to make the rest of the world hate them so much? He noticed along the path, a man cloaked passing out papers to the people, and they read them intently. He couldn't make them out, but presumed as if the answer to all his questions was answered, and the hatred was born not out of something the rangers did, but out of a deep-seated hatred birthed somewhere else, forced through propaganda and attempt that would encouraged all people to hate wood elves.

"This foolish creature came to our walls, to our gates, drinking our drink, eating our food," the captain said, grabbing a torch, and stared at Vircona with menacing eyes. *The bastard!* "She stands accused, if she is indeed a she, foul thing, of burning down Mortha's farm four months ago, and she thought we'd forget? And she has the audacity to eat our food like nothin' at all happened! Tell me, what should be done with *it?*"

It? Erdan snarled. Vircona was not an it. She was an elf, a wood elf, no less, sure, abandoned by her brethren by nature of her skin, unnatural as it was, but she was still an elf, a she. He knew her, all parts, and could ascertain better than anyone that she was in fact a female, capable of acts that would render most men swooning after her. But she was his, no one else's, and to see her like this, chained like a filthy animal sent a rage up his spine, and his hand on his pommel. He was going to kill these men, and if he had any say in the matter, would see this entire fortressed city burned to the ground, and there would be no farmers left to complain.

"Burn it!" a dweller cried.

"Burn it!" a farmer growled.

"Aye," someone dressed in fine clothing said. "Burn the damned elf, show them they belong not in the realm of men! They rose up, and they can keep their blasted forest! Keep it, burn her! They are all evil!"

"Then *it* shall burn." The captain approached the pyre with his torch.

"You people are mad with anguish!" Vircona called. "I've done nothing to any of you. I seek to pass through without molestation."

"You accuse us of molestation when you molested my farm and animals!" the farmer said, straw hat tilted upwards.

"I did no such thing. I've not even been permitted due process!" she wailed. "Why have you done this? Why?"

"Done nothing, she claims," the captain of the guard said. "You are an elf, aren't you? The way I see it, you've been all up in our affairs for far too long, and that is as good enough reason as any."

"I didn't do any of that!" she squealed.

"But you are an elf; your mere existence calls for your extermination!" The guard came closer and was about to throw the torch.

"Burn her now, let her not speak to us with honeyed words so she can talk her way out of justice," a nobleman said.

"Let. Me. Down!" Her husky breath sent shivers even up Erdan's spine, but he couldn't be bothered to wait anymore.

"We're getting her, now!" Erdan bolted from his feet and sprinted towards his love, hoping his friends, if that was what they were, would follow him into this fray.

"Speak not, and just fucking burn her!" a noble woman demanded.

"You drivelous humans, orcs, and dwarves are such unnecessary creatures," she growled, and her head tilted to the sky. A flash of lighting and an echo of thunder clapped against the stone houses, and the rain poured down snuffing out all the flames as the debris scattered across the plateau.

"Hurry and light the flame before she speaks her foul tongue! Elvish, we dare not listen to it," a woman closed her ears.

"Prepare yourself, dark elf," the captain growled. "Beg for forgiveness as you burn!"

"How will you set fire to wet wood in a torrent?" Vircona said. "I've withheld myself for so long, and no longer will I show mercy on you. I will treat you with the same contempt you treat me, and you shall be on your knees!"

Erdan got closer, and he saw a flare of anger in her eyes. Her voice was cold, and her eyes dilated red as she stared daggers of fear into the men who would seek to burn her in this torrential rain. A fear crept inside his heart too, for her prowess of magic knew no bounds as the air around him grew heavy with the rain, and he felt a hand on his shoulder. Nilor stood beside him, carefully studying the disaster threatening to loom over them all. Erdan saw what she could do in Sheris, and he feared what kind of power she had if it would remain unchecked, and what she could, no. What she would do with it was exponentially worse than what she could.

"On your knees," another flash of lightning. Her voice bellowed from the sky like she was pushing a god to answer her call, and she held the gods' leash. "You should be on your knees begging for mercy!"

Opaque clouds loomed overhead, cackling lighting struck the houses, and a violent wind shattered them all like in Sheris. Stones shattered into sand, impaling the citizenry, blood painting the earth and the wood came undone, and they spiraled as Vircona released herself from her chains, and she proceeded to chant in a language Erdan understood not. Men, women, and children fled as the stones of the houses came undone, and collapsed to the ground, violent wails for help escaped their lips as the ruckus of falling debris drowned out their cries for help, and no help would come for them, for there was a great quake in the earth, and Erdan looked below at his feet, seeing the ground split.

He jumped to the side as smoke came out, heart panting again as white webs shot from the ground, and the slab of earth he stood descended into what appeared to be a stair-like formation, and he sprinted up, evading the webs. He hurried, looking upwards, the web protected them from the rain as they attached to other buildings, dragging them to the ground like a raging force, and he heard the sound of clicking. Turning behind him, he saw a cave of the world form underneath that level, and a legion of giant spiders pulled themselves up from the ground, and hurried, scurrying for prey.

"Run!" Erdan shouted.

"Where do we go?" Guri shrieked. "We can't outrun a bunch of spiders!"

"Oh, yes I can," Erdan said, hurrying up to Vircona still chanting.

"We can't!" Nilor shouted. "But if ye can get yer spiders to bring down the walls of this fortressed city, we can finally leave."

At that, Vircona turned her head, and stopped chanting. Tears in her face with regret, he imagined from steps she took to free them all.

"Erdan! I'm sorry," she wailed.

"Run now," he took her hand. "Sorry later. Can we get them to take down the wall?"

"Male," she snapped. He gnarled his lips at that, usually she left that insult for Nilor, the damn prick. "These spiders answer not to me, but to the gods. Not me."

Interesting.

"Just run for the walls," Nilor shouted, barreling down behind them. "We'll figure out what to do when we get there."

"What makes ye think we'll have the bloody time?" Guri said.

"Yes, yes, fearless leader." Erdan could tell Jeritus was rolling his eyes. "I can't exactly serenade our little eight-legged friends to sleep."

"Of course not," Erdan's eyes narrowed.

The ground was being uprooted, pockets of holes with steam came out, matching with the rain. Stone pushed up from the ground like a fountain of soil and roots, and countless spiders clicking. Eight eyes staring at the prey of the buildings coming down in subsequent order, bringing nothing but despair to this once, at one time, prosperous city.

Screams pierced his ears with each level he slid, coming up and down through the maze of corridors. Heart panting, he was certain his exertion alone was going to kill him. When he got to the wall with everyone, the gates of Felldur collapsed, and the webs infested the city. Not a piercing cry for help remained as they jumped over the slabs of metal, sliding outside the confines of the city.

Looking back at it, he saw the walls caving in, the buildings tumbling down, and the webs interwove itself within the crevice of the mountains behind it, and a large nest would be made of giant spiders. In all his years of traveling, he never once came to spiders nearly this large. His hands trembled as they walked further away, wanting to get away from the sight of spiders and web, and Felldur, a place that was supposed to be a refuge, and peace and quiet was now something he couldn't use to describe such a place, especially infested with spiders.

He fucking hated spiders.

CHAPTER 7

The Truth

Erdan took the first watch, the fire was lit in a small clearing just north of Glenwood Road. Vircona was resting on a bed of leaves he made for her, and she was sound asleep, and unhooded. Gazing at the skin, he was drawn to it, enthralled, even for her beauty surpassed all things in this world, and was no pushover like some elves and some wenches were known to be. She was independent, and wonderful, and he watched over her. It would be no mistake, none at all, to say that she was stunningly perfect. A smile crept upon his lips as he looked at her, before turning his ear to some owls hooting.

The flames cackled, and the rabbit stew was licked clean and drank. Nilor and Guri were resting, backs against the trees, but the dwarf was still very, very silent. How could he not be, especially with the way in which the disaster his life had been the last several months. Spent some time in the forges, just a little break from this madness before Felldur all but became a husk for a spider's nest. That very thing still terrified him, and for that reason, he insisted on stopping this evening. He needed to be far away from those nasty bugs, as far as possible.

Jeritus strummed gently on his lute, but it was muffled by his palm, and his gaze eyed suspiciously Vircona. The bard couldn't be trusted, he wanted to leave them in Felldur, and certainly didn't feel right with the group for whatever reason, and also, time and time again, he made a verbal slight against Vircona. It was clear to Erdan's perception that he hated and feared Vircona, as all hatred starts with fear. Fear of elves, wood elves in particular was rampant this side of Alkathos, but never did he think it was ever this horrible!

"Erdan," Jeritus whispered.

"What is it?" he replied, eyes searching the trees for any enemy he might perceive. He still couldn't be certain the spiders wouldn't come this far out of their nest and lay their eggs into one of them. The last thing he wanted was to wake up with his belly inflated with spider eggs. "Speak quickly, you ought to be restin'."

"Well," Jeritus said, and he stopped strumming. "It's really hard to sleep right now with Vircona here."

"This again?" Erdan snapped quietly. "You bring her up every night. No. We're not leaving her, where she goes, I go, it's that simple. What don't you understand about that?"

"What I understand is that she is an elf. Now, let me be clear, I don't hate elves.," Jeritus shook his head. "She has magic capabilities beyond what is reasonable. She pushed a wraith away, and then just summoned a giant spiders' nest. How am I supposed to ignore how dangerous she is?"

"If you didn't focus on what she could do to you," Erdan waved his finger at him. "Then maybe, you'd have nothing to worry about if you didn't antagonize her all the time. She stays."

"You're infatuated with lust, Erdan," Jeritus said.

"No, you're wrong," his eyes narrowed at the bard, appalled he would make that ascertain.

"I'm right, we're going to Malitu where she can raze it to the fucking ground!" Jeritus snapped. "Everywhere we all go ends up in the ground. Sheris. Felldur, and Malitu would be next. Sure. But I can't keep ignoring this, and you shouldn't either."

Guri yawned. "Whatcha two blabberin' about?

"Same typical horse shit," Erdan replied. "Vircona, he wants to get rid of Vircona."

"I never said that,"

"But you implied it," Erdan pointed.

"No, we can't make Vircona leave," Nilor said, standing. "She's too important."

What?

"Why?" Jeritus asked, shaking his head with a twisted face. "Why? Nilor, tell me why you would suggest that?"

"Because of what she can do, she can help me with my errand."

"You're not weaponizing her!" Erdan stood. "Nilor, I've told you this when we met, vengeance goes nowhere, and you're not dragging me or her into this."

"That's really her choice, now, isn't it?" Nilor sneered. "You don't own her, stop pretending like you do."

"No," Erdan said, appalled.

"What—what's all this noise? Silly, I'm stuck with a bunch of *males* ruining my sleep!" Vircona bolted upright, rubbing sleep from her eyes as she stood. "What are you all doing?"

"Vircona," Nilor said. "I've been quiet about this up to now, of course, Erdan already knows. There is someone I'm hunting, and I don't know where he is at the moment, I'm hoping to get more information to locate him."

"Go on." She nodded.

"Vircona, I'll not avenge this man's loss!" Erdan replied, fearful he might lose her.

"Erdan, my love, let me hear his proposal and I might decide," Vircona said. "That his plan and intentions be ill or not."

"Fine," Erdan said, eyes still searching the trees. He couldn't believe he was going to hear this proposal; he wanted no part of vengeance. Nothing good ever comes from it.

"An elf created some disastrous conditions, and some of my family got sick and died. I won't go into complete details to make this request short," Nilor explained. "I'm from Grento, as my accent tells ye, but alas, this elf, I mean to kill him. He is strong, powerful by all accounts in the north, and few match him with the blade. I'm good, but even I'm not foolish enough to suggest that I could beat him in a duel."

What?

"Go on and tell me the identity of the elf whom you wish to kill," Vircona replied. "Should this elf and I have animosity towards one another, I see no reason to deny you, or your spirits for vengeance, despite the tragedy it always leads down. I could start to watch you go mad for my own personal enjoyment."

Erdan tilted his head as he considered the words and tone of which she spoke with such certain cruelty behind those lips. Did the years take her toll? Was she who he thought was. Silly, of course she was. She couldn't be wrong, she was perfect. Beyond comparison to any maiden, beyond any minstrel in a castle, and above reproach. But where was this cruelty coming from? The snarl? The voice cold as it spoke now was just as cold when the humans went to burn her at the stake.

"This elf is Anaergienne." Erdan's heart beat at the mention of his cousin's name. How could he have done all that Nilor is accusing him of? He was far too busy. The Captain of the Rangers' Guild, at least he would have been at the time of the accusation from what he remembered. First the wraith, and now this, and with Vircona, they might succeed in killing him. "He must die. As I can tell from your expression, you've heard his name before."

"Who?" Guri asked. "I've not heard of him before. Who is he?"

"He's the Captain of the Rangers' Guild," Jeritus sighed. "An elf, ruthless as he, sacrificed an entire city to kill a demon before. He's not one you want to cross with. I doubt even the wraiths would stand a chance against him, even the witch out there on the road would be wise to stay away from him."

"And I'll kill him all the same," Nilor growled. "With your help, Vircona, I can bring justice to my family and my land for all his meddling."

"Absolutely not!" Erdan snapped. "That is my cousin."

"Can't be," Nilor said. "He's a wood elf, yer a high elf, different lands."

"High or wood, and even dark, all elves are connected through Carmielle's grace." Erdan scowled. "Though, I will admit these last few weeks have been burdening my faith in Carmielle, but neverthe-less, she connects us all, and we would be fools to think otherwise. Nilor, this won't bring your family back, and I won't let you get my cousin."

That's right, he'd never make it far. Anaergienne isn't even in Malitu at the present time, or shouldn't be, should be in Kinasa somewhere, so this doesn't foil plans of his. For all anyone knew he was dead. In his current state, it would be most unwise to attempt to kill Nilor and prevent this path from being walked on anyhow.

What was he thinking? Murder.

He was contemplating murdering the man whose only crime was to have his family in the wrong place at the wrong time; no matter what actually happened, for even he knew there were two sides to a flipped coin, it didn't justify killing Anaergienne. This was most unlike him, and understanding precisely that was why he shouldn't be the one to kill Nilor; that would make him no better than the drivel of the orcs.

But it didn't have to be him who killed Nilor, did it? No. Not at all, for there was another person who has a personal stake in his cousin's safety. Cardur, captain of the guard at Malitu, and they would be passing right through that city.

Of course, some amount of evidence might be required. No, this was a conspiracy, oftentimes those are done without much evidence at all. Documents, propaganda, that's all any of that ever amounted to, and he could have Cardur hang Nilor instead, and wipe his personal hands clean of the affair.

"That is between me, and Anaergienne." Nilor scowled. "Now, I am going to kill him, whether or not I get your elf's help from this. So, what say you?"

"All this manner of vengeance makes a good story." Jeritus frowned. "But it is one I'll have no part of. If you decide to take this course of action, you are most deserving of your personal doom."

"And what, you take your leave of us without gettin' to Malitu? Seems to be your luck to get caught up through association of." Nilor pointed at Vircona. "Her. We all got caught in that, but without it, we wouldn't have known what she was capable of. And she is certainly capable of killing a Guild Master."

"You may have," Vircona sneered. "Inflated my personal attributes as to what I can and cannot do."

"You summoned spiders from the ground and razed an entire fortress to its knees overnight." Nilor blinked. "Of course, I didn't inflate them, you did that yourself, mistress."

"Don't call me that." Vircona scowled, baring her teeth. "Now, dears, I'd say we've had a long enough road ahead and behind us, it is best that we all try to get some sleep—"

"I'll hear no more of this talk of killing elves, or using them for machinations—"

"Weaponization," Erdan corrected, waving his finger.

"We don't need to be caught up in semantics." Nilor turned to Guri. "Smith, I must tell you that the reason for all this unnecessary hatred of elves can be traced down to Anaergienne. I saw those elvish paintings in your smith, the poetry, the work was mistakenly elvish."

"A gift from Kora," Guri replied. "She is a wood elf—"

"*The* Kora?" Erdan asked.

"The one and only," the dwarf explained with a thin smile. "I last saw her about a year ago, give or take a few months. It was Fall if I recall. Yes, I like elves. They are wonderful creatures deserving of our respect—"

"And what better way to pave a way for them to mingle among the realms of men once more," Nilor suggested. "Then to remove the head of the one who sowed so much discourse throughout all the lands."

"Killing one elf isn't going to solve anything," Jeritus appeased, stepping forward. "I know enough stories to know vengeance always leads to a bloody end, and the blood spilled often isn't the blood intended. Crimson hatred flows through your veins, Nilor, it will kill you before you even get to it."

"I have nothing left." Nilor leaned against the tree, staring at the rustling of the leaves. "What difference does it make? You simply don't understand."

"You're right," Erdan said, thankful that he might not have to consider scheming with Cardur after all. "We don't understand, and I don't want to. Jeritus doesn't want any part of it, and Guri wouldn't want any part in killing an elf either. Forget not, you're in the company of two elves yourself. What are we supposed to think of you when you start spouting off tales of vengeance and misery? Nothing short of racist bigotry."

"We're all guilty of it," Guri explained. "Almost all of us have called for the extermination of orcs and goblins like pests at one point."

"It doesn't help." Jeritus bowed his head, resting at the stump of the tree. "That they ravage, rape, and pillage our cities."

"Humans do that too." Guri's voice went low. "So do dwarves. I've not heard of elves doing it, but we're all mortals with our own desires."

Erdan sat down on the log as the humans and dwarf discussed racial bigotry. Hands shaking as the nerves got to him, the fear, the anger, the anguish, his observations during his travel with them, as well as other observations over the years he now could dare recall. Yes, elves, wood elves especially, weren't welcome in the realm of humans. Perhaps dwarves maybe, but even he doubted they would welcome elves into their midst. The only exception to this bigotry, seemed to him was Malitu, and so too, the danger the elves apparently caused and placed strain on the rest of the world sent ripples so that, he imagined, even humans dared not enter Kinasa, and therefore, go all the way south to Zinasa.

"My love, Erdan." Vircona touched his thigh. "What troubles you so?"

"I must confess I'm still angry," he put his hand atop hers. "I love you, Vircona."

"And I you, Erdan." She sat next to the log, and kissed him on the lips, the flames cackled.

"Vircona." Jeritus walked by the flames towards them. "I'm sorry. I shouldn't have said anything."

"Now, storyteller." Vircona broke the kiss, but didn't remove her face from Erdan's, only sharing a glare to him. "We've all had our frustrations, and my individual hatred for mortality is its own affair. It was not right of you to place blame on me for your particular problems, and there are consequences to the things we say and do. You ought to know that better than anyone."

"That I do." Jeritus bowed. "But I have a silver tongue that sometimes speaks without my thinking, and for that I apologize."

"But it doesn't take away your distrust of me, or fear of me." Vircona scowled, but Erdan felt her lips touch his again. "You are right to be afraid of me, for it's just your carnal instincts that breeds fear into your bones. Leave me and Erdan at peace, as of right now, at this moment, I've no quarrel with you. For now."

"Of cour—"

"*Male!*" she hissed. "Do not test my good graces. You've not seen the depths of depravity or cruelty I've been known to fall into, and must I suggest you don't speak to Erdan of me again, especially when I'm sleeping. Don't you dare—don't dare turn him against me. Or else, your prick might be the last thing that works."

"But of course," Jeritus bowed.

Jeritus walked away and Vircona turned back to Erdan, who wondered what was underneath the heart that she didn't speak. Their foreheads touched, and he gazed into those dreamy eyes, a smile crept upon her lips as she extended another kiss, and her tongue invaded his mouth like a siege weapon.

He lost all interest, suddenly, in trying to rationalize her behavior as his tongue danced against hers in fit of bliss, and he heard the three pairs of footsteps walk away from the fire. Peace, serenity, this moment was all he needed; nothing else mattered to him. No violence, no hope, no depravity, no faith, nothing. Even Anaergienne was a problem that could wait until tomorrow.

CHAPTER 8

Nightmares Realized

The silence was disturbing.

The sun rose like it always did, no storm clouds could Erdan perceive, and his nerves with Vircona at his side weren't picking up any notice for danger. Traveling as long as they did on this road toward Malitu, there was supposed to be wildlife; there was none. No evidence of their existence for they betrayed the natural order of things, and the only sound now was gentle strumming and signing of Jeritus as their boots grew heavy with each step they took. Just the strums, no crickets, no song birds, and even the leaves of the trees hanging above them didn't rustle.

The wind itself seemed dead, and he turned his head to the branches where he beheld nests, or what remained of them, as many nests fell from the trees, straw, and twigs to the ground with nothing inside them.

There was a fluttering of birds, and the sun was blotted out by the constant flocking of blue jays overhead flying at a breakneck pace as if they were fleeing from something. The wind turned and brushed his hood off, and Vircona shrieked as she clutched hers to her face so no one apart from he could see her skin. He grimaced, fearing the worst, and that the rumor of his nightmares were true and Kinasa fell.

Well, that would absolve any and all matter of hatred for the elves if this rumor held any weight to it. But he dared hope against the weight of his suspicions. Hard to hate that which has been exterminated, and perhaps the high elves would have something better to offer the lands of humans for they indeed were devoid of Guilds and conflicts, save for the common everyday problems.

The sun shone again as the shadow passed over them.

"What was that about?" Jeritus asked, strapping his guitar to his back. "I've never known birds to fly in unison in such a large number."

"Where did they come from?" Nilor asked.

"Where do you think?" Jeritus scowled. "Kinasa, something happened."

"In your travels," Erdan began as they continued on foot. "Do you recall anything about Kinasa falling? I've heard rumors when I was in Sheris."

"Erdan," Vircona shrilled. "I'm so sorry, try not to think of it."

"Well…" Jeritus pondered, gazing to the sky. "No, I've not heard of anything, but that would be a hell of a rumor to spread, especially without any backing. If you heard it fell, I assume it fell. Of course, depending on whose lips shared the first spread, that's open to interpretation is what *fell* means in this context. Of course, that elf in Sheris told us that much."

"I see," Erdan said, and yet, still a glimmer of hope remained as the gates of Malitu were in sight.

However, the gates were higher than before with reinforced metal, and armored guards aplenty, more were on patrol than he remembered when he left, and his eyes looked further past that, seeing rangers walking back and forth, many of whom were wounded, maimed, even. Lots of tents set up in the streets right by the pathway, and stretchers carried bodies unable to walk. The wizards of the ward even hurried to bring healing to the wounded. Groans he heard still with his ears, for the silence couldn't distract him.

He stopped in his tracks, and Nilor, Guri and Jeritus walked past him, Vircona still clutching his arm. Was it true? *It can't be! That's impossible. Impossible!* He considered what other context that might call for the Rangers' Guild to be here of all places, and of all times. Rarely did the realm of humans call for elvish intervention. But it did happen. Those were elves, wood elves in there, and of course they were roaming freely, though he could even see a child inside, a young one, terrified as he clutched onto the leg of his mother holding a basket of apples.

"Erdan?" Jeritus turned his head. "You comin'? We can get some rest up there."

"Rangers," he said, eyes gaped open and sweaty.

"I'd think you'd be happy to see your kin, then, no?" Nilor turned his head.

"Rangers, Rangers, they came from Kinasa. What are they doing here!" he exclaimed. "Something happened. Something, I must find out what."

"You must calm yourself, Erdan," Vircona soothed him. "Come, let us find out then, and we'll see what misfortune befell them. Quick now, before the sun sets."

"Agreed," Guri turned, face grave. "Let's find out, gods. What difference does it make?"

"What?" Erdan said. "This is the most singularly important thing we can find out. A nation fell overnight, Sheris and Felldur, okay, Felldur was our fault, but still, places of importance are collapsing. Malitu was attacked before, and likely after I arrived here with Glentor. And my friend. Glenroy! I must see his memorial!"

Erdan sprinted with Vircona past his companions, but he heard them running with him, and the clanking metal of the guards got louder when he approached. His eyes searched the walls of the city, unusually organized and several archers were poised to loose arrows into him, and there wasn't much he could do, save run to the south towards Kinasa, or North to Grento, but then, the memorial? Surely, they wouldn't loose arrows at a high elf.

"Halt!" the dwarf ordered, armored heavily, clanking boots and an ax he had. Cardur. "Erdan, where's your halfling?"

"My halfling is dead," Erdan panted, coming to a halt, and panted. "What, why is the Guild here?"

"You're not privy to that information right now," Cardur spoke quickly. "What happened? Why are you in a rush?"

"I've heard rumors, can you tell me that? Tell me these rumors are false." He felt Vircona grabbing the back of his cuirass and hid behind him. "I heard Kinasa fell. Tell me it's wrong."

"It's right," Cardur grumbled. "We've kept the wood elves safe for now, the injured, we are healing through our ward, I assure you, they're getting the best care we can, but without my head healer, there's only so much even we can do. Already, about a score of elves perished, and we don't exactly know why."

"And—and—" he felt a hand touch his shoulder, and he turned. It belonged to Nilor, who had a sinister sneer on his face. "My cousin. Where is he?" If there ever was a time to start scheming, it would be now. The Rangers most certainly wouldn't permit a man to hunt one of their own.

"I'm not tellin' ye that," Cardur said grimly. "For fear of unfriendly ears, ye understand. But I assure you, as far as I can tell, he's alive."

"So, he's not in Kinasa then?"

"Could be, could be elsewhere." Cardur gazed suspiciously at Nilor. "Now, I've got room to spare—"

"Cardur, what have we here?" a familiar voice said, and an elf with silver hair appeared behind him, hand on her bow, strung for loosing, but there was no arrow. "Erdan? It's been what, sixty years? And who is that behind ye?"

"Oh," Erdan said. "Yun, nice to see you again. This is Vircona, my beloved."

"Nice to meet you," Vircona offered a bow. "It is an honor to meet someone from the Guild."

Yun's smile faded and her eyes narrowed. Her hand tensed around the bow, and the frown turned into a scowl, baring her teeth in much the same way Vircona did when she was angry. Even Cardur traded a look of gross concern when he turned to the Ranger of the Guild. Her hand raised, and suddenly, the wall was manned with elven rangers with bows aimed against them, strings pulled back.

"Erdan, get away from her, immediately," she snapped, pulling her bow out and pointing it at Vircona.

"First Felldur, and now this," Jeritus exclaimed. "What the hell, I told you, Erdan, she is a bad idea."

"Damnit, not this again." Guri scowled.

"Erdan." She drew her bow back, and aimed at him, for Vircona was behind him. "Get away from her, immediately."

"Erdan, don't let them take me like the men did," Vircona pleaded. "Why are you doing this? Why?"

"Vircona," he said, staring at the point of the arrow.

"Damnit, Erdan," Yun swore. "I'll not ask again. Get her away from yourself if ye know what's best for ya!"

"No, Yun," Erdan growled. "What's this about?"

"Are you fucking serious!" She turned her head to one of the archers. "I swear, if you weren't related I'd have loosed ye, and buried yer body in a pit of maggots by now. Kill the bitch!"

"She's a victim here!" Erdan stepped back, providing cover for Vircona. "You can't take her; all she wants is rest. She's not known rest from her own people. She's done nothing."

"Are you fucking serious!" Yun hissed. "Did nothing? Oh, the number of wood elves, and their corpses, blood watering the soil in our sacred forest would beg to differ! Now, I won't ask again, Erdan. I don't care how close you are to Anaergienne, but I won't hesitate to put you down like a dog if you don't step away from her right this instance. Now!"

"Nuh—no, you're lying," Erdan stammered. "She's been with me in Sheris for the last several months. I just found out about your damned forest."

"Don't ever swear about the tree again, you rotten nymph," Yun frowned. "I don't care if I set your body on fire to do it, she dies tonight."

"Yun was it?" the bard spoke, inching himself forward. "I think given the racial provocations within which we all find ourselves adequately entangled, I doubt we'll remove our own prejudices from one another, but I believe it would be in everyone's best interest, yours included, if we dealt with the matter with just a little diplomacy." Jeritus bowed. "I entreat you to speak at least with me about this matter, so we might see some reason in the madness."

"Why would I trust you?" Yun frowned. "I have just as much a reason to kill you as I do this dark elf, this darkling has no place among my kind, not after what they did to us."

"*They?* As in plural? Trust me when I suggest that to you." Jeritus rubbed his hands together. "I believed Vircona here was an anomaly. I may have erred in that assumption, for that I beg your pardon, a thousand times."

Erdan let an escaped sigh through his lips. He was going to witness this bard's silver tongue at work, and hopefully see them through. The things he did for love, for without trials there could be no love, and what greater trial was this, than having his kin point arrows at him with the intention to end his life. But suffice it to suggest even to the weary minds that he had no regrets at all, for the love he felt for Vircona, and he was certain she shared the same, as close as they'd been this year, nothing could break this bond of love.

"I could recount all the things that transpired between the five of us and Sheris," Jeritus replied. "But I assure you, most esteemed mistress of the legendary Rangers' Guild, I was merely a member of convenience of this wretched party."

The bastard!

"You see, I had nowhere to go, and nowhere to get to safety, and it is clear now more than ever I must take my leave of such barbaric fellowship; however, I'd hate to see such unnecessary violence go to waste. The man is hungry for vengeance, the dwarf is filled with grief and greed: I assure ye that both those qualities don't pair well with one another. And this elf is madly in love with this darkling, as you call them, to make any rational decisions. I humbly ask…" He folded his hands together. "…to be let through into this city, for individual passage, and I might travel north to Grento, a homeland. And might I suggest not killing these here adventurers for their stupidity but by all means, don't permit them access through this city's fine gates."

"And what would you have me do with this dark elf then?" Yun asked. "Surely you wouldn't let me let her wander free."

"I wouldn't dare chain her to anything or subject her to torture," Jeritus spoke sternly. "Lest everyone die. And I'm not entirely certain she can be killed. But if you wish to push your luck, by all means? I guess, but make sure I'm far enough away from her so this doesn't bite me in the ass."

"You betray their trust," Yun commented. "Why?"

"Because I'm sick and tired of being in places where history is in the makin'." Jeritus sighed. "These four people, I want nothing to do with, and the sooner I rid myself of them the better."

"Bard," Yun jerked her head to motion him forward. "You may come in."

"Thank you," he bowed before he made it through the gates. Why did Yun have this power over Cardur?

"Erdan, if you ditch the bitch now, you can come in," Yun said. "Otherwise, get out of here and I don't want to see either of the four of you here again, ye understand?"

"I'll take my chances, Yun," Erdan scowled, and took Vircona by the wrist leading her off the path to the south. "You're cold. No wonder the humans hate you."

"And the feeling is not at all mutual, now." Yun scoffed. "Dwarf, man, get out of here, and if I find any of you within a league of this city again, I'll hang ye from the fucking trees!"

CHAPTER 9

"That bastard betrayed us!" Guri growled, kicking a heavy rock with his boot.

"Yeah, well, you didn't speak up for yerself." Nilor sighed. "And it was clear, one way or the other, with Vircona here with us, we're not getting through that city, or any help."

"No," Erdan said, looking up at the dark empty sky. "It's not her fault, don't blame her for this. Jeritus, Vircona made him uncomfortable. Maybe it's her skin, or something else, what she did in Felldur. People often are afraid of power when it isn't in their own hands."

"I love you, Erdan," she whimpered. "Please don't let them take me. They'll sell me to slavery again."

"Of course not," Erdan soothed her. "I won't let you be taken. I promise."

"Well…" Nilor folded his arms as he leaned against a tree. "It's clear you're not gettin' to Paxis anytime soon, with all the activity, and you heard Yun, don't wanna get on any Guild's bad side, really. There isn't much in the way of anything good that can come of this, so, Guri doesn't have much of a reason to do or go anywhere. Vircona is all lovey to you, Erdan, and that's great, I'm glad you found something special."

"What are you suggesting?"

"What's after Paxis?" Nilor asked. "When you get there, what will you do? I don't think the halflings will accept her as she is either."

"They've not known racial conflict for millennia. They don't need to be brought into this," Guri said. "Leave them out of it."

"My employer—"

"Your employer is dead!" Nilor snapped. "Killed by the damned knight in Sheris, we all saw it. You took what was due to ye, and more from the cart he owned. You don't owe him anything, or his family! But Anaergienne, that is something, a place to go, something to do and kill the boredom."

"No. No. No!" Erdan snapped, standing upright. "You'll not kill him; I'll not help you find him. We can part here and now if that's what ye want. Your path of vengeance will lead you nowhere."

"You're right, I'd be a fool to come at him in a fair fight, and even unfair and dirty I might play," Nilor growled. "He'd still dance circles around me with his blades. But with her," he pointed at Vircona, who looked slightly dazed. "We can kill him."

"Why would you think I'd be okay with this?" Erdan snapped, finger pointing at the human in the party. "No. No. No. I've said it before, that's enough."

"Like it or not, you're stuck with me," Nilor turned to Guri. "You? You stayin' or goin'?"

"I've nowhere I gots to be," he grimaced. "But I ain't joinin' no elf hunt. Forget that business. Forget it all!"

"Thank you!" Erdan exclaimed, enthused that he wouldn't have to convince Guri anyways.

"I'm afraid my silence has gotten us in lots of trouble, so I beg your forgiveness," Vircona said, a sneer creeping on her face. "Now that I've got you measly *males'* attention, I must," she sighed heavily. "Erdan, dear, I do apologize and ask for your forgiveness especially. What I might add to this little division in our harmonious little part is that I seek something, something the witch has, and something only she can give me."

"Okay, so now we are on a witch hunt!" Guri threw his hands in the air. "No, last time she was with that knight and his enchanted blade and armor. Almost indestructible he is, and I must say that so. No. I'm not joinin' no witch hunt either."

"What do you seek, my love," Erdan said, ignoring Nilor's grinning face. "If I can get it for you—"

"Unfortunately, this is an item that must be treated with care," she said. Reaching to her breast, she pulled out a chain, and an amulet now hung neatly against her skin. "She has one of these, and I want it. There are seven of these in total, and I want all of them. This one previously shattered in the ground when someone killed the wraith who bore it in Terra Silenti. I am taking it. She's on an island, I think, called Sterilus and it's on our way into Paxis, and I think we should be capable of achieving all our wants. Nilor might have the possibility of avenging his family, I get my amulet, and you, Erdan, get to go to Paxis and maybe live out the rest of your days in peace."

"What?" he shook his head in disbelief. "Are you—"

"You're a terrible lay, Erdan, I'm sorry, but it's true." Vircona scowled. "I had assumed an enemy of the natural world would try to eliminate some capitals and it paid off, and the mist we all saw that night went west. I recognized her, and the legend behind it, she's a witch, Maya Truva. The witch of lust, as was the lust of the blood inside your penis, Erdan, you really need to be thinkin' with the other head of yours."

He felt a weight drop in his chest; his emotions tugged in a way he thought shouldn't be drawn. But it was his heart breaking when he found out she didn't reciprocate the love he gave her, the sacrifices he was willing to make. She was unwilling, and used him for what? To get here? For more information? It didn't make sense, not when she can raze buildings and fortresses to the ground and turn them into a breeding ground for giant spiders. She could do the same to Malitu, but decided it wasn't worth the effort? Even she was stronger than this witch of lust.

"Nilor, if we are to do this, I'll need help," Vircona said. "And whatever happens after our errands, is beyond your control. You will obey me, and don't question anything I ask of you."

"Was it you?" Guri stepped forward.

"Me?" Vircona turned her head.

"Was it you that set the world against the elves?" Guri asked. "Answer me!"

"Guri, trust me when I say, Anaergienne is singularly responsible for the hatred humans have for the elves," she explained. "I'm sorry, but it's true. I don't particularly care, but if it means getting what I want, I'll kill the elf."

"Vircona," Erdan said, voice dropped as the façade of love became undone, and he scowled. "Vircona. I won't let you."

"Nor I you," Guri stood beside him. "This charade goes on for long enough. Jeritus saw an out and he took it. We would have been wise to do the same.

"Yes," she sneered. "Nilor, I'm very much hungry. I implore you to kill both these fools, will you? I'm done talkin', and the elves—"

"It was you, wasn't it? You're responsible for the fall, and the reason why wood elves hated you! That's why Yun wanted to kill you!" Erdan scowled, drawing his sword.

"What happened with Kinasa." She put her hand out. "Has absolutely nothing to do with me, you understand, Erdan. What or who else could be blamed for such misfortune? You've told me before of the wraith, Fakino. Yes, the amulet I have belonged to her. Another wraith, a witch—the five of us saw her. Things are happening that are well beyond my control. and not every disaster can trace their origins to me, but I can very well trace the origins of my anguish to elves. No, this wasn't my doing. But I can't be sad about it either."

"Let us be rid of this, then," Nilor spoke. "It seems, elf, humans are right to dislike you, to distrust you. High elf, wood elf, it doesn't matter, now does it?"

"I guess not now," Erdan sighed. "Come, let us kill each other."

"I've no intention on dyin' tonight, you see." Nilor smiled, sword raised. "I've honed my skills, let us see how well I fare against two, a black smith, and a ranger, though admittedly, not a dangerous one."

Nilor pivoted his body and swung his blade. Erdan parried it, and Guri took his axe swiftly at the man's belly, who jumped back, barely missing. The cloth cut open of his torso, and he pivoted his feet to distance himself between Erdan, and Vircona just watched, arms crossed as she watched the fight. Metal clanged, axe against sword, and sword to sword. They worked together to flank, but the man's footwork was impressive, unable to lose his advantage, the strikes swung true, and the feints with such expertise, Erdan couldn't very well tell the difference from an intended strike, or a feint to draw his weapon close for a disarm.

The forest was silent, just the clanging of metal ringing in rhythmic blasts. Grunting, the dwarf and Erdan tried and tried, but couldn't get close enough to harm the man. Elegant with a sword, he truly was a master of his craft, and say, should Nilor ever meet Anaergienne, he was uncertain who would be better in a fair duel. But there would be no fairness in vengeance. He grunted once more as he opened himself up intentionally, and Nilor took the swing. The blade came down, and Erdan pivoted, his own sword far from his enemy, he threw an elbow as the blade touched the ground, striking the man in the face.

"Gah." Blood came from Nilor's nose as he was forced away.

Erdan took the opportunity to strike at him, swinging hard with a twisting body. Nilor's blade rose up, parrying the blade up, and the dwarf barreled into the man, vines ripped up from the earth, and grabbed him, restraining him to the ground.

Nilor wasted no moment, and before Erdan could intervene, Nilor's blade hacked into the shoulder of the dwarf, twisting the blade as blood pooled onto the soil.

"Dirty."

"You used magic," Erdan replied. "Dirty is dirty! You want to fight fair, you fight fair, but you can't have it both ways!"

His sword came up and struck again. The sword was parried, and Erdan pushed forward, striking as fast as he could, using all things to his advantage, including kicking rocks up in the ground, but to no avail. Erdan backed away, realizing it was a mistake as the fighter took his opportunity to launch his own fury of attacks.

The elf ducked, pivoted, and parried. Only through those motions could he hope to keep him far away from striking anything vital. He panted, the blade heavy in his arms, but as he looked into Nilor's eyes, he saw a blood lust that wouldn't be satiated, and no amount of exhaustion he felt would quench that thirst.

It was a mistake, and he felt something on his ankle. The vines tried for his boot, and he ducked, avoiding a fatal blow, and some of his hair was cut off, strands on the soil. Panting further, he dove to the side before the veins could grab him, and they hurled themselves at him with tremendous force.

He tactically retreated, cutting away at those that would restrain him, and Nilor howled like a blood lusty wolf, and as Erdan retreated into the forest, avoiding all the fauna, he let himself slow down near a bog, trees everywhere. Panting, catching his breath as he no doubt got closer to the forest of Kinasa, though several weeks journey away, he still felt an unusual presence, a coldness, colder than snow was the air as he breathed it in.

He saw a bat hissing as it flew by, and turned itself by a bush, landing itself upside down. Hissing, blood on its teeth. Erdan's eyes gaped open, thinking he knew what it was, and he simply didn't have the heart to even think about dangerous undead creatures in the forest, especially a vampire of all things. But it just looked at him and wiped some of the mess up with his wing like a sleeve, before staring at him again with green eyes.

He felt at peace, and calm now, as he withdrew his blade, and leaned against the tree behind him. He took his traveling pack, and pulled out some water, and drank the last bit of it, but continued to stare openly at the bog.

"Erdan," Vircona's voice called. "Erdan, I'm so sorry, I didn't mean anything by it."

"Vircona," he said, feeling at ease, and he didn't completely understand why. "Vircona, please stop this nonsense."

"Yes, Erdan." She appeared from behind a bush, her skin shining in the moonlight. "I already took care of Nilor, you don't have to be afraid of him." She approached, and he felt compelled to touch the pommel of his blade, but with each step he took, he drew his hand further from it. She touched his cheek, and he hers as he stared into her eyes. "I'm sorry I hurt you."

"It's okay," Erdan said. "I forgive you. Just let's go, leave everything behind and—"

He looked down; a vine impaled his belly and sank into his flesh and wrapped around him. Vine after vine pulled on his limbs and raised him up into the trees. Pain filled his body as blood left it, and he rose in the air, looking up in the sky. Grimacing, the red liquid departed his lips as he felt strained, and the vines pulled on him. Gritting his teeth, he looked down at Vircona who sneered at him, hand in the air.

"Why did you do this to me," he stammered, blood spitting out from his lips.

"Because," she said. "The elves did things to me that made me want to be cruel and harsh to them, Erdan. While I did appreciate your kindness, I wasn't about to stick around for very long for you to stab me in the back. When you see Carmielle in the heavens, unless your soul is rotten and she sends you to the Abyss, tell her that I will smash the gates of Heaven, and kill her!"

Erdan screeched as the tendons came undone, his flesh ripped, and all limbs came free from his torso. Vircona scowled as his body came down, and she released the spell of vines, staring heavily into the mess.

Scowling at the weak, pathetic corpse, she stepped over it gently to ensure her cloak wasn't about to get blood all over it. She turned around the tree and found Nilor tripping over some weeds.

"The biggest problem with losing him is we've no way to find Anaergienne," Nilor panted.

"Of course, *you* don't," Vircona sneered. "But *I* do, which means you best be on your best behavior. We're going to that island first."

Armanis Ar-feinial, in the gritty pits of despair, he comes from: Bridgeton, Maine, a terribly dreadful place. Currently residing in the Greater Boston Area with his family, he studied Criminal Justice, English, and currently dabbles in a little bit of Finance. His unfaltering passion for writing came from his first exposure from the Lord of the Rings, which he drew inspiration from in his first stories, but alas, as all good things come downward into the grimdark pits, adopting tones from Joe Abercrombie. He loves reading, playing games of all kinds, and he is what you call a practicing writaholic. He is personally known for his witty sarcastic unasked for remarks.